CLOSER EAST

A NOVEL BY

ROBERT GLICK

WOODLAND FREE PRESS

For enquires, please visit: www.CloserEast.com

Published by Woodland Free Press, London, England
Produced by The Choir Press, Gloucester, England

Printed in the United Kingdom
First Printing, 2011

ISBN: 978-0-9569602-0-7

CLOSER EAST

To Gordon and Sam. Obviously.

God gave us memory so that we might have roses in December.

—J.M. Barrie

PART ONE

SHADOWS

CHAPTER 1 • एक

The heat was unforgiving. Unyielding. It taunted him, drove him to the limits of exhaustion, of rage, of despair. And it served only to remind him, desperately, relentlessly, of home.

Vikhram Sukhadia had always known the sun's torment. Not that of the fiery Arabian desert to which he had recently come, but the gritty, choking furnace of Bombay. It exuded its intensity like a statement of defiance or a resolute warning. He hadn't heeded, or perhaps he simply hadn't understood, that warning. He thought of it as a fortification to keep out others, not as a barrier to keep him in. A caution to strangers, especially to the venal Western businessmen who had inherited privilege from their colonial cousins and whose enduring presence in India, with their haughty wives and undisciplined children, was to him an abomination.

Yet despite the plaintive protests of his wife Sapna and those of almost everyone in the compound, despite the grinding presentiment he felt on the eve of his departure, Vikhram had set out eagerly for the oil fields of Al-Fadiz. He did so in the pursuit of a success beyond anything his meager means and his scant prospects in Bombay could have afforded him.

Such were the promises of the striking representative of the Gulf Petroleum Company, who appeared that late summer afternoon in the Nayā Bazaar Market. He ignited an imagination Vikhram had long thought extinguished. The man's hardened face and dark skin were those of any of the men in the market, but his earnest demeanor and his handsome attire spoke of a world unknown to these men. His crisp linen suit was dazzling. His patent leather shoes reflected the midday sun like a newly minted coin. The chain of gold on his waistcoat was as thick as a man's thumb. He told tales of riches that many would have thought fanciful, were it not for the impressive figure he cut. He spoke in a measured, confident tone, yet with the inflections and language familiar to all the pitiable and disfavored men to whom he addressed his lofty pitch. Wealth, he proclaimed, was not the preserve of the few, but of the many who worked hard and who saved, and on whom opportunity had shone.

These words struck Vikhram deeply, as if the peculiar visitor were addressing him directly. They echoed his dreams, of liberating his family from the anguish and humiliation of poverty, of seeing his two children educated in the finest Indian schools, where trained teachers, new books and genuine learning were routine, not luxuries.

Two years had now passed since he left Bombay. Two years spent, not in the comfort he had expected, not accumulating the treasure he thought he would salt away, but in conditions every bit as squalid as those he had left behind.

The dormitory rooms in particular, reserved for the multitude of Indian workers, belched a smell so fetid that daily it assaulted him. It was a villainous mixture of cooking grease that wafted down the hallway from the makeshift kitchens, wet clothes strewn across open windows, and the perspiration of a thousand depleted men. The air was as stagnant as the smell was pungent, and often there was too little of it for the two men who occupied each room to breathe comfortably.

Every room was identical in construction and furnishings, varying only by the degree of decay that testified to the neglect of innumerable previous inhabitants. The walls had been painted a sickly yellow that at once mocked and mirrored the punishing sun just beyond, and that lent itself to a particularly rapid deterioration. No personal effects were displayed or even permitted. The single electric bulb was seldom extinguished, providing too little light to peruse the treasured Indian magazines and newspapers brought in by the newest recruits, and too much to sleep, or at least to sleep well. Vikhram presumed that this was what prison must be like, though he had come here of his own volition and was free to leave whenever he chose, as many had done before him and many more were hoping soon to do.

Each man was consigned a single uniform, a curious garment of rumpled cotton ill-suited to the desert conditions, smelling deeply of petrol and of its previous occupant. Vikhram's had clearly been intended for a much larger man. The shoulders drooped almost comically, and the waist would have been too large for a man half again his size. It had originally been dyed a muted orange, in order, he could only presume, to be visible from afar in the blazing oil fields. It was the color of saffron that Vikhram remembered from the spice market near the Jama Masjid mosque in Bombay, though the dye had faded. The cotton had been cleaned so often, or worn for so long, that it retained only the faintest notions of its original color and only the slightest protection for which it was intended.

Saffron was also widely available in Al-Fadiz, and was

a regular part of the sparing food rations Vikhram received each day. But the spices were not used as Sapna would have done, to cure meats or to season the yoghurt, but mixed with peppercorns, turmeric and various seeds he couldn't recognize into *hawayij*, a glutinous blend too fiery for even some of the hardiest of Indians to stomach. It was served on a flat bread the local men called *fatir*, made of toasted barley flour, and which went limp just as soon as it cooled. Even the coffee had saffron and cardamom thrown in, and was stronger, more bitter than anything he had been asked to serve back home.

Out beyond the dormitories, the oil rigs on which he labored were as remarkable as they were intimidating. Giant churning beasts that spewed black mud and rock and venom with a terrible fierceness. These metal behemoths were taller than anything Vikhram had ever seen, soaring higher than he even thought possible. As high as only children could let themselves imagine a structure could be. Nothing Vikhram ever knew was, or should be, taller than the temples in which the Gods dwelled. Even to conceive of building something so towering was to defame and defy the great religion itself. The hateful sound they made only confirmed this. The earth itself clamored with offensive heaves and incessant cries against the violence the dreadful machines inflicted on it.

Vikhram worked these grotesque machines from dawn to dusk, without respite and without complaint. No job was too small or too dangerous. The foremen relied on him to retrieve a tool lost down a pit, or to douse a rogue flame that threatened the rig. He volunteered to take the shifts of men who had fallen ill or who were injured, or of those who had lost the strength or the will required. He made himself useful to the others in any number of ways, from washing their clothes to writing letters to loved ones left behind. Not out of solidarity or compassion. He did so to earn and to save as much money as he could.

He had managed, despite all his efforts, to achieve precious little. His pockets were not lined with silk, his purse not filled with silver. He had scraped together no more than a pittance, and little more than he could have earned and saved working in the bookshop in Bombay. His friend Amit, who bunked below Vikhram and who had also come from the south of India, had warned him to put aside money for his passage home before all else. Too often, the wretched men in the Saudis' employ exhausted their piteous wages on anything that might make their life there more tolerable, from black market whiskey to even riskier and more costly commodities. In this Vikhram had taken good notice, and avoided the temptations for which the miserable conditions and aching loneliness might have provided him an excuse. He stuffed and sewed into the lining of his vest just enough of the silver coins from his weekly pay to provide, for when he needed it, a third-class steamship passage back to India.

There were little luxuries. Not extravagances. Nothing foolhardy. Tokens to send to Sapna and to their two children, old enough to remember their father, but young enough to risk soon forgetting. Hollow tokens meant to demonstrate his incontrovertible success, his growing wealth, his unshakable faith that he would soon be able to provide for his family just as he had promised. An intricate gold bracelet with an inscription in Arabic that, he was told by the pushy shopkeeper, spoke of love in subtle poetry. Two silver-plated carved elephants that looked just like the ones in the book Vikhram had read to his children for nights on end, and that almost always had formed part of the children's own fantastical storytelling. A pair of hand-sewn sheepskin sandals with elaborate stitching and shiny ornaments attached to their impossibly pointy tips. For himself, a gold-plated watch, ornate in design and too showy for such a simple wrist as his. He wore the watch day and night; he flaunted it as if to proclaim to himself and to others that he had at least accomplished this much. In town, he had himself photographed, with the gold watch and his gifts prominent in the frame, straightaway posting back to Sapna the irrefutable pictorial evidence of his triumphs.

But Vikhram knew that even these small victories were illusory. The crush of the days spent on the rigs, the constant pressures and risks, left little room for contemplation. The nights, however, were different. Awake in his stiff bed, while Amit and the other men were able to drift into fatigued slumber, he lay alert, haunted by the shame of his failures and by the thundering distance he knew remained still between his promises and his achievements.

CHAPTER 2 • दोन

The Nayā Bazaar was not among the most noteworthy or the most successful markets in Bombay. Its grimy stalls and storefronts offered little by way of variety or quality. The paucity of goods on display only multiplied the general sense of misfortune, of indigence.

Still, as the market was situated at the end of a busy main road, its outer edges buttressed against the city's central rail depot, it was highly trafficked. From early morning, hundreds crowded the food sellers for their daily provisions, scrambled to the cobbler to salvage ragged shoes, called at the clinic for a balm or tablet to ease some long-suffered complaint. The men queued patiently for a shave or a haircut while their wives or mothers darted frenetically to complete one commission after another. The women often lingered as well in front of the gold dealer's shop, suspended somewhere between fantasy and delusion.

The market's other principal advantage was its proximity to the British Colonial Office and the walled enclave in which many of the city's Westerners and their generally sizable households lived. Cooks, drivers, houseboys, cleaners, gardeners, child minders. Difficult and fastidious in the mold of their masters, it was these household staff who drove the brisk commerce of the market, especially the smattering of secluded, more fashionable shops tucked away in the outlying corners of the Bazaar that catered expressly to the foreigners' needs and whims.

The legions of domestic servants, often accompanying their cantankerous employers on well-choreographed expeditions, carried with them an abundance of money that both pained the many penniless onlookers and sent the voracious merchants into a ravenous frenzy. They purchased vast, wasteful quantities of food. They flirted with recklessness in their procurement of fine cutlery, books, linens and furniture made from chestnut or pine imported from the cold and dense forests of Europe. Most of the market's Indian customers, had they not coveted such profligacy themselves, would have found these expenditures obscene. The Western appetite seemed insatiable, and the greedy merchants who served them were always happy to oblige.

When Vikhram first arrived at the Nayā Bazaar, on Christmas Day 1939, more than four months had passed in his unremitting, grueling search for work. It had yielded nothing, save the occasional local errand for a visiting businessman or traveler met at the railway station – sometimes legitimate, sometimes dubious – for which he had earned but the most paltry of sums. He had scoured the factories, warehouses and markets of southern Bombay for some manner, any manner of job. He presented himself to the foremen and shopkeepers as practiced in whatever trade was being conducted. Skilled in the administration of the modern machines used to manufacture whatever the factory was producing. Willing to take on even the lowliest of tasks with fervor and with commitment.

But these pitches often came across as entreaties, and they strained credulity. Barely twenty in years, his wiry frame and pale complexion gave him an air of urgency, of desperation, of invisibility. He found himself time and again powerless to compete against the army of stalwart, athletic men who inspired considerably greater trust and promise.

Desperation had led him for a short time to join the inestimable ranks of the city's beggars, but even there, he had little success. It was to the children, some not older than four or five, caked in dirt, smelling foul and clothed in tatters, that the passersby extended their rare and restrained generosity. On the streets, too, petitioning the well-to-do in their motorcars and carriages for a trifle, he was invisible.

His arrival at the Bazaar that morning was ill-timed. The streets were crowded with activity. The Christian holiday, of which Vikhram had little understanding, had set off a riot of shopping, a furious search to acquire all the necessary gear and gifts to impress guests and to placate the indulgent requirements of spoiled children. The shopkeepers were busily cleaning up the remnants of the previous day's orgy before contemplating the onslaught of the regular day's business, and had little time for distraction.

Undeterred, he made his usual careful approach to any shop that appeared to offer a prospect. The hint of a friendly smile behind a counter. Maybe an older or infirm man visibly burdened by his load. A storeroom or cellar in obvious, urgent need of a tidying up. He made his approaches, modifying his pitch to appeal to the most pressing need he could see or drawing on the promise of the shopkeeper's kindness or mercy.

By noon, he hadn't had any more success than in the countless days before, as he moved to the second row of shops with fading trust in securing work. As he turned the corner, worn out and deflated, pinching a few ripe mangoes that would serve as his main nourishment for the day from the fruit-seller's sparse stand, he found himself inexorably drawn towards the Victoria Book Palace.

It was not the physical condition of the bookshop that attracted his attention. The building was quite ordinary. No wider than the average teashop in every market he had visited, it boasted a once magnificent staircase linking its two floors, each of which housed a trio of small, discolored windows. Like the other shops surrounding it, the walls were sullied and in many places cracked, the paint chipped and the bold, garish lettering on the over-sized sign above the entrance dulled from years of neglect. Even from the street, Vikhram could see the dust that had accumulated on the stacks of books, rows of which continued improbably until they faded from view into the interior darkness.

Nor was it the proprietor who piqued his interest. Mr. Mukerjee was not an alluring figure. He was stout, unkempt. His arrant lack of attention to the state of his attire, the disdain that permanently inhabited his brow, the shrill voice with which he hollered instructions and orders, were altogether menacing.

What attracted Vikhram's attention had little to do with the bookshop itself. As he approached, he saw a small group of wide-eyed young men and fidgety boys who had gathered around the shop, those at the back of the assembly speaking to each other in muffled tones, but most standing in rapt silence. Vikhram made his way effortlessly to the fore, his sinewy body moving through the throng with little resistance. There, he saw in front of him, a wireless radio, its wooden casing and brass dials radiant in the midday sun.

Though the nascent technology had come to the exclusive drawing rooms and private member clubs of Bombay several years earlier, this was the first time he and most of

the others had ever witnessed the device. None understood
how it functioned. Vikhram thought at first the contraption
might be a new kind of phonograph. He had seen these
machines often, astounded by the vinyl disks that made
them sing. Scratchy recordings of women crooning dour,
grating songs that sounded to his ear like the last, tortured
pleas of a dying bird. But no disks were fed to this machine;
there was no needle to care for, no horn to polish. From the
concentration and the interest of the crowd, he knew that
this was something entirely different, entirely new.

"Who's that talking?" he whispered shyly to the gangly
boy, half his age, who stood beside him.

"It's the Indian Emperor, King George," the boy
replied, in a manner that suggested considerable annoyance. "He wants to wish us all a happy Christmas, and he's
warning us about war."

"Where is he speaking from? Is the Emperor here?"

"Here? Of course not," answered his irritated neighbor.
"He's in his big palace in London. They say he has more
than fifty tigers there, all very fierce, and he's going to set
them on the Germans!"

"Why is he so angry at the Germans, the Emperor?"
said an incredulous Vikhram. "He doesn't seem to me like
he's that cross."

"Oh, but he gets angry often," exclaimed the boy, with
such a confident delivery that Vikhram had no reason to
doubt such news, before their conversation was cut short.
Muffled into silence by the others, straining to hear the
king's message and to understand its complex meaning. He
spoke in a halting tone, in long sentences that lingered in
the empty space around the device.

"To the men and women of our far-flung Empire,"
began the king, "working with several vocations but with

the one same purpose. All our members of the great family of nations, which is prepared to sacrifice everything so that freedom of spirit may be saved to the world. Such is the spirit of the Empire, of the great dominions of India," to which the boys, hearing even the mention of their country, let out a roaring cheer in unison, "of every colony large or small, from all alike have come offers of help, for which the mother country can never be sufficiently grateful. Such unity, in aim and in effort, has never been seen in the world before."

The transmission continued for some time, the king's voice becoming ever richer and more grave. More so than any of the other men and boys there, Vikhram was largely able to follow the king's meaning, though many of the words were complicated, spoken in an English more elaborate than he had encountered before, delivered in a hauntingly deliberate and stilted fashion. He understood that the monarch was preparing his people for the perils of a war to be fought thousands of miles away, a conflict which would come to have such a tremendous influence on these men, and on the destiny of India herself. He had not fully appreciated the call for sacrifice, though he sensed clearly the foreboding in the king's tone.

Mostly, he was spellbound by the medium itself, riveted to the voice emanating from the lustrous device that was, to him, a kind of miracle. He was enthralled with the modernity of it, transported by the idea that distant places of which he knew nothing and desired everything could suddenly be brought here to Bombay. To the Nayā Bazaar. To the Victoria Book Palace. To him.

For three days running, while the industry and trade of the market continued abidingly and without notice around him, Vikhram himself sat unnoticed, an indiscernible figure fixed in front of the bookshop, engrossed in the wonder that was Mr. Mukerjee's wireless.

While the other men soon tired of the novelty, distracted by their responsibilities or burdens, or put off by the narrow limits of their familiarity with English, he remained true. He studied, mimicked the polished voices that so assiduously read aloud the news of each day. Though he could not grasp much of their subtleties, he listened with care to the great variety of programs. Talk of cultural happenings and of London's social calendar. Lively discussions on spiritual matters of the Christian god and his meaning. Gardening and cooking tips, information for travelers to Europe's smart destinations, music with horns and strings and drums every bit as melodious and exciting as anything he had ever heard before. English football matches and cricket games played by clubs whose storied names meant nothing to him. He heard much as well about the hostilities emerging in Europe, and the gathering clouds elsewhere. He came to know the many men and very few women of the British Broadcasting Company's Overseas Service as his friends. And when, as nightfall came and he heard the familiar music of the British national anthem played to signal the end of the broadcast day, exhorting all to save the distant king whose voice he had come well to know, he felt a sense of loss and apprehension, uncertain whether tomorrow would offer him again this splendid gift.

But Vikhram was by then no longer entirely invisible. To Mr. Mukerjee, he had become a nuisance. The proprietor of the Victoria Book Palace, short-tempered and ungenerous at the best of times, had little patience for this exasperating young man, rooted steadfast, unwelcome and uninvited, in front of his establishment.

Though born and raised in the heart of Bombay, not

a few minutes from the shop his father had owned before him, Mr. Mukerjee had little regard, and mostly contempt, for the people of his own India. Educated at one of the city's lesser English schools, he had adopted a sense of entitlement and superiority to which he believed his studies entitled him. Fancying himself above the hardships to which apparently he had been condemned, he had developed an immense admiration, very nearly a reverence for the British people, whose talents and enterprise he believed had brought such illumination to the world and such progress to India.

Like Vikhram, Mr. Mukerjee met each new day alone. His long-suffering wife had died in childbirth some twenty years earlier, bequeathing an only son, healthy and strong, but ungrateful and unkind. A boy who had grown into a hurried young man, whose increasingly radical stance against the British occupation put him at odds not only with the leaders of the country's nonviolent struggle for independence, but with his own father's natural sympathies and political leanings. By the time his impetuous son had manifested his intention to join the militant forces gathering in West Bengal, risking injury or imprisonment, their permanent estrangement had become inevitable.

Mr. Mukerjee had thrown all his thoughts and energies into reinventing the Victoria Book Palace. Refurbishment would provide a welcome distraction from the guile and ingratitude of his son, departed only a few days prior, and bolster his unrelenting efforts to escape the injustices of his impoverishment.

What he envisaged was not particularly grand. It was neither original nor inspired, but it was unique for Bombay, and certain to appeal to the inclinations of his cherished British clientele. For what he proposed was a replica, lesser-grade but faithful, of a refined London bookshop. His model was a quintessential, well-appointed shop located on Curzon Street in the busy Mayfair section of the capital frequented by intellectuals and by the aristocracy. Designed to accommodate its customers' avid enthusiasm for novelty, it was stocked with all the latest journals, books in English and from the Continent alike, intricate writing implements and handmade, embossed papers of silk and parchment. Its walls were cloaked in a vast quantity of exuberant wood panels, garlanded by classically-themed and exquisitely framed ink and watercolor canvases. And set down purposefully in front of the entry, a crystal wireless set with a single-valve receiver and amplifier emblazoned with the name *Falk, Stadelman & Co. of London* and a stamp bearing the inscription "Type Approved by the Postmaster General."

Or so he was taken to understand. For Mr. Mukerjee had never seen the Mayfair bookshop. He had never been to England. Indeed, he had left Bombay only once, to light his father's funeral pyre at the ancestral home in Pune. Even then he had made the trip in only a few short days. He had seen the shop and read its description in a picture book, a superb collection of photographs for visitors to London that catalogued the city's most stylish venues. Noble museums and massive stone churches, exclusive hotels, opulent shopping arcades that showered their customers with a dizzying choice of frippery. The book had been a gift from a well-heeled English customer, a trader who traveled often to India, and who had come to rely on the Victoria Book Palace to furnish him with reading materials to fill the long days of his many journeys home. Mr. Mukerjee had been enthralled by these images, mindful of the disparity between his middling establishment and the superlatives so elegantly presented in the book. He was prepared to risk exhausting his already dwindling savings, and even to accept the unfavorable terms of a loan from the overseas British banking concern, in order to lessen this disparity, to achieve his ambition of creating Bombay's most glorious, most English of bookshops.

A huge array of tradesmen had been engaged for the project, from carpenters to pipe-fitters to local artisans, all of whom jostled Vikhram as they arrived that first morning on site with their extensive gear and paraphernalia. Like their employer, these workers, harried and curt, found the uninvited man's presence to be an irritant, and were not the least bit interested in the noisy radio programs that so captivated him. They appealed to the shop owner to clear this bothersome obstruction.

"Go away, cretin!" shouted Mr. Mukerjee, "This isn't an entertainment hall. Can't you see we're working here? Go get into trouble somewhere else."

"But sahib, I'm not in any trouble. I only want to listen to the wireless," replied a desperate Vikhram, distressed that he might be chased away or that the radio might be silenced.

"I didn't spend my money on that cursed thing for your amusement. It's for my customers. Who you are scaring away!"

Vikhram was flustered, and he was perplexed, since there had been no customers in several days, worn-out by the delirium of the recent holiday and put off by the chaotic construction site.

"Besides," said a diffident Vikhram, "I could make myself useful to you. I can see there's plenty to do."

"Useful at what? I have more than enough cretins scrounging off me at the moment. Look around. I don't need another scrawny drifter around here getting in my way."

"I won't be in your way, sahib. I could make you very fine tea. Or sweep away the sawdust if you like. Or I can fill the water pump."

He hesitated, waiting for a response, any response, which didn't come. Mr. Mukerjee stood rigidly, wiping the beads of sweat from his temples and shifting the dust with the soles of his worn shoes in palpable annoyance.

Vikhram's mind raced to work out how he might gain a position, how he might make himself useful to this irascible man who held his access to such wonderment in the balance.

"I can bring you lunch from the railway station, sahib, so you won't waste any time today. I know where to find the best *chapathis* in all of Bombay!"

Mr. Mukerjee was riled by the young man's insistence and impertinence, a momentary but trying diversion from the rigid schedule he set himself, and from the perpetual supervision of his laborers, many of whom he knew would take the opportunity of such distractions to dither on the job. Yet he also knew that providing for his meals would prove problematic. Since his son's departure, he had no one upon whom he could rely to supervise the shop while its doors stayed open and its contents left vulnerable. So, reluctantly, he armed the boy with a fistful of coins and charged him to fetch a fresh tiffin of rice, dal and curry, wary of whether this young man still unknown to him in name or character would simply abscond with the money, as so many other urchins of his station would be apt to do.

But Vikhram did return, and in haste, to present Mr. Mukerjee with a tiffin, freshly prepared and still warm. And so began his service to the Victoria Book Palace.

In the weeks that followed, the renovations progressed apace. The many fissures on the façade were mended, the repairs masked by two fresh coats of paint. Broken windows were replaced and shined to a pristine brilliance, so that daylight once again penetrated the long-dimmed quarters. The tarnished sign above the entry, informing customers of the miles of volumes to be found within, was re-stenciled with lettering identical to that in the picture book, and lights installed to illuminate it in the evening. Even the once-expensive stone floor that lay cracked and defeated was replaced with burnished teakwood, conveyed obstinately from neighboring Karnataka on shaky ox-carts by six forlorn and underpaid men. Steadily, Mr. Mukerjee's vision of a truly reputable establishment, a place befitting a sophisticated Western clientele, began to take shape. His mood and his demeanor improved appreciably, coincident with the work's advancement and despite the rapid depletion of his reserves.

Vikhram continued to bring meals to the nervous proprietor, but soon began, gradually, almost imperceptibly to undertake additional chores, to render himself quite indispensable to the progress of the project. He swept clean the litter left behind by the workers each evening. Fearless, he dispensed with a swarm of mice that had infested the basement and that frustrated and tormented the laborers. He steadied ladders, sanded wood planks, made huge quantities of tea for the men, ran to the ironmonger's shop for a missing instrument or spike. He was rewarded, infrequently, with derisory tips, barely enough to keep himself fed, but he had secured for himself two great prizes: a proper bed in the shop's storeroom on which to sleep, and unfettered access to the radio and to his distant comrades at the BBC. He considered himself among the most fortunate of men. Even greater prizes, and quite unexpected, were soon to follow.

* *

When, at an early age, most boys of Vikhram's rank left school, they would have benefited from only the most primitive instruction. They would have acquired not more than a rudimentary capacity to read, and only in Marathi, the predominant language of Bombay. Pressed early to find work, each was expected, however meagerly, either to contribute to the family's income or to make his own way. An education was not requisite and was not valued.

But unlike his classmates in the one-room, open-roofed structure that served as a makeshift school, Vikhram alone didn't begrudge study or think of his lessons as squandered time. Above all, he alone had learned to speak and to read a functional level of English. He pored diligently over the well-worn British grammar books, battling to conquer the sometimes bewildering rules and perplexing syntax. He carefully examined the frivolous articles and droll photo captions in his teacher's secondhand glamour magazines from London. He often asked her to help decrypt English-language billboard advertisements or to explain remarks between foreigners he had overheard in the city's markets and on its streets. Untiringly, he badgered his teacher to linger a while after each class and to converse with him in English. She was only too happy to do so, rare as it was for a pupil to show so keen an interest.

His tenacious efforts to study the language were to serve him well, even though at the age of twelve, like most of the other boys, he left behind formal education to find employment.

Work in the booming city for able-bodied children was not hard to find. Industrial tycoons and simple shop-keepers alike, principled or unscrupulous, all had long ago wagered that the city's inexhaustible supply of poor children, pressed into long hours at despicable wages, could provide the cheap, expendable labor on which their own advancement depended.

Vikhram briefly joined the first contingent of workers at the immense cement factory built almost overnight on the southern-most outskirts of the city. There he netted a small amount of rupees each week, until an altercation with another boy, the cause of which he could not recall, cost them both their place. He fared only marginally better at a sprawling textile mill, whose toxic chemical dyes burned Vikhram's skin and eyes, triggering an alarming bout of temporary blindness that meant the docking of his wages for medical attention, and then his discharge.

The mill's long-serving English doctor, who had seen too many such cases to delude himself otherwise, knew that the good-natured boy's dismissal was all but assured. Yet he also knew that Vikhram could speak and read English, and in an act of appreciable benevolence, arranged for him to be engaged as an errand boy in the household of an acquaintance, a minor British counselor official.

Though endless, his duties there were not particularly demanding. He was sent to deliver messages, procure various items for the household, collect the luggage of guests from Delhi or Calcutta at the railway terminus. Each of these missions allowed him to learn something new. He discovered how best to navigate the city's baffling network of backstreets. By learning to haggle in the markets, he understood how to save the officer money or, more often, to pocket the difference himself.

These tasks also allowed him to better his knowledge of English, and for the first time, to use this knowledge in a practical way. For the counselor required, and with patience instructed Vikhram to recognize a host of new English words and phrases in order to execute his duties. He was to note the chalkboard signs at the Club that announced timings for the week's bridge tournament or cricket match. In the upscale markets, he studied the labels on the official's favorite brands of British foodstuffs he was sent to purchase – a mustard's "double superfine compound" or, at special occasions, the custard powder that raved of its "traditional homemade taste." He supplied him every morning with English newspapers – *The Times of India* for the official, sanctioned view and *The Bombay Chronicle* for a rival one more sympathetic to the Indian national cause – in which he caught frequent sight of random English words, especially in the headlines and photo captions that dominated their front pages.

Each new brush with these imported words served as a portal to a world of discovery. Fleeting images of a life of privilege and difference. A life of action, of advantage, of opportunity and of consequence. He could not have spoken of it; he couldn't have explained, much less defended, his interest in the foreigner's tongue, which so many others had by then come to know as an instrument of tyranny. But as the radio also would later reveal, Vikhram knew that here was a kind of enlightenment, a revelation that his inspiration and his ambition need not be limited to the harsh circumstances he'd been so far dealt.

Yet, in his service to the government officer, these momentary glimpses into a more expansive truth were to prove only a pale suggestion of the banquet in store for him at the Victoria Book Palace. There, in the spectral glow of the shop's marquee, while in the late hours the Bazaar and the country beyond it favored sleep, Vikhram began first to survey, then to consume the treasures that lay so casually at his feet. The incalculable accumulation of English books, both new and aged, heaped upon each other in deliriously high mounds, were in the evening's quiet a bounty reserved only for him.

Reluctantly but deliberately, uncertain if the right was his or whether his limited abilities would allow it, he began to examine the hoard. Paying careful attention not to break the spines or otherwise to injure the precious objects in any way, he opened first the books that most caught his eye. He was drawn initially to picture books, travel guides, those works which naturally gave primacy to lavish illustrations and images over the often still impenetrable words. He found in them a universe unbounded by his limited experience, and in their lucid descriptions, painstakingly deciphered, he found license to conceive of another path for himself.

His confidence was fortified as the works of celebrated writers began to be serialized on the wireless, read out in lush, reassuring voices that guided him through the texts he found without difficulty in the shop. Studiously, he followed along with the reader, often scanning excitedly ahead on the page to work out first for himself how the words might be pronounced and what they might mean. Soon he picked up books written for children. Many were the titles that the city's English children and their opposite number in America would have recognized easily. He spent untold hours, weeks on end, untangling the impish exploits detailed in *The Tale of Peter Rabbit* and in *Alice's Adventures in Wonderland.* Myths and fables and epic legends of heroes and menacing creatures natural and supernatural occupied much of his time and his imagination. In their pages, he dreamed of adventures and of distant voyages, the dreams of every young man before him and of every one after him. He aspired to riches and romance and ecstasy, all the things that invariably inhabited the stories he read so zealously.

* *

As the months progressed, Vikhram grew impatient to share his treasures, convinced that they would only increase in value if they were not selfishly squirreled away. He knew that the other men toiling in the market hadn't had the luxury to acquire the skills to read the language as he could, but he knew too that the ease with which they spoke basic English, used it each day to interact with the Bazaar's many British customers, had equipped them well enough to follow loosely the broad contours of the stories, and to enjoy at least the spirit and the heart of the thrilling tales they told.

He found his opportunity on a blistering July afternoon, when the monsoon rains hastily drove everyone to take cover and he found himself in the shelter of the bookshop, in the company of a dozen or so waterlogged men from the neighboring shops and stalls. Confined by an ill-pleased Mr. Mukerjee to the shop's cellar until the rains relented, they proceeded to rib each other, as often they did, in order to pass the time. They maligned the girls who paid them no heed. They long debated and disputed the faculties of their favorite cricketers, none of whom the men had ever seen play.

Suddenly, Vikhram left the cellar, to return but a moment later with a tantalizing book in hand. It was entitled simply, *Peter and Wendy.* The volume, a valuable first edition, immediately captured the men's attention, bound as it was in sumptuous red leather with gold lettering and an extravagantly illustrated cover. It was quite unlike the frayed Marathi storybooks the men were used to seeing. Vikhram knew he had chosen well. Not least, he knew the story would resonate, for the tale of Peter's underground home and his gang of Lost Boys was a kind of peculiar proxy for the very scene in front of him, that of unclaimed boys lost in a Neverland of their own.

He began, unsteadily at first, to read aloud the magical story of a boy who refused to grow up. His voice was somewhat wobbly, for he feared the others might mock or disparage him, but their quick silence and attentiveness gave him the nerve to continue. Because the men plainly couldn't grasp much of the vocabulary, he peppered his reading with Marathi expressions, deviating often from the text with improvised embellishments and local idioms that made the stories both more comprehensible and more relevant. He read through the chapters with increasing emotion and conviction. He began subtly to vary his cadence and instinctively to replicate some of the mannerisms of the colorful characters he was unveiling, filling the frequent gaps where the men didn't understand the meaning of the foreign words with flamboyant, sometimes clownish gesturing.

The remarkable story unfolded swiftly – tales of ticking crocodiles and menacing pirates, of canons and mermaids and poison – to the supreme thrill of the men huddled together in the basement of the refit bookshop. They interrupted sporadically, to ask Vikhram to explain a dramatic passage or to repeat one. He obliged every time. And when the rains stopped and the men were called back to their duties as sweepers or teawallahs or cooks, they did so with great regret. For the telling of the story was not nearly complete. They implored Vikhram to continue the tale the next evening, and the evening after that, with at least the promise that their long, wearisome days could find a small recompense in the awe of his storytelling.

This Vikhram did, in the secrecy of the shop's cellar while its proprietor, at home for the evenings, remained quite unaware. He enchanted the men with account after account of Indian princes and foreign kings. Of poor men made prosperous by chance or by effort. Legends of exceptional bravery and tragic sagas of loss and of redemption. Though they would not have confessed it to each other, his careful listeners craved as well the tales of passion and of romance in which they could imagine themselves substituting for the lead character, now and again breaking up the proceedings with impromptu demonstrations of the valor and the glory being described.

This ritual varied little over time, save for one important aspect. Just as in Peter's story there were no lost girls – too clever were they to go astray – so the small crowd that assembled nightly in the Victoria Book Palace was exclusively male. To have it otherwise would not have suited the men's bravado or their bluster. This place, this shared experience served as an implicit reserve, a timely refuge from the very real troubles and burdens of the life immediately above. Troubles also of love, in which few had been successful and in which even fewer still would have dared to admit an interest. So when Sapna appeared, nervous and uneasy, seated on the darkened stairwell, a silent spectator of the rabble-rousing and carousing that customarily served as an antecedent to the evening's central affair, the men were more than a little displeased.

All but the evening's narrator. For even in the figure half-obscured on the stairs, Vikhram caught a rare and exhilarating flash of genuine beauty.

Sapna did not represent or aspire to the traditional or idealized codes for women in southern India. Her hair was neither long nor plaited, but cropped at shoulder length. She was not especially tall or slender; her skin was not luminous, but bronzed and flushed from hard work and a still early life of ceaseless activity. As she inched cautiously out of the shadows toward the pack of men, anxious to occupy a small, unnoticed place in the proceedings, to share in the marvel and amusement about which her brothers and her neighbors had told, Vikhram was struck by the force of her gaze. Her eyes were penetrating. Graceful, delicate eyes, curiously expressive of both sadness and of cheerfulness in equal measure. She radiated intelligence and compassion, and a humanity incongruous with her woeful surroundings.

Gathering her courage, she marched to the front of the room, past the crush of the men barely disguising their snickering, impervious to their juvenile invectives, to address Vikhram directly.

"I've been listening to your readings for several days. From the top of the stairs."

"Have you? Do you like them?" asked a thunderstruck Vikhram, certain of the answer, but less certain of how to approach this hazardous encounter.

"Well, yes, I like them very much," she replied. Then, hesitating for only a moment, reluctant to meet his stare, she added, "Though why do the men always seem to be rescuing the women in your stories? These women are all so weak and vulnerable. When we tell stories, my mother and sisters and I, it's usually the woman who's doing the rescuing!"

"I didn't write them," answered Vikhram feebly, like a discomfited schoolboy called to the front of his class by his headmaster, unwilling to answer for his trespass. "I only read them aloud. Besides, I think everyone else here likes them. Do you have better ones?"

Just as soon as he launched his question, he regretted it. Of course she would not have better stories to tell. She didn't have access to the resources he did of the bookshop, and likely she didn't know how to read, or to read well. He was ashamed by the discomfort he must have caused her, and uncertain about how to proceed. But Sapna remained unmistakably good-humored, delighted as she was by then to have embedded herself in the evening's activities, and to have so clearly captured the attention of this alluring young man who had become the object of her own growing interest.

"Well, no, of course not, although maybe you can bring along more stories with strong women next time."

At this, Vikhram was enormously relieved. Not simply because he appeared to have extricated himself from the embarrassment of his gaffe, but because he knew then that there was to be a next time. He knew that this woman, who appeared as if from nowhere, who filled him instantly with a rapture he had not before known, would become an integral part of the readings, and perhaps even an integral part of his future. He held a chair for her in the front, silencing the boorish commentary with the unquestioned authority he had established, and barreled excitedly through the next chapter of his book as if nothing had changed. But he knew, or he hoped, that everything had changed.

As the weeks and months progressed, as he brought to the readings the chronicles of Cleopatra and Pocahontas and the bookshop's own namesake, Queen Victoria, the bond between Vikhram and Sapna only strengthened. She waited for him every evening after the readings as he locked the windows and doors of the shop, and they walked together through the streets of the city, not counting the hours. Their unflagging conversation was every bit as rambling, and every bit as romantic, as every new couple's ever was. They stayed generally aloof of others, jealously indisposed to share their fast maturing union. Neither had great prospects, and neither had grand designs, but they found in each other's company a reprieve from the bustles and stresses of a hard life, a joyfulness and a consolation that neither had thought within their reach.

* *

Their marriage was not so much celebrated as it was acknowledged, since neither had the means for even a modest ceremony. Nor indeed the appetite for one. Sapna's sizeable family in particular was relieved to dispense with the rituals and public ceremonials, for even within a scheduled caste that daily endured indignity, to have borne a child out of wedlock brought dishonor to the line. And Vikhram and Sapna had by then borne not one, but two children. Children who were developing strong and cheerful, nurtured in a household filled with affection and hospitality, as yet innocent of their shunned status and the shame their very existence engendered. Vikhram did not see in his children this onus of shame, nor did he mind the financial austerity that their simple but constant needs provoked. He saw in them the abundant opportunities he had seen for himself, and which doggedly, despite his unshakable poverty, he endeavored to imagine for himself still.

Yet even for enterprising, determined men like Vikhram, the always inadequate opportunities for advancement had become even more so as the war in Europe expanded and the Crown's losses mounted. As the conflict reached its climax, these opportunities virtually vanished. Tensions in the Raj between His Majesty's civil servants and the local men and women who served them had escalated irreparably. Barricaded behind their high walls, fearful of losing their comfortable advantages, many of the British holdouts in Bombay had become more noticeably guarded and mistrustful of the locals, and Vikhram sensed he was being treated more regularly with antipathy. The few remaining customers of the Victoria Book Palace, to whom throughout these six years Vikhram had provided loyal service, of late administered only derision, when they deigned to acknowledge him at all. When, at the height of the war, Mr. Mukerjee's foreign bankers called in their loan, despite the near certainty of the liquidation and bankruptcy it would incite, Vikhram's growing resentment of the English, for whom he had once held only the highest esteem, had been transformed into outright animus. With a sorrowful heart for all that it had meant to him, for all the vistas it had opened, he silenced the British radio broadcasts with his own hand, tuning the dilapidated wireless instead into the lackluster transmissions of All India Radio from Delhi.

Even attendance at his now less-frequent readings had begun to dwindle. Many of the men of the Nayā Bazaar who once clamored to hear his riveting tales had long since left to join the British tank and airborne forces in the East and North African campaigns, countless of whom would not return. Untold others had left to join the growing armed opposition to the foreign presence in India.

Of those who remained, the stories roused them still, set them dreaming of glory and conquest and fortune. A fortune they were being promised that late August afternoon, not hazily in the rarified pages of English literature, but in person by the impressive stranger in an immaculate linen suit and shiny black shoes, the dashing representative of the Gulf Petroleum Company.

CHAPTER 3 • तीन

The assistant curator who had arrived that morning from the Victoria & Albert Museum, a pernickety and tedious man, paused for several minutes in front of the elaborate display cabinet so as to examine more carefully the Tang Dynasty figurine on its top shelf. He had already been through the entire house once, combing through cupboards and half-open boxes, meticulously examining jars and bowls of all sorts. He had penciled copious observations in the tiny black notepad he kept close to his chest as if it were itself a precious artifact. By then he had identified five or six pieces of interest, objects the institution might consider welcoming into its renowned collection, but he wasn't an expert on Chinese porcelain, he couldn't assess with certainty the quality or the importance of the piece, and so preferred to have it appraised by a specialist.

But Sebastian Reynolds couldn't afford to wait. He required an immediate verdict. The haulers were to come at week's end, and he would need to decide before then where to dispatch every item in the house. A very small number of articles, particularly those of sentimental value, would be sent ahead to Delhi, in time to meet his arrival in several weeks' time. He would need only a small number of items for the train journey itself, a trunk or two of cloth-

ing and an ample selection of books. He had expended a
vast amount of energy these previous few days agonizing
over the choice of books from his sizable library to take on
board, uncertain whether he would be able to find additional provisions along the way. Other objects, including
the extensive furniture and pictures, he would share out as
gifts to his most loyal editors and assistants, tokens of his
appreciation for their long, dedicated service to his newspapers. The rest then would be left to the museum, for
visitors to admire and to appreciate.

The V&A was a natural beneficiary. At the height
of his success Sebastian had become a patron, invited to
join some of London's foremost citizens on its Board of
Trustees. His name had been put forward not because of
any particular competencies or expertise. He didn't bring
access or status to the institution that it couldn't otherwise
have obtained. What he did bring was considerable wealth,
and a willingness to shower the museum with his generosity, to help endow it against the financial uncertainties of
the time, when too many great British families had been
ruined and their great prosperity had been lost. In return,
Sebastian had hoped to fortify his determined attempts to
enter reputable society, to erase from the public's mind the
enduring association it held between his name and scandal.

In this he had not been successful. He found he was
tolerated, suffered, but not embraced. The respectable,
prideful men of the Board eschewed him, fearing they
might somehow also be tainted with outrage. They avoided
taking the seat next to him at meetings, made unconvinc-
ing excuses to ignore him at exhibition openings and lec-
tures by visiting scholars.

Sebastian nevertheless found other advantages in his
affiliation with the museum, not least in the unhindered

access it granted him to the collections. These past few months, as steadily he began to distance himself from the daily functioning of his business, he had come to spend more and more time wandering the galleries. Untroubled hours lost in lonely meditation or in daydream. He knew by heart the Chinese and Japanese collections that had always appealed to his simple aesthetic, the delicate high-fired earthenware whose traces of amber and paint many centuries old spoke to him of a respect for tradition that defied modern, hurried concepts of time. He cherished too the timeless, epic works in the long hall of British sculpture, plaques and busts whose solid forms of perfectly chiseled Roman stone would stand forever, not in the majestic houses and churches of England for which they were commissioned, but here in the museum, for which they were inescapably destined. Most of all, he was drawn repeatedly to the neo-classical monument by a long-forgotten Scottish artist, a funeral tribute to the early departed Countess Emily of Winchilsea and Nottingham, whose grieving husband had directed such sorrowful words to be inscribed in the marble:

Long since my heart has been breaking
Its pain is past
A time has been set to its aching
Peace comes at last.

These words had been written exactly one century earlier, but Sebastian felt as if their affecting pathos and their grief were his. For Sebastian also, the pain of his heartbreak had passed, though the wound had never quite healed.

Present affairs, however, provided no time for such wistfulness or nostalgia. There were too many plodding, practical matters to attend to – accounts to settle, letters to write, myriad arrangements to be made. Though he would not set off for another week, he had decided to shut up the house early, and to retire to an austere bedroom on the top floor normally reserved for domestics. His house-keeper Mrs. Collins had urged him to make his final week in England more agreeable, to take for instance a suite at Claridge's Hotel where he could be looked after with the appropriate consideration, but he preferred the severity of this almost empty space, very much a reminder of the nota-bly more humble house in the London of his youth. An effortless, happy youth, occupied by the pursuit of simple pleasures and in somewhat naive anticipation of a lifetime of the same.

He had already let the servants go, dismissing those longest in his employ with regret but with a handsome sum and a robust letter of reference that would allow each of them easily enough to find another post. Only Mrs. Collins remained, to prepare his meals, run his bath and tidy the growing disorder. Ordinarily detached in the best traditions of English service, even she had begun to let her emotion show. She had been for many years the only abiding, silent witness to his sorrows, and she genuinely feared the risks to him presented by such an excessive undertaking in such an unfamiliar land. Like his solicitor, exceedingly cautious by temperament and by training, she had unsuccessfully encouraged him not to sell the house, but only to shutter it, an indemnity against the possibility that conditions in India were not as he expected or would not be to his liking.

And this was undoubtedly possible. At the age of fifty, Sebastian would be undertaking his first real adventure. There had been the two years of study at Cambridge, and an unfortunate weekend visit to Cornwall. His professional responsibilities had taken him several times to Birmingham and to Manchester, excursions he made with little appetite and with some impatience. Otherwise, he never had the opportunity, nor sought one, even to leave the capital city.

But India, he reckoned, would not be as dire as so many would have him believe. The heat in the long summer months would unquestionably be a trial. So would the pervasive, acute mendicancy for which he was instructed one could not be adequately prepared. He might lament the loss of so many of the comforts he had come to take for granted, but these comforts, which had served to soothe and to console him, he had not sought. His prosperity had been an outcome of his labors, not an object of them.

India, he was convinced, had surely become a vibrant, optimistic place, mobilized by its hard-won independence secured not one year before. Even if it were not, it could not be a lonelier place than was his England.

Over the course of an eminent career, he had made the acquaintance of many people. A few had been gracious and welcoming enough, and he had for some time taken them into his narrow confidence. Most, however, would show themselves to be scroungers, scavengers feeding on his power and on his influence for some advancement or advantage. Fewer still had been willing to disbelieve or to overlook the gossip and the rumor that preceded him always. He had been deceived often enough for it to have soured irrevocably his sympathy for others. Loneliness had become its own comfort, a callous luxury he began purposefully to seek.

On the frequent, ambling walks Sebastian made these final days between his solicitor's offices, his own office and his mostly-bare house, he had time to ruminate at length on the years of solitude that in his youth he could not have conceived would be his. He thought of how great was the chasm between what he had wished and expected for himself – a life replete with friendship, with familiarity, with love – and the melancholic, solitary one he had come to know. Like the city of London itself, alive with renewal after the trauma and wreckage of war, this undertaking would be a kind of renaissance for him, too. He would start again a life in India. A life abounding with a new sense of purpose and expectation. With hope. With her.

CHAPTER 4 • चार

Even if the furnishings were somewhat outdated and much too prim for such an unassuming young man, Sebastian had chosen these new rooms in the college because they opened onto a lesser courtyard, and so he imagined they would be quieter than his previous accommodations. Without doubt the lodgings he had been given in his first two years at Cambridge were charming. Those rooms had provided him with many conveniences and his first real taste of independence. With their superb appointments and substantial volume, they were among the finest quarters available to a student of such limited funds. But their large, generous windows gave onto the only street that served the town's central market. The commotion and the bustle that came with such a position, notably at day's end when so many were rushing to satisfy their daily requirements, served only as frequent distractions for someone still so easily prone to them.

These new rooms, however, would hardly prove any better. The courtyard was undoubtedly more secluded. Its single access through a close arch of chipped red stone provided tardy students no shortcut to the dining hall or library, and unlike the many inspired buildings at Pembroke College, its sturdy but unimaginative architecture drew no unsolicited visitors. Yet what he hadn't anticipated was that its very seclusion also provided an ideal setting for every brand of assignation, particularly after dark, when the dons had retired to their ablutions and their secrets, and a hush had descended broadly over the rest of the campus. From his window Sebastian was soon witness to a seemingly endless stream of unwelcome and often illicit activity. Flirtations with attractive, eager girls from town. Good-humored scuffles and outright brawls between jealous, argumentative rivals. Rowdy conferences of ambiguous intent.

Still in only the second week of the new Michaelmas term, there was even more of a tumult than was usual for such a gentle autumn night. Many of the other students had not yet shaken off the merriment and abandon of their blithe summer holidays, and brought to the courtyard an infuriating degree of revelry and near debauchery, abetted by plentiful drink, as if they were still frolicking untroubled and unsupervised on the Continent or in the private, manicured gardens of their sublime country houses.

The unrelenting racket had disturbed his already volatile slumber, something that had always come more easily to others than it had to Sebastian. Even as a boy, the night had brought agitation, as he drifted in the frozen hours before sleep toward a vivid replaying of the events of the day just concluding, and intense anticipation of the one to come. This evening, with the interminable fracas and fuss being played out just below his window, he was particularly bothered. For his convulsive night was possessed also with the question as to whether tomorrow would be the day he would at last manage to ask Olivia for her hand.

Surrendering to the disturbances, and defying his

acute longing for rest, Sebastian attacked the morning at daybreak. He had resolved to approach this day just as faithfully as he had done each of the previous two, but hoping that this time his nerve would not again fail him. He was determined to win Olivia's consent, and in preparing for the day mechanically and with attention to every detail, he sought to distract and to steel himself against a lingering doubt that, as unlikely as it was, she might still find reason to decline his proposal.

The routine he was to undertake was a rigorous and a lengthy one. After a light breakfast, all his fragile nerves could bear, he would visit the barber for a close shave. Hurriedly making his way home, he would buy a fresh carnation in the waking market to place later in his lapel, as was the fashion of the day, hoping it would not end up wilting on his armoire as had those he bought the two previous mornings. Returning to his lodgings, he would take a brisk bath, press his best cotton suit and a freshly laundered shirt, choose a stylish and bold tie that might telegraph a false message of poise and composure. He would then stare intently into the antique mirror above the mantelpiece and practice aloud the lines and the expressions he had so often rehearsed. Finally, he polished again the simple ring his mother had that summer helped him choose, placing it in the pocket of his vest but inspecting it nervously throughout the long day to sustain himself.

He would not meet Olivia, in front of the Fitzwilliam Museum, until early in the evening. He wasn't interested in the exhibits, just as he had to feign interest in the botanic gardens the day before during their lingering tour of the lake and glasshouses. He would have been unable to concentrate on the Dutch paintings or the medieval manuscripts. It was, however, a practical and convenient place in which to meet, and as he knew the collections well, the museum was somewhere he could impress and charm her.

* *

Olivia was unquestionably the most exhilarating woman Sebastian had ever known, and quite unlike the other women of privilege he had met since coming up to the university. Too young during the war to join the nursing corps and not content to sit at home knitting socks for soldiers in the trenches, she had pleaded with her parents, minor English nobility, to let her study at Girton, one of the only colleges to which women were admitted. Sebastian had noticed her on several occasions during his first months at the university, scrutinizing *The Times* at the café opposite the library, cycling headlong down the uneven cobblestone path in front of Pembroke, haggling lightheartedly or conceivably flirting with the fruit-seller in the market. She exuded an intoxicating blend of conventional femininity, conspicuous self-possession and irresistible charm. More than a little intimidated, he hadn't been bold enough to approach her.

Her opinions on politics and on topics of the day were strong, cogent and well-informed, delivered respectfully but with the unusual force of her convictions. She had established herself as one of the few women who regularly attended, and took an active part in, the proceedings of the Student Union. It was there, in the drab meeting hall of the Union, that they had first met, following a raucous debate entitled, "This House Supports the Treaty of Versailles." Sebastian, as always well prepared and confident in his delivery, had argued strenuously against the established British position in the negotiations. He was overwhelmingly, and not surprisingly, outvoted by the congregation, though not before Olivia bravely stood to support his view, and added her own eloquent, if equally unpopular statement. Their relationship was forged in shared opposition to orthodox thinking, in an instantaneous, mutual understanding.

Olivia's father, Lord Granville, a shrewd and highly-accomplished peer, had this summer privately given his approval for the marriage, despite Sebastian's lack of title and utter want of income. He acceded to the request, and willingly so, having made discreet inquiries of Sebastian's Director of Studies, through colleagues at his London club and in person during one of his frequent visits to his daughter. He was assured that the young man was as gifted a student as the Director had known, hard-working and driven, principled, appreciated by both his fellow students and by the faculty. With energy and industry he was destined for a successful career in the City or in government service. Perhaps a seat in Parliament and even a place at the Cabinet table, if providence were to allow the Liberal Party to remain in power until his maturity. Lord Granville knew as well, of course, that with two older children, his line was already well assured. Not least, and grudgingly sympathetic to what he considered to be his wife's somewhat overwrought romantic tendencies, the result of too much idle chatter and dreamy literature, he knew that his youngest daughter was very much in love.

In the two years since the initiation of their courtship, the couple was seldom to be seen apart. Together they marveled in what the other was studying, challenged and supported their respective efforts, shared silent and talkative hours alike reveling in each other's company. They explored the inimitable history and architecture of the campus, lazily took meals in the gardens or in town, made secretive weekend escapes into London for shopping and forbidden amusements. Having early been introduced and embraced by each other's family, they rejoiced in being able to entertain their parents during weekend and end-of-term visits, and savored the invitation to visit each other's home during the long summer months. Their blatant exclusivity had become a minor source of annoyance to their classmates, laced undoubtedly with a touch of jealousy, but this did not discourage them, it only made their connection stronger.

In the space of these two wondrous years, they had become more than companions. They had steadily but indisputably become what each other had always craved most. For Sebastian, he saw in Olivia the very picture of tenderness and refinement, a woman with whom he could share his dreams and, with her by his side, would be all the better placed to achieve them. Olivia understood and shared in those dreams. Not least, she found in Sebastian an enthralling, charming escape from the conformist and stuffy world her parents inhabited, and for which until she met him she had been preordained.

Still very much youthful in attitude and experience, neither was practiced in the art of passion, knowing only of such things from the books they had read and from the boastful, mostly invented yarns they had been told by friends. Though neither was brave enough to speak of it openly, each was certain that theirs would be a jubilant life together of pleasure and of cheer.

Sebastian trusted that this euphoric life might begin in earnest this very evening, when at last he would declare his intentions. Yet with his morning regimen concluded, he had still the daunting outlook of a full day ahead of him, an eventful one filled with study and with numerous other responsibilities that separated him from his paramount commission. He decided he would confront the day in manageable increments, and confine the fearsome idea of his proposal until closer to the appointed hour, although he continued absentmindedly all morning to fiddle with the polished ring still burning in his pocket.

As this was a Friday, he had two principal obligations. The first was to complete his assignment for the new term's first edition of *The Cambridge Ledger*, the weekly student newspaper for which he had been writing since virtually his arrival at the university. As the British athletics team had done exceedingly well that summer at the Olympic Games in Antwerp, Sebastian had been asked to write a profile of the gold medal winning champions, two of whom were recent graduates of the university and who were to be invited back the following week by the Chancellor as honored guests. Like most of his fellow students, Sebastian had that August followed with great interest the reports in the London newspapers of the drama and performance of these sporting heroes. He had become familiar with an entirely new vocabulary – free relay, steeplechase, tug of war, bantamweight, single sculls and Eights. All of these terms told of skills and of competitions about which he knew very little. Still, these men had instantly achieved momentous popular acclaim. They had been received at the Palace by King George and Queen Mary. Sebastian was intrigued not only by the men's singular achievements, but by the ability of the newspapers to manufacture this instant celebrity, to shape so immediately the public's perception of events so distant. He aimed to find a new, a different way to tell their stories that could likewise grip the attention of his readers.

His other main undertaking for the day was to prepare for his weekly literature seminar, and in particular to complete the Latin essay he had been asked to recite that afternoon to his classmates. These seminars formed the core of his instruction at the university, and were sought after highly. His colleagues, almost all cut from the type of glittering cloth of money and private schooling of which he had been deprived, were among the most able and clever at Cambridge, and his association with their number served well his own reputation. All shared a keen interest in literature and in the power of the written word to provoke and to thrill. Together for close on two years, they had spent scores of hours poring through the traditional canon, working to clutch the subtle use of phrases that had startled and regaled so many generations of students before them. They made close readings of the classical texts, dissected their artful allegories, surveyed the origins of words in ancient and modern languages. They conferred and debated as to why certain knotty phrases had been chosen when others more simple might have been considered. They pondered the immeasurable influence these texts had made on liberal humanism and on the utilitarian philosophy so prevalent and so popular.

Sebastian treasured these sessions. He drew inspiration from the other students, most if not all of whom, though unmistakably superior in class and background, had long since accepted him as an equal. He treasured too the interaction with Professor Harkins, as idiosyncratic and eccentric an instructor as the university could plausibly offer, whose warmth and consideration, and especially whose intemperate devotion to the subject matter, were legend.

Sebastian had known Professor Harkins well before even envisaging his own admission to the university, something that for a boy of his circumstances was not to be assumed or even contemplated. As a schoolboy, he had entered a national writing contest on modern literature and the arts. Although he did not that year take home first or even second prize, and his effort did not win him the bursary to a local sixth form college as he had hoped, his inventive composition, with its elegant use of metaphor and its lush imagery, stood out nonetheless, and was recognized with a special mention.

It was noticed most of all by Professor Harkins, who led the jury that selected the winners, and whose presence at the awards ceremony at London's Royal Society of Literature lent the event an even greater air of gravitas. His scruffy appearance – unshaven beard, tousled hair, trousers and jacket that appeared locked in a quarrel with each other – were all very unconventional and might have expressly been designed to upset the conservative audience. It couldn't help but delight Sebastian.

After well-received remarks, in which the professor explored themes of classical texts and made unexpected and intriguing parallels to contemporary work, Sebastian, not the least put off by the flattering crowd, marched directly to the front of the mob and proceeded to unleash question after question about what he had just heard, what he had most recently read, and what he was thinking next of writing. The professor, who had so admired the student's submission, gave this precocious boy much of his attention.

On his return to Cambridge, the professor invited Sebastian to pursue a correspondence, a gift that would only encourage the student's desire for study and feed his limitless opinion of this learned man. In return, Professor Harkins, who had come to see in Sebastian the raw passion for knowledge he had once known in his own youth, had a hand in promoting the young man's application and bursary to the Faculty of Arts. He took special pride in welcoming Sebastian to his seminar, to take his rightful place among the brightest of his students.

These seminars took place in the professor's chambers, rooms that teemed with strange curios. Souvenirs of expeditions to unnamed lands and gifts from many unnamed admirers. Often the students were interrupted by the professor's striking wife, who came to offer them chocolate biscuits and black tea, but who was mostly interested in meddling. These rooms seemed to Sebastian more like a home than a hall of study. He felt entirely gratified here, having found in these beguiling pursuits, surrounded by other discerning, capable men, an early idea of the intellectual enterprises for which he was fated.

* *

He rushed that afternoon to finish his Latin essay. It was a revised version of the composition he had prepared for his application to Cambridge in the winter of 1917, "*Quam terribilis est haec hora,*" which he had loosely translated for his admiring parents as "How fearful is this hour." He had written it when the Allied victory was still anything but assured, and spoke with eloquence of the fear and trepidation of the men of his generation. A fear that, like the many promising men whose lives had been cut short by their service to the nation, they might also be called to such forfeit. He wrote of the uncertainty with which he and others were confronted, whether they would be able to enjoy the advantages and opportunities of study to which they so aspired, or whether they might be cut down before their time. It was in large measure on the strength of this poignant work that Sebastian's place at the university had been assured.

Having made the definitive revisions just as the bell in the courtyard rang a quarter to three, he quickly gathered his papers and scrambled across the immaculately trimmed grounds to Professor Harkins' chambers, impatient to deliver a recitation he knew could not fail to impress. He did so with even more enthusiasm, as he knew that this was the only commitment still separating him from his approaching, decisive meeting with Olivia.

Arriving a few minutes late for the start of the seminar, Sebastian was not met at the door by his classmates, as was so often the case. Often they would converse lazily for a few moments in the entry until all had assembled, talking of the week's assignments and of the other more mundane matters that monopolized the life of the student, before proceeding as one into the main room. There Professor Harkins would arrive, often winded and disheveled, sometimes apparently mid-way through a sentence he had begun in the hall to no one in particular.

Sebastian casually hung his flimsy overcoat on the rack, and observed that the rest of the wooden pegs were already in use. The other students had as usual all arrived on time, and had proceeded to the session before him. He glanced at the gaudy clock above the fireplace, and confirmed his tardiness.

Opening the main door, Sebastian saw immediately that each of the others had taken his habitual place. The rigid, battered chairs had been arranged, unfailingly, in the same familiar constellation. So too the drapes were but half-drawn, as was the custom, either to keep out the reflexive, prying eyes of onlookers or, more likely, to keep the students' occasionally fleeting attention squarely on the subject at hand. Curiously, tea had not been prepared, much to Sebastian's chagrin, as the affairs of the day had left him insufficient time to take a proper lunch. Even more improbably, not one of the students had a book or text open to make his usual final, rabid preparations before the seminar began.

Most disquieting, as he made his way toward the empty chair that was routinely his, Sebastian noted that none of the students would directly meet his stare. They appeared intent on taking no notice of him altogether. Such a churlish, hostile reception was a stunning, unwelcome surprise to him.

Before he could question any of the students on the meaning of this peculiar treatment, Professor Harkins quietly entered the room, and asked in an almost inaudible voice to speak in confidence with Sebastian in his private office.

When they had arrived into the office, and the door was shut behind them, the Professor's customarily affable countenance had altered. He had taken on the stern, uneasy look generally reserved for a student's dim answer to a straightforward question, or as a piqued sign to his intrusive wife to withdraw.

"I'm afraid, son," whispered the Professor, in a sober tone and with a look of decided discomfort, "you won't be able to attend the session this afternoon."

"Why ever not?" asked a bemused Sebastian. "I've done the week's readings, and I've prepared my composition just as you asked. I think you'll be well pleased with the revisions I've made. I've taken the liberty of re-drawing the main argument in a more modern . . ."

But the Professor cut him off with a curt wave of his hand before he could finish the sentence.

"I'm not interested in your work just at the moment, Sebastian. I'm interested in your conduct, and in your character."

"In my conduct, sir? With respect, Professor, have I done something to offend you?"

Stepping back a few paces, scratching awkwardly with his finger at the burnt residual tobacco in his pipe and taking an exaggerated deep breath, the Professor continued gravely.

"It is not I who is offended, young man. It is the standards of this university that have been offended. Standards that have built the matchless reputation of this institution over centuries, and that none of us can afford to have blemished by the vile incident in which I am taken to understand you have been involved."

Sebastian was very much taken aback, quite unrehearsed for the episode swiftly unfolding, and entirely unprepared to respond.

"Sir, I assure you, there has been some mistake," he said. "Of what am I to be accused?"

"Don't be impertinent with me, unless you want to add insubordination to the list of your crimes."

"Impertinent?" countered Sebastian, in a tone of voice that belied both irritation and alarm. "I'm certain I don't know what you mean."

He paused to measure the effect his aggressive attitude might have on the professor. He saw at once it had none.

"Please, sir, tell me, what is the supposed offense in question?"

"Nonsense, I am not amused by this game of feigned ignorance," Professor Harkins said with clear annoyance. "You have been denounced not by one, but by several of your fellow students."

With that, the Professor began to catalogue, in specific and graphic terms, the offenses for which Sebastian was to be charged. He delivered uncomfortable details that made both men blush, details that must have been a great deal more difficult to say aloud than they were to contemplate in private. Transgressions of a scurrilous nature that would shock polite society, and would shock even many whom society had long since rejected.

Sebastian could not help but immediately appreciate the gravity and the magnitude of the allegations. He was dumbfounded, aghast. And utterly speechless. As he flew through a mass of disordered thoughts, all in conflict, all in disarray, he found he could bring himself neither mournfully to acknowledge the accusations, nor emphatically to refute them. He had no words at all. He tried to gather his shattered wits, struggling to settle on a suitable course of action, a manner in which to respond that would end this frightful scene as rapidly as it had begun. In vain.

"The Disciplinary Council will meet shortly to discuss your case," continued Professor Harkins, "and to consider possible sanctions. I needn't tell you, if they are not pleased, if you can't bring yourself to account for your involvement in this incident, then you risk being sent down."

"Will you . . . help me?" Sebastian managed to murmur, rattled by his own question and the obvious fragility it betrayed.

"My only charge is a simple one, to inform you that you are to report post-haste to the Dean's office where the Council is meeting. They require your presence immediately."

"Professor, I'm sure this misunderstanding can be explained. Will you come with me to see the Council?" asked Sebastian despairingly, with a look of mounting panic dominating his features.

"I cannot. This is something you alone have done, and the consequences of which you alone must confront. Now please go, I have a seminar to conduct."

Professor Harkins retired into the antechamber, shutting the door firmly behind him and against the disconsolate expression that had come to govern Sebastian's face. Behind the closed door, however, away from the glare of Sebastian and of the other students burning to learn of what had just transpired, the Professor stumbled slightly, overtaken by emotion, and by his concern for this young man so full of promise and for whom he had developed such a genuine fondness.

Over the years of their acquaintance he had seen Sebastian mature, deftly guiding him from a raw, scattered intellectual innocence into a confident embrace of serious scholarship. He had invested heavily in the schoolboy's progress, drawing a path for him that would reveal unimagined insights. In so doing, the eager student reopened the professor's own eyes to the wonder and spectacle that teaching had once promised him, and could promise him still. A wonder that, with the perpetual tedium of his career, had lately begun to wane.

To even imagine Sebastian's fall from grace, to contemplate his brutal exclusion from this hallowed place, was too painful to consider. Yet despite the profound attachment he had to his student, the care he had come to develop for his welfare and for his success, Professor Harkins knew he was impotent. He knew by heart the rules that had long since been laid down. That the dons would neither expect nor tolerate his intervention. He knew as well that the boundaries he had always set between himself and his pupils, boundaries that spoke of a genuine but mostly impersonal affection, that frowned on personal entanglements that could distract from study and compromise his impartial guidance, he could today only regret.

* *

Sebastian left the Professor's chambers entirely shaken at these repellent events. Neglecting his overcoat and books, he staggered out into the quadrangle as if cast out to sea, propelled by a force that was no longer his own, driven to move himself speedily away from this torrid scene. He began to tremble, to shudder against the faint wind, though the air was not cool. He envied the life of the university around him that continued unabated and unconcerned by his affliction. The minutes passed without notice and without incident, though how many he would have been incapable of telling. He knew only that every minute that elapsed drew him closer to the Council, and to the terrible possibilities of such an encounter.

Uneasily, he made his way across several colleges to the Dean's imposing offices. Twice before he had been invited to meet this learned man, the first time to be awarded a commendation for his student journalism, the second as part of a hand-picked delegation representing the student body put together, rather expeditiously, to meet the Earl of Balfour, the university's new Chancellor. On both occasions, he found the Dean to be formidable yet fair, someone Sebastian presumed would be amenable to reason.

Arriving almost breathless on the second floor that housed the Dean's offices, he was not received immediately, as he had expected and as Professor Harkins had led him to believe. Rather, he was commanded by the Dean's private secretary to wait in the dimly lit hall until the administrator was ready to receive him. Sebastian soon understood that the Council had been convened already, surely with his case the main item on what he supposed was a crowded agenda.

From the hard bench where he took his seat, he had a clear line of sight to the Council's meeting. Repeatedly, as the doddering secretary struggled to open the wide doors, to bring in tea or chaotic piles of papers, he stole a hint of anger in the men. He saw a podgy, formally dressed man bang his fist with authority, and another rise in a fury.

Shaky and agitated, Sebastian sat patiently in the hall, desperate to end this deferment and to be called into the inquest, or at least to be shown some sign of humanity from the indifferent secretary. Neither was forthcoming. He sought frantically for ways to assuage the mounting apprehension as best he could. He studied the long row of portraits of the Dean and of his predecessors, men who seemed in these representations to be competing in a show of solemnity. Generations of men who had risen to the height of their profession, uniquely talented men fêted for their erudition and ennobled by the monarch, and who had since been consigned to oblivion. The portrait of the current monarch was also displayed prominently, the definitive, official portrayal of the king in all his preposterous military glory, flush with splashy medals he had awarded himself, bulging gold epaulettes and diamond crosses presented by subjugated peoples affecting gratitude for the protection and advantages his Empire afforded. Sebastian studied as well the threadbare Persian rugs that littered the floor, the patterns of which were irregular but repetitive, as if they sprung from a complex mathematical formula or formed a puzzle to be solved.

None of this kept from his mind the disconcerting, still-vivid images of the episode with Professor Harkins.

Nor did it serve to prepare him any better for the difficult interview that was shortly to come. As if fighting an invisible enemy, Sebastian didn't know where or how to prepare the attack, or the defense, for that interview. He thought of the men in the trenches, the men he had evoked in his essay that had confronted such fearful hours, and thought that this too was as fearful an hour as ever he had known.

He began to imagine the lecture that, as the head of the Council, the Dean would be required to make. The show of authority, of scorn that was his right and his responsibility. He would preach in almost religious tones of morality, the kind of sermon to which Sebastian and his friends were weekly subject at High Table, and for which afterward they would mock the speaker for his hypocrisy and for his bombastic delivery. Empty phrases about the grand traditions and principles that underscore this noble place, the primacy of Christian values and proper virtue, what is right and, more frequently, what is wrong. The Dean would surely call on the memory of the sainted men recently fallen in battle, exemplars of probity and honor, lost in a distant fight that did not interest or affect these often insincere, sheltered dons.

Sebastian was transformed by these accidental thoughts. No longer was he confined to this stifling corridor in this soulless building. He was floating, high above this cold, trivial secretary, above these inconsequent men, above himself. Briefly he would hover, then he would soar away, far away to somewhere more convivial, more safe. He knew then that a confrontation, that a plea, was futile. It would be impossible, unthinkable that even a strong man could recover from such ignominious accusations. And he wasn't a strong man. He had understood that, whether false or accurate, the university would be obliged to dispense –

heartlessly and instantly before the contagion could spread – with anyone or anything that could bring even the suggestion of scandal to its hard-won reputation. Defending himself was useless. His guilt or his innocence was immaterial.

So Sebastian rose and began to retreat down the long, suffocating hallway, past the file of baleful portraits, past the detached assistant and the hypnotic carpets, not looking back. Calmly, he descended the central staircase, and in a moment he had left the Dean's offices behind.

As the dusk began to unveil its weighty cloak on the university, he ambled without direction and without purpose, lost in reflection, but in the evening air and open spaces, the detachment with which he had left the Council's chambers began to fail him. It jarred disturbingly with the ineluctable knowledge that his fate was being disputed. The boundless hopes of his family, who had denied themselves so much in order to see Sebastian succeed where none before him had, these hopes lay unsteadily in the balance. Those he had for himself, notions of a brighter tomorrow to which Cambridge had granted him certain access, would be crushed if he were to be sent down. His name and this vile incident would forever be linked as one.

And then there was Olivia. Her family, the very embodiment of convention and cautious pride, would hardly accept the discredit and dishonor that such an association would engender. As readily as Lord Granville had agreed to the alliance, so too would he call off the wedding before even it had formally been proposed. Sebastian would return the ring, still sheltered carefully in his pocket. Or possibly, in a more reckless and aberrantly melodramatic display, he would throw it into the River Cam.

At the very depths of his hopelessness, despairing of the reaction of so traditionalist a family as Olivia's, suddenly Sebastian came to understand something vital that had until then eluded him. Condemnation would not be, could not be the reaction of the Council, men as proud and as haughty as any noble family in England. These were the very same professors, he recalled, who had fought for and orchestrated his entry into the university, a fight that had not gone unnoticed by their colleagues. These guarded men had taken a gamble on granting Sebastian a place. They had seen him as someone with an incontestable aptitude, but also as someone whose background and lack of traditional training did not fit the standard mold. His candidacy had provoked impassioned, heated arguments among the admissions officers, and had left scars behind. These same men had then been overly interested in taking credit for his successes. They had sponsored his progress, elevated him, and had so publicly lauded his achievements. Their judgment would be in question as much as would be his own. His fouled name would eternally be their burden, too.

For men for whom status was all, who had slaved all of their days to construct and to advertise their famed reputations, a sentence of guilt for Sebastian would mean dishonor for them all. This, he understood, they would not allow to happen. He would be given a caution, be called back to the Dean's office for a private dressing down, and the alleged incident would be buried and forgotten evermore.

After the harrowing developments of the afternoon, of these last few hours lost wandering almost unconscious with fear, Sebastian at last began to feel relief. His thoughts went again to Olivia, who in only a short while would anxiously be awaiting him in front of the museum, unaware of the trauma he had today suffered. He would not speak of it to her. He would proceed undeterred with his original plan which, though diverted, would lead him still to so dear a prize.

Having left his overcoat at Professor Harkins' chambers, and with his suit soiled from the afternoon's long, directionless walk through the town, he would need to return to his rooms and change quickly into a fresh set of clothes. As he scurried across the campus, he thought that his pale blue shirt with the white trimmed collar and ivory buttons would be clean, and had the advantage of allowing him to wear the same tie over which he had so long fumbled this morning.

Crossing the courtyard in Pembroke, he raced up the stairs. As he reached the top of the landing, from the staircase he could see a letter fastened to his door. The envelope bore the seal of the Office of the Dean. His name had been written hastily with a black fountain pen, and was smudged at the edges. The letter itself, which ran to two pages, had been typewritten, and smelled still of fresh ink. Sebastian could not bring himself to read the contents in their entirety. He focused only on the one word that drew his full attention. Expelled.

CHAPTER 5 • पाँच

"What *is* this slop?" Vikhram asked his friend Amit in the cafeteria, just loudly enough so that the cook, carelessly dolloping out the evening's meal onto the men's empty plates, could overhear. "Were the dogs not hungry this afternoon?"

"My guess," replied Amit, "is that the dogs, and even the vermin, would rather starve than eat this rubbish."

"Is that so, you brutes?" shouted the incensed cook. "What do *you* know about cooking anyway? If it's not your damned lentils and yoghurt, you bumpkins think I'm trying to poison you. Some days I think about it, mind you. I think about it seriously. What a relief," he continued, gently slapping the back of Vikhram's close-cropped head, "what a blessed relief it would be for me!"

Vikhram recoiled in an abrupt, extravagant motion, summoning all the theatricality he could marshal to affect a grave injury.

"He struck me, the villain! First it's his poison, then it's just bald violence. I'm done for! Tell my children their father loved them..."

Predictably, this flippant, playful exchange sparked a round of banter in which the rest of the men happily took part, as they did most evenings, teasing and mocking each other, discharging at least a small degree of the many stresses to which this and every day they had been subjected.

When at last they had exhausted this frivolity and they had finished their meal, the men marched as one along the dormitory's long corridors, filing off in pairs into identical rooms. Despite the naked electric light that hounded them, most soon fell instantly into a profound slumber, hastened by the tremendous exertion of another long day.

Yet while nearby this army of weary, broken men drifted off to sleep, in the late evening hours Vikhram and Amit would steal together an hour or so of privileged, quiet moments in the room they shared. Within the protected confines of these austere quarters, the two men had formed a deep attachment, a bond forged over two hard years of common experience and close proximity that had become a kind of deliverance. They had come to rely on each other for more than just empty chatter or simple companionship. Each offered to the other a measure of salvation, a prized if fleeting letup from the desolation that defined this mostly cheerless existence.

These favored evening hours gave the men the chance to discuss, timidly at first and eventually unreservedly, both the banalities of their collective routine as well as their more private experience.

They spoke in English with the better part of the workers transplanted from the northern provinces of India and with their Saudi and British overseers, something that came easily to Vikhram, though Amit struggled with it still. Only with each other, and only in their native Marathi, did they find the words precise enough to express faithfully their most consequential and their most personal thoughts.

Freely and with sometimes bawdy humor, they would

deride the ticks and affectations of their boorish colleagues, curse the despotism of the site supervisors, talk at length of their respective families and of the promises each had made to them of better, more joyful days. In a casual gesture that the other men might have found questionable, they would hold each other's hand as they conversed, a substitute for any other available physical contact. Between them there was no pretense or posturing. They had learned to understand each other well, knew the same worries and the same anguish, nursed the same ambitions.

Regularly in the hushed evenings, when they knew they would not be disturbed, the men took down from their single wardrobe the hidden lock-box in which they kept their earnings, and allowed themselves to imagine what each would do with his respective share. Vikhram, who despite his best efforts had been able to save only a very modest amount, spoke often of ambitious projects that even he knew to be fanciful. By contrast Amit, who had come to Al-Fadiz almost four long years ago, had banked a superior sum. Yet despite the heftier amount he had come to put aside, Amit's ambitions were decidedly more unassuming. He would use his savings, maybe even by this year's end, to buy a simple home in which to raise his family and to ensure that his aging mother, without other resources and without other support, could be kept comfortable in her declining years.

They reveled as well in each other's tales of home. Though the younger of the two men, Vikhram's learning, the important store of knowledge he had acquired through years of careful reading, lent him a relative sophistication, and it endowed him with a genius for telling stories that his friend couldn't help but admire. Amit marveled at the spectacular tales of Bombay, a city he had visited only once and only in passing, when he had made the long march from Ahmednagar to join the other fervent, hopeful men departing from the acclaimed Gateway of India for Kuwait, and from there to this withered heart of the Saudi desert.

Time and again, Vikhram employed all of his refined skill to describe the city of his youth in some detail, some of which was quite conventional and some of which was quite fabricated. He enraptured Amit with his portrayal of a place alive with, and exemplified by, its contradictions. Of immense, crippling need and of enormous affluence. The gleaming marble and the silk tapestries that bedecked the lobbies of the foreigners' hotels, and the filthy alleyways behind each of them that harbored heaps of refuse through which the destitute would sift for any scrap of food or discarded item that could be bartered or sold. The constant bedlam of dueling pushcarts and motorcars, of children noisily begging and hawking their crude goods, and the majesty of a flawless sunset over the Arabian Sea viewed from on high on Malabar Hill.

Vikhram's flair for storytelling, of making immensely colorful the many impersonal and otherwise insipid anecdotes he had over the years overheard or read, did not at first translate into a willingness to discuss more closely-held matters. He had come to be deeply suspicious of others. His friends in Bombay were few, his neighbors had snubbed him for his rather belated conversion to the prevailing anti-British sentiment and, most of all, for the disgrace of his children born before his marriage to Sapna.

Only over time, and only in minute increments, did he allow himself to share confidences with Amit, to trust in him unconditionally, to appreciate that discussing aloud his biting heartache could itself bring some release. Only very gradually did he come to understand that this odyssey on which he found himself could be less perilous if traveled with a companion. In talking more frequently and openly over the passing months, particularly of the family he had left behind, he had progressively let the wall he had so laboriously erected come down. He spoke more often, more effortlessly now of the achievements and the disappointments of his previous jobs, and mostly of the Victoria Book Palace, of the dreams he had there constructed and of the dreams that had there been thwarted.

Amit had always been more forthcoming. He spoke most often and with animation of his wife, an attractive, strong-willed and determined woman who only with reluctance and cajoling had agreed to his leaving home. Their marriage, as was so often the case, had been arranged, but their rapport had developed quickly into something more substantial, something authentic, and something more than either of them could have anticipated. But he had left their home soon after the wedding ceremony, too soon to establish familiar habits and much too soon for either of them to be at ease with such a separation, especially one in which the term of his absence was undefined and in which communication between them was to be so limited.

Amit did often write to his wife, with Vikhram's help, for like most of the Indian men recruited from the ailing rural farms where the state's compulsory education was patently ignored, he could neither read nor write. On this evening, as on so many others, he wanted to compose a letter, but as had become routine, he shrunk from doing so, protesting as usual that he had little idea of what to say and even less so of how to say it.

"I'm not even sure she wants to hear from me again so soon," uttered Amit reticently. "I know I've nothing of interest to report."

"I think you're right," sneered Vikhram, tiring of this inevitable, tiresome charade. "She doesn't want to hear from you. What a bore it must be!"

"Really? Do you think so? I'm so ashamed. She must think it so childish of me."

"Oh don't be so daft, *of course* she wants to hear from you," said Vikhram reassuringly, adding in a mildly sarcastic and sardonic tone that was mostly lost on his listener, "Women are desperate to be reminded of how much they matter to their men. They don't ever tire of it. Every book I've ever read is filled with pages and pages of women's weepy pleas for attention and for signs of adoration."

"Is your wife desperate that way?" asked an astonished Amit.

"Well, no," came the embarrassed answer. "Sapna might get tearful every once in a while, sometimes for reasons I really can't understand and which even *she* can't explain. Or won't explain. Mercifully though, she doesn't require me to make repeated declarations of my commitment. I think we understand and trust each other enough for that."

"I envy you then, Vikhram. I can't even say I know my wife all that well, though she's the only woman I've ever loved and, God willing, the woman I hope will one day, in God's own time, bring me many sons."

"Then why don't you just tell her that?" Vikhram blurted out. "Tell her what's in your heart. If you do that, you can't fail."

"What's in my heart? But it's so black. More than anything, it's just how unhappy I am, Vikhram, how much I despair at being away from Ahmednagar, the revolting smells of this place, the way they treat us. The shame of it all."

"Amit, my friend, she knows all of that already. We've

written to her, I've written with this same hand, I don't know how many letters that say just that. Do you think it eases *her* suffering, *her* solitude, to know how much *you're* suffering? I think it can only distress her, and sadden her more than just your absence does already."

"What then, what shall we write about? I can't do this like you can, Vikhram, I am empty."

"Of course you can! Why don't you talk about something more unexpected, more unusual? Let's see. Can you remember something special about her, something that may be secret that only you would know, the memory of which would surely make her laugh?"

For a long moment, Amit paused. He thought hard, his forehead wrinkling in apparently deep reflection. A glazed look came to possess his eyes as if he were being physically taken back to India, back to his adored wife, away from the battles and throes of his lonely reality.

"What would make her smile?" continued Amit. "What about her smile itself? When she laughs, and she's quick to laugh, her nose sort of curls up and her mouth opens at one side. She looks like the crabby old tax collector from Ahmednagar who had a stroke a few years back, and I just love teasing her that she's also having an attack. That we have to rush to find the doctor to save her. The more I tease her, the more she laughs, and the more her face becomes contorted. It's just wonderful to see!"

"Yes, let's write about that," exclaimed Vikhram. "She's not interested in how sad we are, or whether a new well came in this week, or how it's so hot we can't think straight. She just wants to hear, Amit, that you're thinking about her. That you're devoted to her. That one day, and maybe one day soon, you'll come back to her."

"Tell her just that I'm thinking about her?" replied a

surprised Amit. "But that's *all* I do. I can't think of anything else."

"Well, we'll tell her that, shall we?"

Scrupulously, taking care to consult Amit for compelling details that would allow it more genuinely to reflect his own voice, Vikhram constructed a letter whose very simplicity was an eloquent testament to his friend's devotion to his wife. A tasteful, poetic tribute to his fidelity.

Amit was pleased with the result. Ardently, he lent his simple signature, a flourishing, elongated letter A, to the bottom of the single page. As he sealed the envelope, he turned his back discreetly to bestow upon it a furtive kiss, a pointed, heartrending act that Vikhram glimpsed sideways in the wardrobe's mirror, and about which, out of respect, he would keep silent.

* *

In the morning, the men arose early, reminded in their barely wakeful state that the day promised to be another drawn out, arduous one. Too soon reminded that, out on the sweeping, forbidding oil fields, they were nothing.

They knew well that each imported worker was indistinguishable from any other. They were expendable, replaceable at a moment's notice, or with no notice at all. Their overbearing superiors might on occasion half-recognize them, acknowledge with a detached nod their backbreaking efforts at the end of a difficult shift, but not with anything resembling praise, and certainly not with anything resembling affection. Even to their fellow workers, to those who suffered the identical circumstances, each man was inconsequential. Another unremarkable, repeated face in an infinite series of trying, repeated days. A competitor perhaps for the most treacherous and thus the better-paid work, rivals for the scarce hot water for bathing or for a fresh uniform that reeked less violently of petrol or of sweat.

This utter lack of even simple recognition was to Vikhram the sharpest manifestation of the debasement to which the men were regularly subjected. They were somehow less than human, unseen and unnoticed. They were nothing.

As he had been for much of the preceding week, Amit was randomly assigned one of the more undignified jobs, cleaning and maintaining the steel-sided workroom the men referred to as the doghouse, cantilevered out from one of the most active rigs. This small, practically airless space was the focal point for all activity on the field, and bustled with chronic, feverish activity. Surveyors consulting their complex charts, scrawling notations and distinctive markings that baffled the untrained men. Engineers fiddling with their testing equipment and who, day and night, sampled the crude as it was extracted from the adjacent wells. Laborers queuing to pick up their tools, stored haphazardly within its cramped cellar.

Amit's deceptively simple mission was to keep the walls free of the soot that gathered so persistently, to scour the floor of the ample sludge tracked in by the push of workers, and generally to keep order where, amid the disarray, little seemed possible. His task required no particular skills, but to keep ahead of the mayhem, commanded a great deal of stamina and fortitude.

This morning, Vikhram was again appointed to work alongside Amit, but in what had become a well-rehearsed dance, he cajoled and flattered the duty manager in an effort to obtain a task that was better paid, frequently with the aid of a cut of his wages.

Wearing down the supervisor's resistance, Vikhram

today achieved for himself a more lucrative assignment. It was also one of the more onerous and laborious jobs on the site. Together with a small number of others, he was tasked with cutting pits into the earth, cavities dug at the wellhead that, once lined with a dense canvas or cloth, would capture the surplus fluids discharged from the borehole just below. Digging these enormous, shapeless pits was exhausting work. It left the men covered with dirt, with slippery grease, and with the escaping oil that assaulted every part of them. The wages, however, were almost double what he would have earned in any other assignment, and so it was welcomed.

This day was made easier than many for Vikhram by the patchy cloud cover that, although it would not bring the relief of a rain shower, would nevertheless shield him from the worst of the sun's intensity. Over these past two years, the sun had wreaked great injury on his relatively fair, increasingly scaly skin, burned so often in the desert heat it had become a noticeably darker shade. The skin on the back of his neck had thickened into coarse, deep wrinkles, while the bruising on his forearms and blisters on his hands refused to heal. He had developed dark patches on his face that only highlighted the redness and obvious irritation of his eyes.

His only reprieve, particularly from the ravages of the mid-day sun, was the brief lunch break he would most often share with Amit in the wispy shade of the rig. There the men would chat idly of their morning, or fall instantly if only momentarily into daydreams, at least until the sharp whistle blew, rousing both men and summoning them back to their respective stations.

As was his custom after lunch, Vikhram walked first for a few minutes out onto a disused portion of the field, a patch of desert that had already been raped of its usefulness, to limber his legs and to prepare his stiff body for the afternoon's exertion. In the distance he saw Amit returning to the doghouse, and greeted him with an affectionate, hearty wave that fortified both men for what was certain to be another slow, tiring shift.

As Amit turned to open the rusty door at the front of the small structure, both men heard a tortured, penetrating noise emanating from the steam-powered pump at the bottom of the derrick. The pipes and valves underneath let out a shrill cry, an unholy wail that anyone who had clocked time on a rig would instinctively dread. The noise quickly grew only louder, more riotous, more ominous. In an instant, before the workers had time to react, and well before they had time to decamp, the pressure from the pipes hidden underground exploded with the terrific force of a blowout, sending dirt and rivets and splinters of wood from the soaring booms that elevated the assembly into a hundred different directions.

A colossal fireball, fed by invisible gases, shot high in the air, then descended just as swiftly, and with equal fury. Emboldened by the oil that everywhere beset the ground, the fire greedily began to engulf everything within its hungry reach. No longer supported, the structure's main mast began slowly, deliberately to collapse in a measured movement that, had it not portended such carnage, could otherwise have been considered elegant. Its collapse caused the pulleys to give way, and for their tangle of ropes to flail about uncontrolled as if they had become hysterical. The concrete block that held together those ropes and cables, which but a moment ago had sat proudly at the top of the derrick, no longer had anything to prop it up, and itself came crashing down into the doghouse, slicing cleanly through its thin roof.

The entire site descended into chaos. The emergency crews, in which the miserly owners had invested little, were slow to react. When at last, wrested out of their listless haze, they did arrive, their immediate priority was to douse the rapacious flames, for fear that the fire would spread rapidly across the huge area and set off a series of other fires in neighboring wells that would be infinitely more difficult to contain, and infinitely more damaging to the facility's production. The workers organized themselves in a chain to throw mud on the flames. Their courage and nerve bought them enough time for the specialist teams to arrive who, assessing the situation, took the dramatic and risky decision that the only way to extinguish the fire was to deprive it of oxygen, preparing and detonating a series of controlled dynamite explosions at the wellhead.

The blasts had immediately and spectacularly achieved their purpose. The flames had been entirely snuffed out. But in the smoky debris, what soon became clear was that the explosives had not only destroyed what remained of the rig, but they had obliterated the doghouse as well. The metal structure had been reduced to a burnt pile of rubble, its broad lines still discernable, but it contents, open onto the field, entirely exposed. Charts and graphs were carried by the wind in all directions, the tools and equipment from the cellar had been tossed into a jumbled pile on the scorched floor, and in the corner of the building lay the charred, lifeless bodies of the two men who had been trapped inside. The foreman, identifiable by the dull yellow helmet still strapped to his bleeding head. And Amit, alone on the cracked stairs, crushed under a smoldering pile of wood and mangled steel.

CHAPTER 6 • सहा

Though the blaze had been smothered, the plume of gray-ish smoke from the explosion lingered, visible from miles around. It besieged the landscape. The remnants of the blast, gorging the skies in a rage of sand, dirt and the saw-dust of the spent dynamite, lent the air a foul stench, some-thing akin to curdled milk or to rotten fruit.

The scene was one of apocalypse. Those of the men who still believed in a God, despite their grievances in this loathsome job, could only see in the devastation a divine judgment rendered on this annihilated wasteland. Retribution for the injury to the land they were them-selves bankrupting, and for unsettling the fragile balance of nature.

As Vikhram surveyed the wreckage, stumbling over the searing and chaotic shambles, he thought he heard the earth continue to rumble beneath him. He pictured the copper coiling and the miles of pipes that yet waited under-ground aching to be emancipated, and he feared another blowout at least as violent as the first. His instinct, even as he considered the danger to his own person, would have been to alert his friend Amit, and together retreat to safety. Yet a second discharge was not to come. The pent-up pres-sure had been fully released in the first terrifying eruption, and so another would have been impossible. Both the pressure and the young man had been expended.

Distraught, Vikhram stood for a long time immobilized, oblivious to the frenzied activity unfolding around him. Everywhere the men set about clearing the shards of metal and glass that had deluged the site. They attempted to put right any beam or pole left intact, collected the scattered tools, raced to retrieve the engineers' plans and drawings strewn across the dunes and of which not one of them could have judged the relative importance. The fire brigade had begun to pull back, while the emergency medical teams surveyed the men for injuries. With a disconcerting detachment, they began as well to retrieve the scorched bodies from the decimated shell of the unrecognizable doghouse, wrapping them clumsily in nearly translucent white cotton sheets through which profuse stains of blood were clearly visible, and that only gained in size as the two dead men were moved to the waiting carts. Wagons that would soon take them, sluggishly and somberly, away from the scene. Instinct told Vikhram he ought to approach the inert body of his friend, but he found he had neither the strength nor the heart to stir.

When the bodies had at last receded from sight, the scene that but a moment ago was one of upheaval transformed with miraculous speed into one of industry and of order. The rig on which Vikhram had been working that morning, very nearly annihilated, would need to be salvaged and likely reconstructed at another point on the field. Under the watchful eyes of the English and Saudi supervisors, the workers on adjacent rigs soon took up their stations and resumed their incessant drilling.

Within minutes the deafening wail resumed. The alarming, violent sound of rocks being blasted. Gurgling mud pumped in gargantuan quantities. The chilling ruckus of combustion and steam engines releasing their stupendous power into the drills, piercing the earth's crust and extracting the viscous liquid from its bowels.

All around him Vikhram observed that the rhythmic, crushing routine on the oil fields had recommenced, as if the tragic accident just unfolded were to be ignored, or denied. He imagined that in the dormitory, the men who would together take up the next shift were busy as usual preparing for their duties, while others lounged absent-mindedly and indifferent in the common areas. The cook would continue without pause his slapdash preparation of the evening's shabby meal. Provisions were surely still being delivered, and the day's waste being noisily carted away. Nowhere amongst all this frenetic movement and motion would Amit's absence even be noticed. Likely no one but Vikhram, among the masses of workers with whom he and Amit had lived and interacted for several years, would even mark the loss.

No, Amit would not be missed, and he would not be mourned. Not by his colleagues or by the town's shopkeepers who, despite his regular custom, had barely noticed him. Not by the supervisors who could instantly replace him on the rigs and give his place in the dormitory to yet another anonymous, eager recruit. Not by the women in whose company Amit had a handful of unhappy times, and for a small fee, taken some comfort to ease his agonizing loneliness.

He would be lamented here only by Vikhram, his only friend in this foreign land, and for whom the idea of returning to the half-empty room they shared had suddenly become a curse. He would be grieved for by those he left behind in Ahmednagar, his cherished mother and above all by an adored wife, at home in ignorance of the events that had just befallen her only love, her only hope.

Vikhram had never met Amit's wife. He had never known the commanding charm and quiet intelligence that defined her. He hadn't seen for himself the tantalizing smile and the wildly expressive eyes that had instantly captured her husband's heart, the memory of which so often by itself had sustained Amit. He didn't know the pleasure of the succulent *idli* cakes and coconut chutney for which she had, according to her own accounts, won such singular notoriety, and about which Amit would often rave. The long letters from her that Vikhram had read aloud, and those in return that he had written in Amit's name, were a poor surrogate for seeing, for knowing this dearly loved woman.

Vikhram considered those many letters, but with a jolt, he remembered the one he held even now in his vest pocket. He knew that the responsibility to inform his friend's family of the accident that robbed Amit of his future would lie only with him. A representative of the Gulf Petroleum Company might in due course send notification of Amit's demise, but this would be slow in coming, and Vikhram couldn't abide the thought of what he assumed, what he knew could only be an impersonal and detached telling of the events, devoid of any kindness or of anything but false consideration. Likewise, it would no longer be possible to dispatch the letter he had planned to post this afternoon. Its contents were obsolete and, were they to be read after the news of his death reached her, would constitute an unforgivable affront.

But Vikhram's attention was soon deflected to other concerns. For in long considering how best to inform Amit's wife, how to organize and send home with haste his friend's few personal effects, his thoughts were drawn to the lock-box hidden in the wardrobe in which they had stashed their savings. The small black box that held within it the mounting stacks of coins that provided both the permit to leave this unhappy place, and the key to unlock brighter opportunities for both men.

Only Vikhram knew precisely the extent of the cache and, importantly, the outsized share that was due Amit, earned and saved through the many years of diligence and of sacrifice. The two men had avoided speaking of this stash to the other workers, for fear it might be pilfered. In letters to his wife, too, out of modesty or out of an instinctive disinclination to boast, Amit had not once mentioned the actual sum he had put aside.

Even among the very few Indian laborers who had, against the odds, succeeded in securing the distant promises that had first drawn them to this cataclysmic desert, it was an impressive sum. A figure to which Vikhram could only aspire and that, taken with his own, considerably lesser savings, would more than suffice to achieve the most urgent and even the more audacious goals, setting out impatiently from Bombay two years ago, he had set for himself.

It would allow him to go home vindicated. To prove indisputably to Sapna that his long leave, to which she had always been opposed, had been warranted. It would mean taking his two children out of the contemptible classrooms that the state provided in favor of an English-run school in which they could be educated properly, and that would place them in much better stead to break the iniquitous cycle of poverty into which he had been ensnared. It even let him conceive of a dream more grand, that of opening his own bookshop. It would not of course be as grandiose as the once glorious Victoria Book Palace, long since appropriated by the merciless British bankers, and lying today derelict and abandoned, but he could imagine a dignified place of commerce and of culture, and from which he could provide for his family.

Vikhram rushed back to the dormitory. Past the fragments of the blast that were quickly being all but erased. Past the legions of dispirited workers persevering in their tasks, with exhaustion and with indifference. Past the shops and cafés in the town center where ordinary life continued, without regard for Vikhram and for the grim developments of the morning, nor for those he was certain were soon to come.

He bolted up the stairs to their room, and secured the door behind him. With a ferocity that bordered on rage, he tore open the wardrobe and rifled through its contents to retrieve the box, which he opened with equal fervor. There in front of him, in jumbled piles, was the mass of shiny *riyal* pieces of silver and nickel. Coins of every denomination, vintage and condition. Some newly minted, having been little traded. Others clearly heavily exchanged, their Arabic numerals and letters extolling the King of Hejaz, indecipherable to him, barely visible.

The cumulative effect, the combined result of more than three hundred weeks of hard-earned wages, was breathtaking. He sat frozen, assessing the stash. He counted out the sums again and again, terrified at how lightly he might forsake any principled commitments to his friend, but also energized by the knowledge that paradise might at last be his.

He schemed about how credibly to explain to Amit's widow that her husband's savings had disappeared. Perhaps he could send to her only a small portion of those savings, and he spent many hours calculating the amount she might need as a dowry for a second husband, telling himself that a new spouse might assuage his responsibility and his guilt. He questioned even why this terrible responsibility should be his, as surely the Company, which everyone knew to be deceitful, could be blamed for the evaporation of Amit's savings.

Unaccompanied, Vikhram had traveled the thousands of miles to this sullen, barren outpost. He had given up witnessing much of his children's growing maturity, the innumerable and almost imperceptible, quiet pleasures of daily domestic life, for the sake of his family and of their prospects. He owed no obligation to any man, had no loyalty nor compulsion to anything but a steadfast, single-minded focus to succeed. And to return. To end this dire interval as quickly as practicable. To resume a life he knew only to be suspended.

Laid out in front of him, with a luster that derided the stark light of the dormitory, was an unexpected rejoinder to his silent pleas for mercy. His friendship with Amit had been an unanticipated gift for both men, the one redeeming aspect of their sentence. This sudden legacy, then, could be the one final, grand bequest of that friendship, an endowment he had earned by his fellowship and by his faithfulness. His commitment to Amit, the compassion and the decency he had shown his friend, would serve to exonerate him. It gave him both the justification and the apology to keep these funds for himself.

But this tortuous reasoning, this scheming and duplicity, was not in Vikhram's character. Despite the indubitable pull and the lure of temptation, by morning he knew his path was a clear one.

* *

Before the other men had arisen, he bathed, dressed and, poaching a stale *fatir* from the kitchen for sustenance, waited for the first transport to take him to town. Once there, with the wages he and Amit had earned bulging in his coat pockets, he crossed the grand lobby and entered, for the first time since his arrival in Al-Fadiz, the main office of the oil firm that was his employer.

He waited patiently to see the manager, a displeasing, corpulent man who sat unhurried within Vikhram's sight, casually smoking and leisurely taking the remains of his breakfast. At last, the man signaled to have Vikhram brought forward. As he rose, Vikhram faltered, lopsided as he was from the uneven weight in his pockets. And from nerves.

"Good morning, sahib. My friend Amit, God rest his soul, was killed yesterday on the rig."

"Yes, I was told about the accident," replied the manager. "Damned thing, it's going to take us weeks to get that well back on line. I never did get a decent barrel out of that wretched thing!"

"Sir, I'd like your help with Amit's affairs."

"Who's Ahmed?" said the distracted administrator, lighting another cigarette with the butt of the previous one, all the while fiddling with his tattered tie.

"Amit, sir. He was my friend, the one killed on the rig."

"Well, what do you want *me* to do about it? There's surely plenty of other men you can work with. Look at them out there on the street, those miserable men who'd be grateful for a little extra work. Is *that* what this is about? You want an extra shift? Look here, boy, I'm not in the habit of doling out assignments to any scamp who manages to crawl his way into my office..."

"Oh no, sahib," said a flabbergasted Vikhram. "That's

not what I wanted to say. You see, sahib, Amit left behind a wife in India. I'd like to send her this money."

With that, Vikhram emptied the piles of coins he had crowded that morning into his pockets onto the desk, sorted by denomination and crowned each with scraps of paper on which he had tallied their amounts. The loud, distinctive thud of so many assorted pieces of metal meeting the desk had attracted the attention of the entire office. Even the manager, for whom seeing large sums of cash from the weekly payroll was customary, could not help but be impressed by this display.

"Where did you get all this, young man? Who does it belong to?"

"It belongs to my friend Amit, may God rest his soul in peace. It is the money he earned while working for you for many years, and which I want his wife to have."

"Well, I'll be damned," said the incredulous manager. "I've got to say, this is the first time I've seen *this*. Most of you lot would have stolen this money for yourselves."

"This money is not mine, sahib, it does not belong to me. I was told that the Company could arrange for it to be sent home, in cases where one of your workers expires on the job."

"Well yes, we have the facility. Can't remember the last time we used it, though. Most dead folks don't care much about money."

Suddenly, a slightly malevolent smirk emerged from the side of the manager's mouth, as he came to realize the opportunity in front of him. He added, "Of course, you know we have to take a cut for the paperwork? This is going to cost you. The standard rate is, let's say, twenty-five percent."

Accustomed to the greed and corruption that pervaded every strata of the business and tainted almost every inter-

action he had with its representatives, Vikhram had anticipated such a reaction, although he was staggered by the
brazenness of the request. Without other recourse, however, he reluctantly agreed to the manager's terms, handing
over the entire amount along with the name and address
of Amit's widow, careful to have the transaction observed
by others in the office and, stubbornly, waiting for written confirmation that the transaction had been completed
before leaving the premises.

Yet Vikhram also decided, despite a resolution he had
made earlier that morning, not to send his own savings
home to Sapna, which might have otherwise been convenient. It would have relieved him of the lumbering bulk of
so many coins and, even more importantly, provided him
a measure of security against the constant threat of theft.
But he considered the terms excessive. With still so little to
show for his efforts, he could ill-afford or ill-stomach relin-
quishing so much of his savings simply to satisfy the avarice
of a corrupt administrator.

Rather, he left the firm's office and crossed the wide,
dusty street with two immediate goals in mind. First, he
entered the main branch of the town's largest bank, and
within a few moments had converted the residual silver in
his pocket, all his own savings, into Indian rupees, into a
stack of crisp banknotes that he placed carefully back in
the pocket of his coat. A transaction for which in advance
the commission was sign-posted, invariable, and in his
judgment, fair.

He then set out to the central market. Wedged between
the chemist's shop and the shirt-maker, at the end of a road
that in many respects resembled every congested, heaving
alleyway of the Nayā Bazaar, Vikhram entered the offices
of the town's only travel agency.

With the little money he had remaining, he purchased from the agent passage back to Bombay. The ticket gave him access first to a bus to Kuwait City – a difficult journey across the entire expanse of the Arabian Desert – and then in four days' time to a boat direct to Bombay. It was the reverse of the same journey that had brought him, with such anticipation and with such expectation, to Al-Fadiz.

He had set off some two years ago to this untamed land, seduced by the vague, careless promises of wealth and achievement, and had left behind all that he knew and all that he loved. The cost was more than he could have known, and the rewards notably fewer than he had anticipated. He had toiled tirelessly. He had relinquished amusements and recreation, time with his family, nearly all joy, in dogged pursuit of an elusive goal. He had not been a failure, but he had certainly not been a success. By Indian standards, his takings were respectable, and with enterprise would allow him to make a fresh start. They could hardly, however, compensate for the gloom that now bedeviled him. Amit's death told him plainly what already he knew, that the price he was paying was too high. The desert, with its strange foods and unfathomable dangers, which offered him no physical amenity and only inexorable loneliness, was no place for him. The time had come to own up to this defeat. The time had come to go home.

CHAPTER 7 • सात

The bronze knocker, the ornately sculpted lion's head that for close on a century had adorned the otherwise ordinary front door of Sebastian's townhouse, had recently been replaced with an electrified bell. Its multi-toned, clamorous chime echoed loudly through the rooms, trailing off only slowly, and long after the waiting caller had released the pressure on its lighted switch. The postman, tradesmen and other visitors, unfamiliar with the device, and mischievous neighborhood children all too familiar with it, would lean vigorously on the square, brushed-steel encasement, allowing the irregular tones to continue until at last the door was opened and calm could be restored.

As the housekeeper, it naturally fell this morning to Mrs. Collins to answer the bell. Hastening up the stairs from her room where she had been listening, as she did most Sundays, to the "Woman's Hour" broadcast on the wireless, she half-expected to encounter an unwelcome salesman flogging his wares. So when she opened the heavy door, not without some effort as a result of her various ailments, she was quite startled by what she saw. For standing in front of her, at what she estimated to be more than six feet tall, was an elderly, dark-skinned man, capped distinctively by a striking, bulky turban.

The man's headgear was nothing short of exceptional, and unlike anything Mrs. Collins had ever seen, apart from in newsreels at the cinema about the recent unrest on the Indian sub-continent. Layers of brilliant orange cotton were bound tightly into an off-center crescendo, covering a brown strip of thicker cotton that bound his forehead. Its effect was to provide the man the appearance of even greater height than he already had. The colors complemented perfectly the russet tones of the man's skin and the shock of white hair that constituted his pronounced beard and moustache. The harmony continued in the simple clothing he wore: a well-pressed, cream-colored linen jacket with a high, straight collar, a loose-fitting garment that served as trousers and that rustled in the soft breeze, and a loosely-knit chocolate brown scarf thrown around his neck, despite the unusually warm London weather. The thickset bracelet of silver on his right wrist reflected the mid-morning sun, and drew the house-keeper's eye.

"May I help you, sir?" said Mrs. Collins as she stepped out onto the landing, intrigued by the pageantry and the mystery of the visitor.

"Mr. Sebastian Reynolds, if you please."

"Whom shall I say is calling"?

"Mr. Sebastian Reynolds, please," repeated the man in a low, gentle voice.

The Englishwoman surmised, or at least hoped, that he was more likely not to have understood the language than not to have understood the protocol.

As he stepped forward, in apparent anticipation of an invitation to enter, he drew a package from the ragged goatskin satchel he carried on his back. A package wrapped in elegant red silk, on top of which was affixed an envelope upon which Sebastian's name and address were clearly visible.

"Won't you please come in and wait in the hall," she continued, with an exaggerated waving of her hands that indicated to the stranger he should enter, and precisely where he was to wait. He obliged immediately. "I'll inquire as to whether Mr. Reynolds is receiving visitors this morning."

Cautiously, for she had long since learned that Sebastian preferred not to be disturbed while in his library, Mrs. Collins knocked lightly on the frosted-glass door and entered the room.

Seated in a broad, timeworn leather chair, with his back to the window and deeply immersed in his reading, Sebastian looked up with a cordial grin that granted the housekeeper an invitation to speak.

"Sir, there is a man here who wishes to see you. He has something for you. A parcel, I believe."

"Do tell him to leave it in the hall with the rest of the post, and please give him a shilling, Mrs. Collins, for his troubles."

"If I may, sir, he is a very unusual man indeed. I am not even certain he speaks English. I think he must have come from India, sir, and from the looks of him, I would say he has just arrived!"

"From India, you say? Well, that *would* be unusual. It isn't every day we receive such a visit, and from the *Republic* of India, I might remind you! He hasn't come to exact his revenge on the British people, has he?" teased Sebastian, a joke lost on his hard-faced housekeeper, one of the many traditional English men and women who made no secret of their dismay that so great an imperial prize had recently been lost.

"Well, do show him in."

The old man made his way down the long, carpeted corridor from the entry to the library. His deep-set eyes remained fixed in front of him, unblinking and undistracted by the impressive objects that typically were the cause of such animated observations from other guests, placed at strategic points in the hall for precisely this purpose.

As he entered the room, the visitor was struck by the opposition between that narrow corridor and the library's mighty dimensions. The light, too, streaming in from the two levels of windows along the length of the far wall, contrasted appreciably with the dimness of the confined hallway. He paused for a short while, in awe of the power and the prestige that such a room implied, and to what he presumed to be the importance of the man he had been charged to seek out. Once he had situated Sebastian within the fullness of the space, he stopped and bowed as deeply as his aged frame would allow.

"Mr. Sebastian Reynolds?"

"Yes. What can I do for you?" replied Sebastian, as impressed by the man's unusual appearance as had been his housekeeper, but better equipped by the forewarning to conceal his astonishment. And his pleasure.

"From Miss Olivia," replied the visitor, extending in his tremulous hand the silk box he had shown to Mrs. Collins a moment ago.

Delighted by this surprise, Sebastian reached for the box, but even as he did so, the old man had begun his withdrawal from the room, walking backward with elegant, controlled, almost silent movements. Sebastian bid the man to stay, to explain where he had come from, to share a meal, to accept some gratuity for his pains. The visitor refused these gestures, and was gone just as quickly as he had come. Mrs. Collins, too, after accompanying the taciturn gentleman to the front door, returned to her room where her radio program was by then concluding.

Sebastian carefully examined the parcel. The box was small in size, and no thicker than his closed fist. The magnificent red silk, studded with what he took to be rock crystal or glass beads, had been tied tightly, draped with an elaborate bow of the same fabric, and fastened in the center with a silver clasp. The effect was mesmerizing. From underneath the bow, Sebastian retrieved the envelope on which was written his name and address. He recognized at once Olivia's distinctive, florid handwriting.

Despite the supreme temptation to do so, he decided he would open neither the letter nor the parcel immediately. Not because he had any pressing engagements. Not because he feared its contents might be upsetting, but precisely because of the captivating anticipation of it, and his wish to extend the excitement of the uncertainty for as long as he could. He allowed his thoughts to wander aimlessly in considering, from the most banal to the most elaborate, what the letter might say and, not least, what the box might contain. The gift had arrived so unexpectedly, he wanted to respect the long voyage it had made, and to savor the ultimate moment of his discovery.

In a trial of self-restraint, Sebastian placed the parcel with the rest of his papers on the solid oak desk in the corner of the library, and returned to the volume that he had been studying that morning, a densely written and superbly illustrated catalogue of recent acquisitions of sculpture at the British Museum. He had soon settled back into his reading, into the cozy armchair and embroidered footstool nestled by the marble fireplace at the far end of the room, just as he had been before the brief interruption. But his thoughts rarely wandered far from the red box on the table behind him.

* *

The room itself, the tremendous library that was the very heart of the large townhouse, was in some respects unremarkable, in that it had been built according to all of the standard conventions of the day. Though uncommon to find such a room in London rather than in a great country house, it followed the same, predictably strict codes of architecture and design. Wood paneling. A cast-iron spiral staircase leading to its second level. A protruding balcony that extended right around the length of the shelving which offered the rare visitor a view of the entire, sprawling space. Even the nineteenth-century stone mantelpiece and crystal chandelier were modeled closely on those found in the library at Apsley House, the Duke of Wellington's London residence, which Sebastian had often visited and admired.

Where the library was most notable was not in its structure or furnishings, but in the extent and quality of its collected works, particularly of the English novel, with which Sebastian had always been so enamored. Over some twenty years, and with the help of a succession of curators and of one unflinchingly loyal buyer, Sebastian had amassed a uniquely consequential set of volumes. He had purchased thousands of novels, of both little-known and celebrated authors alike. He acquired encyclopedia, new and previously owned, from Britain and from the Continent. Outstanding books on art and photography and travel. Compendia of English poetry and history. It was by any measure a truly significant collection.

He hadn't stocked his library as a showpiece, and

indeed, few were ever granted access. He had done so simply as a tribute to his voracious love of books, as physical objects and as vessels of knowledge. He had built it as well as a refuge from the convulsive bustle of his office and from the chaos of London's streets, and as a retreat from the caustic judgment of others that, even some thirty years since his expulsion from the university, stung still. He could not measure the wonder or count the jubilant hours he had spent in this room. He could scarcely count the time spent building an exemplary career that had subsidized such extravagance.

It was a career executed without fault, and though it was rapidly advancing to a close, it had long since become fodder for mythology among practitioners of the newspaper business. Even as a student at Cambridge, writing mostly trivial pieces for *The Ledger*, he had begun to understand the power of the medium. The power to persuade. To engage. To manipulate. It was a skill he would rapidly come to master, to exercise with unique control and, ultimately, to govern with unquestioned supremacy. It was this skill, too, that allowed him to overcome what might otherwise have been the serious handicap of his expulsion from the university, easily securing a position within the capital's press corps. Since apart from the Tory editors, so closely connected with the Establishment that they dared not overtly flout the popular gossip, most of Fleet Street's hugely competitive elite were interested only in talent, and cared not a whit about scandal.

That scandal would even, in time, come to serve Sebastian. For on leaving the university, on having so brutally taken from him the things he held most dear, he faced a stark choice. He could spend his days hounded by regret, bemoaning his loss of access to study and his life with

Olivia. Or he could use that trauma to drive himself to succeed, to vanquish and to defy that early, terrible blow. His choice of the latter was swift and it was clear.

Shrewd judgment had also played more than a minor role in his success. As a young editor, his notorious purchase of a long-failing, once-revered London newspaper for just pennies on the pound, assessed to be a ruinous decision by most of his contemporaries, had proved the cornerstone of his rapid ascent. Straightaway, he set out to change everything about the tired publication, keeping only the masthead and the fabled name. He took extensive risks. He brought a new, controversial focus on famous personalities, interviewing not only the country's leaders, but also the social luminaries and film stars of the day, providing them a much-appreciated platform from which to enhance their reputations and their fame. He proposed political comment and opinion in an unembellished manner, which his growing readership found easier to understand and more relevant to their concerns than that of his traditional, stodgy competitors. He identified and recruited skilled but unknown writers, photographers, copy editors, salesmen, not from the country's famous universities that were the industry's standard feeding pool, but from nonconformist and surprising sources, including most contentiously from abroad.

Almost immediately, he turned the paper into one of the capital's most respected and most widely read. And most profitable. He would repeat the exercise, applying each time a formula almost identical to the first, a dozen times, up and down the length of the country, until he had amassed a network of newspapers that became the envy of his peers.

All this he might have forgone for the chance at something like love, for affection, enduring friendship or even for genuine consideration. His had been a mostly reclusive life. Despite his growing wealth, and the high-profile generosity it afforded, Society had been less than kind to him. London's infamous cliques in particular, those confidential worlds of private schooling, of exclusive drawing room entertainment and intrigue, had never forgiven the wrongs ascribed to him. In his professional capacity, he had been welcomed within the most eminent salons, but he knew their interest in him was all too transparent and all too superficial, limited to extracting from one of the country's most powerful pressmen any advantage his papers and his influence could impart.

At the same time, the anonymity of the city had provided Sebastian a cloak of secrecy and discretion behind which, unimpeded by the damning opinions of his patrician counterparts, he could undertake simple, agreeable pursuits. His working-class background, with its characteristic accent and distinctive, bawdy vocabulary, meant he could at will leave behind the imposing world of high culture and business in favor of the familiar, colorful London of his youth. It was here, nameless and ordinary, that he thrived.

Whenever the rigors of his professional responsibilities allowed it, he would take leave of his office. He would ride the city's underground, listening in surreptitiously on snatches of conversations, observing the changing fashions, noting what commuters were reading and discussing. He frequented the popular cinemas and the music halls south of the river, charmed by their snappy songs and off-color comedy. Most of all, he enjoyed spending his Sunday afternoons, and many evenings as well, at the Crown and Pail, a lively neighborhood pub in a disaffected part of Lambeth he had discovered as a boy, which because of his youth was then barred to him, but which he had come to frequent ever since.

Appreciating as he did a plump roast or smoked bacon pie and more than a pint or two of beer, he would linger for hours in the smoky pub with the regulars, listening attentively to descriptions of their exploits, and sympathetically pondering their woes. The other patrons, who over the years had grown quite accustomed to his amiable presence, knew him only by his Christian name, and he theirs. They knew him to be unusually articulate and well-informed. They knew nothing of his position or of his status. Just as Sebastian preferred it. For the veiled, escapist nature of these outings was the defining element for him. The discovery of his stature and of his wealth would have drained for him the simple charm and chief lure of the excursion.

Today was one of those Sundays. A warm, blusterous day, one so unusual in the fleeting English summer that Sebastian would have considered it a transgression to forsake it. Leaving his townhouse in Pimlico, armed as usual despite the fulsome sunshine with an umbrella in case the weather were abruptly to change, he set off by foot for the public house. He strolled leisurely through the streets, busy with crews of workmen razing or rebuilding the blistered shells of the capital's many bombed-out buildings and with boisterous children, playing ball games or conkers or an improvised version of Five Stones. He made his way through several of the city's many parks, bursting again with activity and filled ever more with tourists who were only just beginning to return to the city from France and Belgium, and from even farther afield.

When at last he arrived at the Crown and Pail, parched and tired from the day's long walk, his entry was noted above the din with shouts of salutation. He took his usual seat among a small crowd of burly men, relishing as he did an afternoon absorbed in the entertaining company of the working, local men from the neighborhood.

This afternoon there was a new girl tending the bar, scantily dressed in a tight-fitting blouse and too-short skirt calculated to provoke. The stable of barmaids in fact changed often. Local girls mostly, looking to earn a little extra on the weekends. Girls who either quickly fell out with the pub's tetchy owner or who were clever enough to soon realize they could earn almost as much on the dole as they could at the bar. It was not unknown for Sebastian to make brazen advances to these pretty, transitory women. Advances that were not always summarily rebuffed, and on more than one occasion he had conducted a brief affair.

"Hello, darling. What can I get for you?" she said, pinching his cheek in a flagrant flirtation that made Sebastian blush redder than the tatty leather booth in which he was sitting. He would have given her ten guineas right then to repeat the gesture.

"Just a pint," he replied diffidently. "And maybe a ham sandwich, if you can conjure one up."

"Conjure? I ain't no magician! But I'll see what I can do for you."

As she turned, walking away slowly enough for the men to admire her assets fully, those sharing Sebastian's table pounced on him mercilessly.

"She's a little out of your league, wouldn't you say so?" said the man seated to his left. "I'm bettin' she's young enough to be your daughter."

"Daughter?" said another. "You need new spectacles! I'd say granddaughter is closer to the mark. There are laws against that in this country, old man."

"Is that so?" retorted Sebastian, in a defiant tone. "You lot think I can't win over a girl who looks as good as that? Well, I've just been keeping my charm under wraps! The next round says I can have her under my spell in no time."

"That's a daft bet, old man," laughed the youngest of the crowd. "I hate to take money off a dimwit, but times *is* tough!"

Sebastian rose from the table and slowly made his way to the bar, buying himself time to devise a strategy or a few seductive lines that might beguile or flatter the target of the wager. He decided, given the odds stacked so significantly against his favor, that what was required what a bit of ruse.

With a conspicuous swagger and just a slight tilt of the head, his back turned to the men whose attention was fixed on his every movement, he addressed the barmaid.

"Listen, luv, can you do an old chap like me a bit of a good turn? These miserable, sad gentlemen behind me are out to make a fool of me. They're convinced that a pretty girl like you wouldn't pay any attention to a washed-up man like me. And probably they're right. But it *would* be something to prove them wrong..."

She needed no more convincing, and showed herself more than willing to play along.

"Nonsense," she said, "come a little closer, handsome," and she planted on his lips, longer than probably the charade would have required, a most pronounced kiss. He went even redder than he had before.

Instantly, pandemonium broke out at the table. The men, quite untroubled by the loss of their bet, banged their tankards in uproarious approval. Sebastian returned to the table as slowly as he had approached the bar, savoring this most agreeable of victories.

* *

By the time Sebastian left the Crown and Pail, twilight, so slow to arrive this late in the season, had begun to envelop the city. He was by then shaky on his feet, unsteady from the better part of a sluggish afternoon spent drinking generous quantities of beer and whiskey. He needed assistance even to install himself in the back of one of the city's newly refurbished black taxis.

As the vehicle jostled awkwardly along the uneven cobblestones and the paved streets so long neglected, he closed his tired eyes. He let his mind drift away from the pangs and the distress he knew were everywhere around him, distress that blighted the city so disfigured by war. Away from the narrow-minded scheming and maneuvering that dominated his work. Away from the tedious gossip-mongering and cruel invective that followed him far and wide. Only half-awake, he was elsewhere. He was somewhere more forgiving. More tolerant. Where his history and where the opprobrium that plagued him didn't factor into people's estimations of his person or of his worth. A place where he could retell, reshape his own story. Where he might re-invent himself.

England, he knew, could not be that place. His renown was too great, his roots too deep. Yet he had not managed to find the time, nor indeed had he ever found the motivation or the resolve, to leave its shores. He had never for himself partaken in the delights and the pleasures of travel abroad.

He did, however, hold one undeniable advantage over his compatriots who had themselves not traveled. He had read extensively about some of the world's most remote and most mysterious locations, and not simply in trawling through the vast volumes of his library, though his collection was beyond question a constant source of instruction and enlightenment. He had learned most, gained a personal and authentic picture of so many distant places, by way of the voluminous, and of late more frequent correspondence he had these many years received from Olivia.

She had begun this correspondence against the express wishes of her father, Lord Granville, who, as expected, had called off the engagement just as soon as news of the troubling events at Cambridge reached him. She did so without the sanction or even the knowledge of her husband, who would not have approved of her maintaining communication with someone he considered beastly, and whom he knew was once, and could conceivably be again, a rival for his wife's affections.

Olivia's marriage had been arranged in short order after Sebastian's expulsion from the university, designed in large measure to extricate her from disrepute and to bring her conclusively back into the comforting fold of class and affluence that her emphatically conventional parents considered both her birthright and her obligation. The match would not be a happy one. Her husband was an imposing figure. A solemn, officious man, the scion of a legendary family that had made its name and its extensive wealth in the service of its country and its king. A high-ranking member of the British Colonial Service, he brought as much ardor and enthusiasm to the execution of his official duties as he brought a lack of it to their marriage.

They had lived in the distant colonies since almost the first day of their union. Indeed, their honeymoon was celebrated not on an amorous tour of European capitals, as she might have hoped for and expected, but on a steamship bound for Ceylon, where her husband was to take up a post overseeing administration in the north of the country.

It was from there, largely confined to their sprawling, well-staffed house, bored and weary after months of idleness, that she began to write to Sebastian.

At first he received only postcards. Comical or even outlandish photographs printed on cheap, starched cardboard on which she had written just a line or two, a witticism or anecdote that began, as these notes had accumulated over time, to paint a picture of the country – the environment, the culture, and of her life there. Even the stamps, chosen with care to amuse or to provoke him, told a distinctive story, and set his imagination alight. Soon these pithy missives were replaced by proper letters, from Rhodesia, South Africa and from each of the other countries in which she briefly lived. Still quite terse, but much more evocative, and progressively, much more explicit.

She wrote of the other European ladies in her circle, women she thought maddeningly complacent in their subservient, docile role as hostess and guide. She parodied and ridiculed these women. But many of the letters also bore witness to her growing affection for the people of the country in which she then found herself, who had showed her many kindnesses and had taught her many things. She recounted the bouts of malaria and typhoid that ravaged villages, and of which she lived in continual fear. She told of the ubiquitous adversity of the people, which she felt she had an obligation to ameliorate, but which again and again found herself powerless to do so. She wrote as well, first ambiguously, but then with growing candor, of the inattention, the infidelities and the temper of her husband that flirted on the border of violence.

Free from the rigid confines of English decorum, a master on his estates and in the sparse government offices, he had revealed himself as a brute, bullying his employees and the household staff. And bullying her. She had come to know only constant trepidation, that he would strike her, betray her, banish her, leave her. For days on end he would vanish, lost in what she knew to be a stupor of drunken excess and loose women, only to return, unannounced, with no scent of repentance or apology. For too many years, for close to three decades by her count, she had endured this humiliation, and as a result the tone of her letters had become steadily more desperate, and increasingly more fraught.

* *

The letter that had been delivered so dramatically that morning was, for the first time in their long correspondence, accompanied by a parcel. As the taxi drew ever closer to his townhouse, stopping often for errant children who darted out in front of it or for absentminded pedestrians, he found the anticipation of discovering its contents had become almost unbearable. His curiosity had consumed him. On reaching his home at last, sobered from the drive across the city, he hurried through the entry and shot down the narrow corridor to the library, practically toppling a number of the costly objects on display.

He was not disappointed. Tearing through the smooth silk wrapping of the parcel, he opened the lid of the wooden box it contained. In its center, anchored by a ravishing velvet lining, was the most brilliant gemstone he had ever seen. A sapphire of astonishing size and, even to his untrained eye, of astonishing quality. Flawless, the stone was a magnificent color and clarity, a dark, deep purple with only the slightest hints of violet and green, hues that rose and fell in emphasis and intensity as he turned the gem to meet the flare of the room's massive chandelier.

Perfectly round, the stone seemed almost to be layered, in an infinitely repeated geometrical pattern that had no beginning and no end. In its core, the layering continued and only intensified, with faint, almost indiscernible spikes rising from the center in a spectacular petal-like formation.

The stone had been bonded onto a slim silver base and set as a pin for a man's tie, roughly the size of a shilling coin, in a style that had seen the height of its popularity amongst modish English gentlemen at the end of the last century, and which had newly seen a resurgence. At a lecture not a fortnight ago at the Victoria & Albert Museum, which itself housed a fairly reputable collection of gemstones, Sebastian had spied just such a pin being worn by the Earl of Hereford, though it was not nearly of such brilliance or distinction as the one he held in his hand.

He knew nothing of the origin of the stone, nothing of its history or its significance, but given its size and its quality, he instantly began to imagine the folklore and the legends that might have been attributed to it. Possibly it provided restorative energies to those who wore it. Powers to heal and to fortify. Protection against demons and unknown dangers.

The letter, he thought, would surely reveal both the gem's origins, as well as Olivia's purpose in sending him so extraordinary an object. He tore open the envelope with some dispatch, desperate now to learn of her intentions.

Mohan Bagh, New Delhi
22 July 1948

My dearest Seb,

It has been many months since I have written to you last. Please forgive me this long interval. Much has happened since.

Just this week, Eleanor and I returned from a difficult but marvelous trip to Rajasthan, the second of our visits to the wid-

owed maharani of one of the smaller princely states there. Since
the coming of Independence, though still revered among the
people, her power has evaporated, and I suspect, as must she,
that her influence and stature can only follow. Mostly, she is
concerned for her young son, a fine-looking boy of just seventeen
with obvious ambition, but whose path could not be less certain.
At the request of the High Commissioner, on whom Her Highness
had called for assistance, we were dispatched as part of a small
contingent to help facilitate a discussion, one that might see the
young prince matriculate at a university in England. Happily, I
was able to win over the maharani to the merits of Cambridge,
and the deal has been done. The boy will leave for England at the
end of the summer.

As an expression of her gratitude, Her Highness took the rather
unexpected and startling step of presenting me with the sapphire
you see before you. It forms only a trifling part of the royal family's quite remarkable collection of jewels. In the palace, there is an
immense cabinet replete with such jewels, many of which I assure
you would put the one she has offered me to shame.

This particular sapphire, mined in Kashmir, is an exceedingly
rare one they call 'midnight indigo.' I have had it fashioned into
a tie-pin, as I am told this is in vogue in London. I have done so
in the hope that you may wear it often, and that you may think of
me. May you admire it, Sebastian, at home in your library, where
I suspect you are even as you read this letter, and as you consider a
great journey that I have decided to request of you, to implore you
to undertake. I do so after much consideration, and not without
profound hesitation. It is a journey I ask you to make to Delhi.

I cannot say, my dear friend, that all here is well. My health
remains robust. Yes, of course, the house continues by and large to
run itself. The garden, of which you'll remember I sent you a photograph last year, is in full bloom, despite the corruptions of the
summer heat. But it's I, not the house or the garden, who suffers

most, who is wilting under the strain. For, as he considers his next posting, in Malaya or Burma, I have taken the tumultuous decision to leave my husband.

After much too long, I will leave him to his drinking. To his mistresses, whose number I can no longer count. To his gambling and licentiousness and decadence of which I have so often written you before, and that are everything I loathe.

Like the maharani, from today I too must contemplate another path. A return to England, to its petty intrigues and its false morality, where I might be secreted away on the family estate after a lifetime already of exile, seems unimaginable. I want no part of that too-small island. Besides, I have come to think of India, free from the shackles of our rule and brimming with regeneration, as my home. Every day I learn more about the customs and traditions of this radiant place, a place I assure you is full of energy and determination. I have found a role for myself here. For the first time, I have truly found a way to make myself useful.

Still, I am not strong enough to manage this place alone. Why learn of its secrets, why partake of its gifts, if these cannot be shared? And it is with you, my dearest, you who have remained most faithful and most loyal, only you who has long buoyed me and consoled me, with whom I wish most of all to share these splendid rewards.

Though they tore you from me once, I never gave up on you, Sebastian. I never gave up on us. You must see this to be true. Even if the distance and the years between us have been immense, I haven't really learned to live without you. I loved you once. I love you still.

I cannot pretend that I don't recognize what I am asking of you. I know the audacity of my request, but this much I also know: you are in the closing stages of your career, a glorious career spent in an England that has not been a friend to you. I, too, am at a crossroads. I ask you then, I entreat you, let us meet these crossroads

as one. Come join me here. Let us start a new life, a happier life,
together.

Take this jewel in the same spirit in which it was given to me,
with affection and with gratitude. Keep it with you as you allow
yourself to imagine a voyage that will take you to India. To me.
It is a voyage that might just save me and, I am persuaded, might
just save you, too.

    With much love,
    Olivia

Sebastian let the letter drop from his hand, over-
whelmed by a bewildering array of sensations, from alarm
to exhilaration, all of which arrived concurrently. That
Olivia had found herself in such a calamitous state, that her
misadventures had left her so despondent, filled him with
anguish. That she would turn to him as a redeemer, that
after all of the years of separation she could look to him to
release her from such injury, could only gratify him.

He was not by nature a spontaneous man. Every move
he had made, every decision he had taken in his long and
eminent career, had been carefully appraised and played
out in advance, like an intricate game of chess. A game he
was not certain still to have won or to have lost. His deliberate approach had been vital to his professional success,
beyond anything he could have anticipated or hoped for,
but it had not served him well personally. It had not translated into contentment or satisfaction beyond the attain-
ment of the material success he had never sought. Perhaps
spontaneity, perhaps decisiveness was at last what he hungered for. It was surely what the extraordinary situation
called for, and called for loudly.

He knew as well that both he and Olivia had changed.
That the intervening years, the challenges and ordeals each

had faced, had altered them incalculably. That any bond between them, between any two people driven apart for so long, would today be entirely different, maybe disappointing, to one or even to both of them. But change was what he wanted, and what she required. A change would mean that fresh, new place he had dreamed of, where he could reinvent himself and seek another chance at the happiness he had long been denied.

Within the week, the inventory of his house was complete. The servants had been dismissed. And his ticket for India, for the long train ride that would lead him to the renaissance he sought so urgently, that would convey him to his beloved Olivia, was in hand.

PART TWO

PASSAGE

CHAPTER 8 • आठ

"Zoom."

"Zoom," repeated the young Indian boy kneeling on the seat directly in front of Vikhram, keen to draw the man's attention. With both hands he pushed two toy cars along the top and the sides of the worn seat cushion as if it were a racing track. Though they were hardly racing cars.

The toys were second-hand, discarded souvenirs from another child's long-forgotten trip to the British Isles. Remnants of a family's likely expensive holiday, where indulgence and immoderation would have been routine, and where mementos were acquired as effortlessly as they were neglected. One was a replica of an iconic London bus, missing its front grill and number plates, but instantly recognizable by its familiar double-deck construction and by its vivid red color. The other, convincingly leading the chase across the seat-back, was a model of a London hackney cab, painted its trademark black, with four working doors that opened only stiffly, front wheels that turned begrudgingly on a single axle, and the distinctive yellow trademark "Taxi" sign above the windscreen that once would have shone bright, but whose bulb or whose zinc battery had long since burnt out.

"My name is Sunil, and these are my cars."

"It's nice to meet you, Sunil. I'm Vikhram. Those *are* fine looking automobiles."

After just a single day and night into what promised to be a protracted campaign, a crossing by bus of the sterile desert that had become despairingly monotonous, Vikhram was eager to converse with other passengers, any passenger, to break the chronic boredom, but suspicious, withdrawn or simply exhausted, few in the bursting carriage had greeted him, and fewer still were disposed to engage. So the young boy's interruption, which might otherwise have been vexing, was a welcome recess from the crushing invariability.

"That taxi must go very fast. I hope it's not dangerous."

"Dangerous?" said the boy, with a genuinely startled look. "That's just silly. Of course it's not dangerous. *I'm* driving it!"

"Oh, well then, I feel much better about it already. Especially considering your great speed. How far are you planning to go?"

"I'm driving these people all the way home. To Madras. It's going to cost them *a lot* of money. Then I'll be rich," he said, already imagining the infinite treasures that such a pharaonic fare might afford him.

"You know," said Vikhram, in a murmured whisper expertly calculated to pique the boy's interest. "I rode in a taxi just like this one once."

"Really? Where was that?" exclaimed the boy with obvious curiosity. Even as he did so he lowered his own voice, having already been scolded by his irritable father, dozing uncomfortably next to him.

"In Bombay. Maybe ten years ago. I met a man there, a very pleasant man from England, who thought he could sell a lot of these taxis in India. I remember, he was very tall, with dark, wide eyebrows that pointed up at the end so he always looked like he was surprised by something, even when he wasn't! He was going to get rich, that man was. Just like you. So he brought twenty or more of these on a ship all the way to Bombay. It took weeks and weeks to cross the seas. When they arrived, he had himself photographed as the shiny new cars came on shore. It was in all the newspapers. The very next day, I got to take a ride in one of them, with the very distinguished man I worked for then. We went from one end of the city to the other in that taxi."

"Did you like it? Did you buy one?"

"Well, it *was* an unforgettable day. I can still remember most everything about it. Where I sat in the car. The route we took through the streets. The English man trying to explain things about the engine and cylinders and tubes and the power of horses that none of us could understand. As we drove through the city, people stared at us. *Really*, they did! They pointed at the car, and thought we must be very important people. Or very wealthy people. I *did* feel important. I felt like a millionaire that day. But can I tell you something, Sunil, can I tell you a secret?"

"Yes! What?" shrieked the boy, bursting with anticipation, eager to be taken into the stranger's confidence.

"It was a hideous, unnerving ride! It was bumpy all the way. It was sweltering, too, both inside the car and outside. Hotter than a lizard's breath. It was even hotter than on this bus, if you can imagine that. So scorching that the taxi kept overheating. The driver had to keep jumping out, like a frog leaping out of a boiling pot, to pour water in the engine. That car was even thirstier than *we* were! It must have drunk an ocean that day. We all said it would have been better just to take a rickshaw. This happened over and over again. It happened to all of that poor man's taxis. And do you know, in the end, how many he eventually sold?"

"No. How many? One hundred? Two hundred?"

"He didn't sell even *one* of them. He had to send almost all of them back to England. That man never did get rich."

"That's a pity. He should have taken some of them to Madras so I could buy one. Do you think I can get a ride in one back home?"

"I don't see why not. Although I don't think it will be as nice as this one. Where did you get it?" asked Vikhram, surmising by the pitiable state of the boy's clothes and shoes, a state all too similar to his own, that neither the boy nor his father were likely to have traveled all the way to England. That together they had come as far as the Arabian Peninsula was already exceptional, as bringing children into such hardship was generally ill-advised and seldom attempted.

"My father bought it for me in the market before we left Madras. That's him there sleeping," he said, pointing to the hunched figure beside him, trailing off his voice into a more muted tone as he again remembered the earlier admonition.

"I was only five then. Now I'm six and a half!" he continued, pushing out his chest in an instinctive, ritual sign of pride at this supreme accomplishment.

"Why, that's almost the same age as my son, back in Bombay. I bet he likes cars, too, just as you do. Though I don't really know for sure. I've been away for a while. But there is one thing I *do* know for certain he will like. Would you like to see what I got for him?"

Sunil nodded excitedly, as a broad, expectant smile emerged across his exultant face. Vikhram reached above his head to the rusty, exposed steel rods that served as a storage rack to retrieve the canvas sack that constituted his only baggage, and that contained the sum total of all his belongings. Sorting through the bag's neatly folded contents, he pulled out a small packet swathed in newspaper and tied irregularly with twine, unwrapping it in a tantalizingly slow manner.

"Maybe he can ride one of these in Madras as well as in your taxi . . ." said Vikhram, as he revealed from the newspaper one of the pair of beautifully carved, silver-plated African elephants he had purchased in the bazaar in Al-Fadiz.

The young boy was speechless. Had he been old enough to name it, he might have spoken of his astonishment at both the prodigious strength and the quiet grace that the object somehow communicated. It was the very same paradox that had attracted Vikhram's notice to these particular carvings, stowed deep among the heap of characterless keepsakes and tawdry handicrafts competing in the city's markets for the tourist's piddling budget.

The majestic animal had been fashioned in exacting detail. Its broad ears stood upright, as if it were straining intently to heed a mournful cry. Its massive trunk, cocked high in the air, might have been poised to intone a song or a secretive call that, if he listened hard enough, the child alone might hear. Clothed in the likeness of a weighty tapestry of silk and jewels, it radiated the simple but unassailable power of this most noble of creatures.

The carving's thin silver plating shone into the boy's wide, admiring eyes, reflecting the brilliance of the sun's harsh rays streaming through the open windows of the bus. This did not in the least disturb him. He writhed in excitement at the sight of so splendid an article. He held out his hand instinctively, anxious to know its texture, to assess its weight, to hold it as his own, even if only for a moment.

As the boy played with the silver elephant, seamlessly integrating the mammoth beast into his racing game without any of the sense of contradiction or incongruity that would have stifled an older person's creativity, Vikhram turned away. In an instant, unannounced and unexpected, he was afflicted by a potent, grievous remorse. For he heard in the child's laughter, he saw in the boy's easy, effortless joy, distant echoes of his own children. His two young children who for more than two painstaking years he had not seen. A son and a daughter who might have grown beyond his recognition. Whose inevitable amusements and short-lived predicaments of youth were perfectly unknown to him. Children who after all this time, after the plethora of privations in the desert that had darkened not only his skin but his disposition too, might not recognize Vikhram as their absent father. Would they understand the sacrifice he had made? *Could* they understand it, when even Vikhram himself had trouble doing so?

His agony was only exacerbated by the hard truth that he was returning to his family with his ambitions unfulfilled, with his word having been broken. He had given assurances to his wife Sapna, an oath that his leaving, cruel and testing as they both suspected it would be, was necessary and it was right. It would, he had pledged, yield security. It would at last provide them a new life, free from the want and the adversity that weighed on them so heavily. It had done nothing of the sort.

His homecoming, the approaching reunion that had for so long preoccupied and sustained him, was to be bitter-sweet, for he had accomplished very little. He had failed to secure the success he was promised and had in turn promised his family. He had suffered much degradation, had put up with ignoble conditions, and seen the brutal loss of his only friend. For this and more, he had not very much to show. There was no one else to blame, no artifice behind which to hide. The decision to go abroad was his. The failure, too, was his.

From almost the very beginning of his service, Vikhram had chosen to conceal from his wife the extent of his disappointments, convinced that every setback and every loss was but a temporary hurdle on his relentless path to fortune. But that fortune proved stubbornly elusive, and the longer it proved so, the more vigorously he found himself compelled to mislead her. Ashamed of his shortcomings, conscious that Sapna had from the start been suspect of the entire undertaking, he had in his many letters home intimated that success would soon be his. He had chosen an innocent deceit to ease the inordinate strain of responsibility, and to justify his continued absence. Triumph, though ill-defined, would always be close at hand, and with it, vindication. It was not.

Doubt now seized him. Violent, fierce doubt. Uncertainty as to whether the errors of his abortive venture to those bleak oil fields could have been foreseen, and whether he ever could or should defend his obstinate conviction to go. Trepidation about how his patient, indulgent wife would receive him. If she would consent to absolve him, or whether on his feeble return she would hold him in contempt. As increasingly he held himself.

* *

Vikhram's descent into this dizzying morass of self-doubt was interrupted only by a minor but raucous scuffle, as a shock of new passengers, picked up at one of the lost, remote outposts positioned seemingly randomly in the

middle of the empty desert, jockeyed for a seat near a
window, a precious commodity in the kiln that was the
jammed, rickety bus.

Apart from the young Sunil, his father and Vikhram,
booked in three days' time on the same boat bound for the
sub-continent, there were no other Indians on board. The
rest of the travelers, whose numbers swelled to more than
thirty, were Arabs, although from which part of the Gulf or
even from the Maghreb, Vikhram was unqualified to deter-
mine. He detected differences in what he assumed to be
dialect or accent. A tendency among some of them to more
heavily emphasize a final syllable in a word or a final word in
a sentence. Unique expressions or salutations to each other.
He had not learned, or even attempted to learn their language during his time in the region, beyond the minimal,
requisite formalities and the mostly insincere, formulaic
greetings exchanged with shopkeepers and company officials. Traditional greetings such as *"assalaam alaikum"* to
address friends and strangers alike, and to wish that peace
be with them – the one expression Vikhram had found so
congenial that during the day he often manufactured flimsy
excuses to use it. Or the precise phrasing he memorized to
let those strangers know that he didn't speak Arabic, though
with his dark, southern Indian skin this was largely superfluous and would have stunned them otherwise. The language's elongated vowels and diphthongs were alien to his
ear, and he despaired at the complexity of the grammar,
once described to him, by a member of the ship's crew on his
initial crossing to Saudi Arabia, as analogous to an algebraic
equation. As he knew no algebra, nor even what algebra was
beyond some loose association with the calculation of sums,
he found neither the drive nor the interest to study it in the
way he had studied English so passionately in his youth.

Still, he could manage to communicate with the other passengers, especially those who could make themselves understood in some loose approximation of English. Notions of the language would have been required for many of them in order to perform the litany of menial tasks and bleak jobs for the Westerners who day by day were decamping in ever larger numbers to stake a claim to the region's burgeoning oil wealth. So, as Sunil drifted into sleep, resting his head softly on the older man's shoulder after exhausting his energetic games and himself in the process, Vikhram decided to introduce himself to his fellow travelers. Had it not been for the crippling tediousness of the trip, he might not have been so forward.

He discerned among the passengers a diversity of motives for undertaking this racking trek across the infinite desert. Directly across the aisle, Vikhram presented himself to an older couple, both the man and the woman clad in loose-fitting, ankle-length shirts of black cotton. He was able to decipher, not without some difficulty and mostly by way of the bountiful samples they proudly showed him, that the aim of their expedition was to sell a selection of handmade wares to affluent Kuwaitis, only lately becoming prosperous from the commercial exploitation of crude. They were taking to the markets an extraordinary, and what looked to him like an indiscriminate assortment of gold and silver decorative jewelry, sandals, saddlebags and other skins, most festooned with elaborate geometric designs or with religious inscriptions rendered in what he took to be delicate calligraphy.

Behind Vikhram sat a retiring man, absorbed by a deck of playing cards that he simply shuffled again and again, almost to obsession. This solitary man, if not unfriendly, then at least withdrawn, explained that he was charged with retrieving an automobile that had been sent from Coventry for his employer in Sana'a. A Daimler Saloon that, he was instructed, cost more than the man was likely to earn in his natural lifetime.

And huddled tightly at the back of the bus, like cattle in an abattoir, was a cluster of men who together were traveling on to Baghdad, at least another half-day's bus ride from Vikhram's own intermediate destination. These men, each more abject than the other, were traveling to the thriving capital of Iraq in a desperate search for work, particularly among the many Jewish-owned tanneries and textile mills that prevailed over the Kingdom's flourishing economy. One young man hoped to take up a place he had been promised at one of the city's booming cement factories. Still others were hoping to find employment aboard the luxury trains that frequently left from, or stopped in Baghdad on their way to cities across the Asian and European continents. The rowdiest of these men, slight of build but with a voice that was as brassy as his words were vulgar, boasted of the dozen or so trips on these trains that he had undertaken already, and had, or so he asserted, in gratuities alone amassed a considerable amount of money. Vikhram found this one account particularly suspect, for surely no one with any wherewithal would have chosen to travel on a bus in such squalor, but he found the tale, one that he might himself have invented, amusing and distracting enough that he held his tongue.

* *

As the discussions waned, and those around him drifted off or spoke amongst themselves, Vikhram became impatient to withdraw. It wasn't that the stories his companions told, stories of perpetual aspiration that closely mirrored his own, were not compelling. Nor that the conversation, difficult as it showed itself to be, was not welcome. Rather, Vikhram was eager to seize the opportunity, and the little of the day that remained, to read.

Returning to his seat, he removed from its careful wrapping one of the several paperback books packed away in his canvas bag. In Al-Fadiz's only foreign bookshop, he had a few times these past two years permitted himself the purchase a book. He had bought a number of cheerful, jaunty American novels. He found a book from the previous century that irresistibly described life in the rural English countryside, written by a woman but, confusingly, published under a man's name. A collection of Australian stories that illustrated seductively the vastness of an open continent and its settlement, apparently, by castaways. Even rarer still, the odd second-hand Marathi book left behind, no doubt, by a literate Indian worker who had long since left these shores.

To read, to devour the sensational and affecting stories he loved most in English, was for Vikhram still, just as it had been at the Victoria Book Palace in Bombay, more than just a pastime. It was a potent reminder that he had already once achieved an implausible goal. Learning to read, and in a language that was not his own, served as credible proof that he was capable of achieving more than might have been expected of him. It was a reminder, too, that another, a better day was possible on the other side of this agony. He had no pretensions to superiority, sought no advantage from his achievement or drew any arrogance from it. He had only a conviction, and in his treasured books he had irrefutable evidence, that any one of the lowly people with whom he shared his invidious fate could, with industry and with perseverance, one day shake it off. Just as he might still do.

He read for what seemed like hours. He would have liked to continue doing so this evening for some time yet, to have propped up the failing sun so he could saunter further through the lush fields of his enthralling novel. But the light faded more quickly than he had anticipated, so imperious was its power during the day that it seemed improbable it could be so utterly extinguished at night. As the radiant moon slowly ascended in its place, cooling the land as it shrouded it in darkness, he was at pains to distinguish the words on the darkening page. Resigned, Vikhram neatly put away the large volume, and fixed his wandering stare out toward the unbounded plain.

He paid no attention to the murky landscape, almost wholly clothed as it had become in obscurity. The minutes and the miles passed, quite ignored, as he found himself hypnotized by the strident, perpetual repetition of the turning bus wheels. Every one of those turns lulled him, deeper and more profoundly, into something close to a meditative trance. In this dulled state, suddenly he saw that every new rotation, raking up the loose gravel in an eruption of brutality and leaving in its wake a towering curtain of sand and dirt, was bringing him closer and closer to home. Somewhere between waking and sleep, he began at last to imagine it, to see his home more lucidly than he had done since leaving it. That, too, brought him only greater and greater relief.

Almost mechanically, he took from his jacket pocket, and then clutched with both hands, the boat ticket that he saw as a kind of amulet. An ordinary, double-folded piece of printed paper that held in its gift the promise of return and of renewal. The ship's name was written in bold characters on the front of the ticket like a celebration. Christened *The Artemis*, she was then one of only a pair to make the crossing, once every six weeks at best, direct from southern India to Kuwait. In reverse, it would call at Bombay, Jaffna at the tip of Ceylon, Madras, and then on to the Burmese capital of Rangoon.

It was the very same craft, ceaselessly shuttling cargo and men from east to west and back again, that had first brought him to the Gulf. Built two decades ago, it was one of the last to be produced by the Middle River Shipyard Works in the United States, before the company collapsed from a lack of orders, and with it the men to properly maintain her.

To Vikhram, familiarity with the ship was immaterial. As he was to travel third-class, and the poorly maintained ship itself was little more than an aging ruin, she held for him no pleasure or amusement, save for the fresh sea air on the decks that he would so welcome and for the obliging company he hoped to find below. He knew the return journey would be as disagreeable and as deafening as was his coming. His only interest was in the vessel's ability to transport him swiftly home to his family, and away from his many errors and misjudgments. He would have suffered even the foul punishments of toiling in the ship's fearsome engine room if it had meant delivering him there more quickly.

* *

Soon the evening's light had faded so entirely that driving the weather-beaten bus, fraught even in the raw brightness of day, when one could actually see the many obstacles and detritus that encumbered the clumsily-paved route, had become foolhardy. The blistering engine, assaulted from the small hours by the uncompromising heat of the desert, like the tired passengers and the driver too, needed to rest. They all needed fuel as well, and so, as they had the night before and would do so the next and final night as well, the disparate group of drained men, women and one careworn child disembarked just as soon as they had reached the next way-station and the engine had been cut.

It was an austere and desolate place. Constructed principally of sand, gravel and rock, the station might once have been painted in a broad palette of colors, but had long since assumed the same pallid complexion as the heartless desert that threatened to swallow it whole. Two identical, rusty petrol pumps stood guard under a broad stone canopy, bounded on either side by faintly charred columns of gratuitous height. The top of the canopy bore in dulled paint the vestiges of an inscription in Arabic, welcoming no doubt the fatigued traveler to this providential sanctuary, but it had deteriorated beyond recognition over time and by obvious indifference. A large portrait of an unsmiling, dispassionate-looking King Abdul Aziz, masked by a thick layer of grime, hung crookedly on the posterior wall, lit up by a single, bare bulb that cast an unnerving pallor over the whole structure.

Behind this wall was a small room that served as a workspace and storeroom, and sleeping quarters for the owner. Farther back still there was a small, cluttered shop stocked with canned goods and other packaged provisions that could withstand the infrequency of visitors. Each room claimed large windows covered by a steel grill and a narrow door-frame, though none actually had, or had any longer, a proper door. At the end of a short, run-down passage, the station also proposed two stark bedrooms for hire, each consisting of a single bed too small for most, a set of matching straw-backed chairs, a sink that most days supplied running water, and the complete want of any decoration or embellishment.

These rooms, one of which was reserved for the driver, were meant to provide the odd paying visitor shelter from the cold and exposed night, while the others would have to make do with sleeping out of doors as best and as securely as they could. None of the passengers on this journey could muster even the trivial sum required for the second room. Conscious of every last penny he had in his possession, and anticipating the outlays he would face for his short stay in Kuwait City and then on the ocean crossing itself, Vikhram preferred to brave the elements than to squander his shriveling capital on a night of only relative comfort.

Despite the sordidness of the establishment, its proprietor proved good-natured. As the bus pulled up he was to be found sitting under the canopy, dressed in a sweat-stained, sleeveless cotton shirt, untucked at the waist, lazily smoking one of the distinctive, fragrant clove cigarettes that Vikhram had encountered and enjoyed on only a few occasions since leaving India. Attracted by the sweet smell of the tobacco, Vikhram made his way directly to the paunchy man and asked if he could spare or would sell him a cigarette.

"Why, you needn't worry about that, there's plenty more where this came from," said the proprietor, pointing to the shop where many of the passengers, who appeared to know the layout of the grounds, were heading already.

"I'm much obliged," said Vikhram, using one of the overly formal phrases he had been taught in the British Colonial Service, and which had since become an unwitting part of his standard English repertoire.

He struggled to keep up with the man who, like the new recruits, was pressing now to make his way to the shop, anxious to sell as much as he could, but equally anxious to ensure that none of his stock went missing by any sleight of hand from the ravenous crowd.

"How much does it cost for a carton of these cigarettes?" asked Vikhram eagerly, more out of curiosity than from any real intent to purchase them, since he had long since forsworn such luxuries.

"Probably more than you think, and I'd guess more than you have," came the unexpectedly frank, and the unexpectedly astute answer. "These are all hand-rolled, and imported from Java. From Indonesia. They taste a little like licorice, which I'm not particularly fond of but which a lot of my customers seem to like."

He pronounced this as if his customers were numerous and as if they were regular, conjuring up chimerical patrons who would have had to brave the uninterrupted miles of oblivion, to trudge across the parched wilds, expressly to seek out his trade. Vikhram thought this to be highly unlikely, and even slightly fantastical. He was unsure if the station owner was delusional or whether he was enjoying a laugh at his visitor's expense. He very much suspected the latter.

"There are plenty of other things here you might need on your way. I expect you're going all the way to Kuwait, yes? You will need supplies; there is almost *nothing* between here and the city."

Vikhram found this last remark particularly comical, as the station seemed to him practically nothing already. He wondered what less than nothing might look like.

"How about some caraway seeds?" said the proprietor. "Or a bunch of almonds? That ought to see you through."

In fact, casting his eye around the cavernous room, Vikhram could see that the shop contained a striking quantity of foodstuffs, stacked tightly, and defiantly high. There were lentils and chickpeas by the pound. Tinned meats and beans and cooking oil. Baskets of pitted and unpitted dates alike, most covered in a thin layer of dust, and nuts of a phenomenal variety for so small and so remote a location. Boxed lemon juice, dried milk and coffee grounds on the crammed, sullied shelves. There were many other items that would have made the days and the nights of his journey that much more bearable. There were bars of lye soap, toothpaste in collapsible tubes such as Vikhram had never seen before, portable flashlights and countless other items that he either could not recognize, did not need or could not have paid for.

When Vikhram had selected the few purchases within his means – less than he would have liked but perilously close to what he could not afford – the shop owner leaned over the low counter where he had weighed and wrapped the goods.

"Here, my friend," he said. "Here's some chocolate for your boy. My treat."

Vikhram, perplexed, hadn't until then noticed Sunil shadowing him in the shop, grabbing surreptitiously at the lower shelves he could reach, and helping himself to the odd date or biscuit. Even at his young age, he understood well enough that his own father, washing the accumulated dirt off his clothes and face in the common lavatory, would not have the means to purchase these items. He understood, too, that the punishment for stealing would not likely outweigh the benefits.

That the boy could be confused for Vikhram's son was understandable, given their general physical similarities, at least to those who knew little of foreigners and who saw even less of them. This impression could only have been amplified by the search for approval in the boy's eyes, a look of anguish as Sunil turned desperately to Vikhram for his consent to allow this gracious gift of a sweet he so desired, as naturally he might have looked to his own father. A small gesture that Vikhram was only too happy to oblige.

With Vikhram armed with his provisions, and the boy with his sweet, the pair made their way back to the courtyard, but not before Sunil, grateful for his unexpected windfall, offered to share the bar of chocolate with his new friend. He broke it in two and presented Vikhram with the larger half. Something he accepted with pleasure, even if he didn't quite care for the bitter taste of the local varieties. This simple expression was to him deeply poignant. He saw in this tender act, just as he had during their racing game, a flicker of the bond he might hope to renew with his own son. A son he would once again see in just over a week's time. And in an instant, that thought eclipsed what he knew would be the testing night ahead.

* *

In another place, at another time, he might have been keen to explore the site, to investigate the uncanny ferment emanating from the invisible corners that dotted this mystifying nocturnal landscape. He would have liked to wander toward the unfamiliar, drawn to the discovery of this forbidding world, listening for the secrets of the desert and for clues to its soul. He might have reveled in observing the staggering beauty of this night, more vibrant than any he had seen before. The sky he had come to know in Al-Fadiz had been thoroughly disfigured by the incandescent fires of the rigs. The skies of his youth in Bombay, where night and day were nearly indistinguishable, and where the always brilliant lights and insidious pollution of the city blurred out almost entirely the drama of the stars and planets, were all but obscured.

But this was not the place, and this was not the time. His attention was focused not on such ethereal considerations, but only on his purposeful, unalterable advance toward home. In this moment, he needed not to contemplate the distant heavens, but to survey the solid ground in front of him for a suitable place to rest. To prepare himself for the next day's challenges, and for the rest of the difficult journey that still lay ahead.

One by one, each member of the traveling party was making his or her preparations for the night's rest. The bus was shut and locked, despite the obvious flaw that the windows had no glass, and no one was allowed to spend the night inside it, lest everyone attempt to do so. The quicker ones found their place beneath the vehicle, where the wind was less fierce and where it could less easily penetrate.

Some of the passengers, especially those who had made the trip more than once, were better equipped, and had crude sleeping gear at the ready – a blanket of some form or another, and warmer clothes to serve as protection from the rapidly cooling air. Others, including Vikhram, had prepared less well, if they had prepared at all, and had to make do with only improvised arrangements. Another layer of clothing, wrestled over the tight jacket in which he closely guarded his money and his boat ticket, would serve as his only fortification against the cold. His canvas bag, stuffed with clothes and gifts and books, would be his pillow.

He had become used to sleeping in hard and irregular conditions, to stealing moments of respite whenever the circumstances would allow it. Tonight then, despite the cold, despite the unsettling echoes and the nameless others crowded around him, he managed to fall speedily and profoundly to sleep.

The night, however, was a short one. The morning sun peeked over the horizon with remarkable pace, and with it began almost straightaway the preparations to leave. Still drowsy and drained, not one of the group would have wished to linger, intent as they all were to reach their destination, still at least another day and another night from this lonely place.

Besides, the driver was compelled to keep to a rigid timetable. Any deviation or delay would not be forgiven, even if it could be explained. Like an army drill sergeant directing his somnolent troops into formation, he bellowed terse instructions to the mob to assemble their few effects and to board the bus in haste. Accustomed by this time to his brusqueness, and suspecting rightly that he would show them no clemency in leaving behind any laggards, the group promptly complied. Within minutes they were off. The station owner, roused from his nervous sleep by the sudden commotion of the impending departure, raced to the bus in one last effort to sell to the group any supplies they might need or desire for the next leg, but he was too slow off the mark, and as they sped off in a squall of shouts and dust, he could only offer a lusty wave.

The passengers settled into their seats calmly, many taking the very same positions they had vacated the night before, as if by some unspoken rule. All but Sunil, who was searching frenetically under the seats.

"Vikhram, Vikhram! I've lost my taxi. I think I left it at the station. I *know* we left it behind!" he cried with alarm and with dread.

"Surely you have it. Have you looked in between the seats? What about in your bag?"

"I've looked *everywhere*. I had it last night before I went to sleep, but we left so fast this morning, I didn't have time to check." His sobs made it difficult for Vikhram to understand the boy's mumbled words, though their meaning was clear.

The boy's father appeared indifferent. Even mildly annoyed. He suggested that Sunil play instead with the red bus he seemed to like just as much, or with the sculpted elephant his neighbor had yesterday shown him. Yet for Vikhram, there was something desperate, something primordial at play. With his own son and daughter foremost in his thoughts, even the loss of a cheap, insignificant souvenir meant he felt his heart break for the young boy, and in a way, for himself. He had come to realize, still only at the start of this journey home, that his being so long away had surely meant his own children had been deprived on so many counts. Not simply of toys or of sweets, but of his affections. Of his attention. He had withheld his presence too long. He could never fully make amends, and he certainly couldn't do so simply by salvaging an inconsequential toy for a boy he hardly knew. But here and now, he might at least be able to offer support. To be considerate. Useful even.

He rushed to the front of the bus and set about convincing the driver to go back. Asking, pleading with him to turn the vehicle around in order to retrieve the lost toy. The driver showed no inclination to do so. He had targets to meet, a schedule to obey. Still, Vikhram remained insistent, as if the world depended on it. He appealed to the man's sense of sympathy and decency, qualities the latter had little displayed these past two days. He appealed most of all, and in more persuasive, more personal terms, to the man's sensitivity as a father, having spotted a discolored photograph of a young family dangling askew from the vehicle's rearview mirror.

To his great relief, the driver at last relented, and to the disapproving howls of the other passengers, made a wide turn off the gravel path. In no time, they had returned to the way-station. Vikhram, charging off the bus, found the toy car in short order, covered in sand and turned on its side, precisely where Sunil said he had left it. When he handed it to the young boy, the child melted into irrepressible tears. As too, more discreetly and with his back turned to the rest of the group, did Vikhram.

CHAPTER 9 • नऊ

It wasn't the impression that the landscape and the architecture had changed so dramatically that most surprised Sebastian, but that they had changed so suddenly. By the time the train had steamed its way to the eastern periphery of France and deep into the intricate web of minor towns and bucolic villages of northern Switzerland, the dependable brick and concrete masonry and unvaryingly flat, slate-roof houses that had thus far reigned over the countryside had yielded almost entirely in favor of prouder, more intrepid wooden structures. Many of the elegant homes he observed sported sloping rooftops, covered in polished, tightly-stacked stone tiles in various shades of grey. Sturdy, meticulously crafted overhanging eaves provided protection from the harsher elements in the demanding mountainous terrain. But they also gave their occupants both the license and the opportunity to parade more ornamental, sometimes flamboyant expressions that had been all but absent from the previous architectural homogeny.

The topography had altered as well, so that the gently pitched and scarcely billowing fields gave way to powerful cliffs littered with a riot of ancient stones and dense, deciduous trees. Closely packed trees whose milk-white flowers and bright orange fruit lit up the hillsides like beacons. So too did the brilliant, virgin snow that blanketed the commanding mountain peaks, even as the summer heat continued to dominate the valleys below, through which only the thinnest of paths had been cut for the train's tracks.

Sebastian was surprised even more by the change in the air, which in the higher altitudes through which they were passing had become noticeably thinner, and the pressure markedly lower than he had ever known in England, aside from the highly charged moments just before the onset of a particularly violent thunderstorm. He had not anticipated the different atmospheric conditions, nor the fickleness of the weather so prone to arresting variation from hour to hour. The men of his professional circle to whom he only belatedly had confided his travel plans had spoken to him at length of the various landmarks and monuments he might visit as he traversed the continent. They hailed or reviled the food, deplored the cacophony of languages and the often impenetrable cultural practices. They had neglected, however, to speak of the crispness and the purity of the Alpine air, which evoked for Sebastian something akin to a flavor he could taste and which, though he suffered some of the fatigue and unsteadiness one might have predicted at such heights, he found to be most agreeable. There was none of the choking smog or the rank industrial pollution that had long since come to characterize the air in London. Nor was there any of the unending blare of the capital's streets to which he had unwittingly become too accustomed.

At the dawn of his third full day on the train, he was gradually settling into the long voyage. Away from the tumult of the last fortnight and the endless preparations for his departure, and further still from the doubts that tugged at him even as he saw the Dover Cliffs recede across the Channel, Sebastian at last began to bask in the travel itself.

The perspective from his cabin windows could hardly have been more advantageous. He thought of the passing, storybook scenery as if it might have been contrived expressly for his entertainment. As if he were watching fragments snatched from one of the films he so often watched back home, the constantly changing spectacle like a false movie set constructed just in time for his arrival, and dismantled just as soon as he had passed. The unspoiled villages were irreproachable, their suspiciously perfect church spires shimmering in the morning sun, the lush pastures that encircled and fed them too immaculate to be real.

Apart from his sea crossing, as brief as it was turbulent, the voyage had been remarkably smooth and unproblematic. Like a wide-eyed schoolboy earnestly taking on a research assignment, Sebastian today closely tracked his progress against the stylized and rather approximate map of Europe that decorated his cabin, just as he had done on the previous days. Many of the names of the stations he encountered were recognizable. Historically or culturally significant, they recalled noteworthy events of times recent and of times past. Others, announced on platform name boards and in stations scarcely larger than the train itself, were entirely unknown to him. Their pronunciation often confounded and almost always amused him.

At none of these stations did he disembark. He wasn't planning to leave the train. He hadn't bothered to explore any of the legendary cities through which his itinerary was taking him, as other passengers had done and as so many had recommended he do. He might have lingered for a few days in Paris, where he didn't know a soul, but felt he nonetheless knew the city and its unmatched treasures, especially by way of the substantial literature it had produced and through his own reporting on French politics and arts over many years. He could have strolled through the Tuileries Garden, taken a leisurely meal on the Left Bank, or more ambitious still, traced the Sun King's footsteps at nearby Versailles. Vienna, where the train would stop for only a short spell, promised similarly enticing attractions for the cultivated and educated traveler, from its palatial Hapsburg residences to its baroque Opera House. He might have dined with the director of that city's Museum of Fine Arts, to whom he had been introduced some years prior, having played a role in securing for the V&A in London a loan of several paintings by Raphael and Brueghel from the Viennese institution. The two men had continued to correspond even during the most terrible moments of the war, though they had never met.

Even the promise of such a meeting was not to be contemplated, for it would have meant leaving behind the train and idly awaiting the next one, in several days' time. Nothing – not the prospect of renewing an erstwhile acquaintance, not the potential to pay a visit to the famous sites that largely defined a continent and had so unexpectedly defied the wounds of its most recent conflict – would distract him from his only objective, to join Olivia in India as quickly as he could manage. And he hadn't a moment to waste.

Only a few short weeks had passed since he had received her melancholic plea, but many years had passed since they had parted, since they had been ripped apart by scandal and by an obdurate, insular community that offered an opposition stronger than either of them could even have attempted to resist.

In that sustained interval, he had long since resigned

himself to a permanent condition of loneliness, of seclusion. He had abandoned hopes of reclaiming the joy and the passion that marked his time at Cambridge with Olivia. Despite their extensive correspondence, in which traditional codes of civility were rigidly respected and where discretion predominated over forthrightness, he could not have known, and would not have suspected, that she too longed to regain that joy. That suddenly, and only after so many years had much altered each of their circumstances, he would find himself on a luxury train, tearing along freshly cleared tracks over the broad expanse of two alien continents, having been summoned to her side. No wonder he could ill afford to deviate. He had already spent an eternity astray.

* *

He would allow himself only one outing, but one that would not set back his firm timetable. When tomorrow the train reached Budapest, the narrower gauge of rail farther east required that the engine be replaced in a prolonged and, for the untrained workers in particular, a sometimes risky exercise. He would use that interruption to meet with his friend and former editor, Salamon Gaál, a gifted newspaperman of Jewish heritage who had the foresight to leave Hungary for London at the start of hostilities and had only recently returned to help rebuild the country he had once lost and the capital city that had come so desperately close to being obliterated.

Their appointment at the stylish Café Prater, scheduled for noon the following day, had been confirmed in one of the two telegrams presented to Sebastian at the station in Vienna by the train manager, a rare enough occurrence even for the many moneyed passengers on the line. As was customary, the cable contained no extraneous words. It contained no suggestion of the great eagerness both men felt in expectation of their imminent encounter.

The second of these telegrams came from his solicitor in London, and brought various pieces of news from home.

THE WESTERN UNION TELEGRAPH COMPANY, INC.
CABLE SERVICE TO ALL THE WORLD

Received at: Vienna, Austria via London, England. Paid.
Sebastian Reynolds, en route Delhi, Care Conductor, Bright Star
Line, Train 103.

"HOUSE SALE COMPLETE STOP FUNDS WIRED N. DELHI ARRIVE 14 SEPT STOP PLS URGENTLY INSTRUCT LIBRARY CONTENTS & COLLINS SEVERANCE 12 MONTHS AS INTENDED STOP FIRST TEST AUS BY 8 WICKETS STOP E.S.G."

He received the news of the sale of his London house with something close to indifference. It was of little import to him, except in the sense that he knew it meant, or suspected it did, that his return to England had become even more unlikely. He knew that his solicitor had also understood this, and would have dictated the news of the rapid sale with more than a touch of regret, for the lawyer had opposed from the start what he thought of as a reckless decision. He had tried with all of his practiced powers of persuasion, honed for years in front of cowering witnesses in the box and sardonic judges on the bench, to steer Sebastian away from this path. To no avail.

Sebastian felt compelled, before the train left the station at Vienna, to construct a reply that confirmed the payment of severance to Mrs. Collins, his abidingly loyal housekeeper. His present buoyant temper inclined him towards being even more munificent than had been previously agreed. He felt less compelled to provide an immediate answer to the matter of disposing of his library, an issue that required more careful attention, and over which he vacillated considerably. The collection, impressive as doubtless it was, was not in his estimation of enough consequence to merit a bequest to the British Library or to a similarly venerated establishment, and it was unthinkable that he would confer it on any of England's academic institutions for which generally he retained a pronounced antipathy. Yet it was substantial enough not to be presented as a mere token to an acquaintance or to an associate, who might not appreciate its value. He would consider it more, and in the days to come he would waver still.

Yet it was the cricket score, the result of the first of five Test matches between England and the visiting Australian side, which served most to amuse him. To have included this was a spot of fancy on the part of his solicitor. Before his speedily arranged departure, Sebastian had studied the batting line-ups for weeks; he knew the match schedules, and he knew in detail the tourists' unassailable record. If he had stayed in London, he would surely have partaken in the general fanfare and euphoria that greeted such respected and such feared competitors. But he was today half a continent away from England, and a world away from the affairs and the copious minor preoccupations that had there held sway over his days. Cricket matches were entirely discordant with the hoary Austrian mountain peaks on which his gaze from the cabin windows was firmly fixed, and growing only more insignificant as the train drew him farther and farther away.

* *

The cabin, comprised of two adjoining rooms, was not notably spacious. The width of the sleeping quarters hardly exceeded that of its double bed, whose tight fit implied it had been constructed or at least assembled in place. As the bed butted up against the narrow room's sides, its occupants were required to perform a somewhat awkward and decidedly inelegant maneuver to climb in and out of it. What the room lacked in size, however, was more than offset by its splendor. The erratic jolts of the train aside, no fashionable hotel in Paris or New York could have offered the visitor any more opulence or luxury.

The bed, firm and high, was headed with a profusion of plump, goose feather pillows and draped in Egyptian cotton sheets of an impossibly high thread count. At its base sat an oversized armchair and matching footstool that incited its inhabitant to idleness, to languorous moments measured not in minutes but in hours. The small writing desk, flush against the opposite wall, was burnished to a terrific sheen. Fashioned out of the same wood as the panels that encased the room, the desk seemed to have emerged from those panels rather than having been built against them. On the desk, the passenger was awarded with a medley of finely-crafted writing implements and thick paper that bore the railway line's distinctive emblem proudly as a watermark, and in a surprising bid to nostalgia that was largely superfluous, given the extensive electric lighting in the room, a crystal-and-brass oil lantern.

The room's other ornamentation was similarly lavish. Over the desk hung a circular, silver-gilded mirror, placed directly opposite the windows and at precisely the right height and tilt to produce the effect of dramatically enlarging the limited space. Its reflection, bringing into the cabin the colors and forms from the shifting environment without, lent the room a certain sense of harmony, as did the predominance of the single grain of wood throughout. Likewise, the bed's coverlet, cushions on the armchair and curtains all were made of the same cream-colored silk, bearing a distinctive pattern that fell somewhere between a fleur-de-lys and Scottish paisley. Sebastian presumed the silk to be of Chinese manufacture, an impression he formed not least by the hint of the grand, ancestral portrait of a Chinese nobleman suspended above the bed. Seated in almost regal pose, the anonymous official held a delicate parchment scroll in his palms and bore a contemplative, enigmatic stare of both wisdom and serenity that itself added a patent sense of calm to the room.

The sitting room adjacent, bounded by a full bath, provided the same glittering splendor. It was only marginally larger than the bedroom, but had an altogether different disposition. The room's plush sofa, large enough for several people to sit comfortably and flanked on either side by a leather club chair, had been positioned directly in front of the ample panes of glass. The same wood paneling pervaded, complemented by rich furnishings and highly decorative paintings of undetermined ancestry, and by the ornate map of Europe. The view from the sizable windows was unhindered, as if the room's designer wished to compel the passenger to concentrate his full attention on the superb display outside, to be so completely engaged by the transitory manifestations beyond, so much at ease by the simple amenities and simple indulgences of these rooms, that one needn't ever leave the carriage.

This, in fact, was precisely the posture Sebastian had increasingly come to adopt. He was content to spend his days in solitary. Lazily admiring the ever-changing vistas. Producing lengthy correspondence for those at home to whom he had not provided a sufficient explanation for his sudden departure, or for whom he hadn't found the appetite or the nerve to do so in person. Meditating on what the breach into which he had leapt so impulsively and so irrevocably might deliver. And, not least, spending long hours devouring the many books he had brought aboard.

He read extensively, uninterrupted by the minor stirrings that in London were common in his household and by the disruptions that were endemic in the city beyond. He had long hesitated about which volumes to pack in his seldom-used red leather trunk, and had finally decided on taking a number of the more substantial works of fiction that somehow he had never found the time or the peace of mind to read. He had largely selected illustrious novels that told stories of travel and of nervy adventure that he thought, somewhat fancifully, might loosely resemble his own adventure, and would serve to hearten and to fortify him. Chief among them was the rousing tale of the *Count of Monte Cristo*, in which he saw in the aggrieved young sailor's invention of a new persona and a new life an echo of what he was intending to set out for himself, absent the exuberant swordplay and the ruthless vengeance. He brought, too, the *Rime of the Ancient Mariner*, the stirring ballad he had read first as a boy, but whose tale of an heroic voyage through the South Seas Sebastian felt would today resonate even more, flattering himself into thinking it had parallels to his own, audacious expedition, where many tests would surely await but where redemption was all but certain.

Engrossed in his reading, he stayed alone for hours. He stayed in his cabin as well so as to ration his interaction with the other passengers, and most particularly to limit his communication with the irritating Prescott family who had been assigned as his regular dinner partners. In the first-class dining car, where the service and the decor were impeccable, he was robbed of what might otherwise have been cheery interludes, condemned instead to share his meals with this voluble, irksome English clan.

This small family, from their roaring voices to their brash, lurid language, were little more than lamentable caricatures. A mercifully aberrant perversion of proper English society. The family's patriarch in particular, a portly, pompous, self-made businessman, father of the two spotty children opposite, was the very picture of the vulgar tourist abroad. The condescension and the disdain with which this surly character treated the train's wait-staff were insufferable. For them to hear him speak of the unfriendly, unclean foreigners he had so far stumbled upon, to listen to his infinite bemoaning of their unseemly comportment and of their alleged discourteousness, was to question why a man so innately beset with protest for the unknown and the unusual would have undertaken to leave his island nation in the first place.

Every sanctified temple or monument Alfred Prescott had inspected, every local food he was compelled to endure, was judged against its equivalent in England, and judged unfavorably. Similarly for Mrs. P. – for that was how her husband familiarly referred to her – nothing compared kindly to what she knew at home, a limitation only compounded by her unqualified lack of interest in these very same discoveries. Her small talk veered constantly toward empty tittle-tattle, largely about people unknown to Sebastian. What she lacked in inquisitiveness about the places she had visited, she counterbalanced only by a vigorous, gossipy interest in Sebastian's person and in his circle.

He had half a mind to affect an assumed name, to introduce himself as an arbitrary character from one of the novels he had in his possession, and had considered the choice with his usual assiduousness. He thought it might be especially amusing, and most appropriate, to choose a certain Cyril Fielding as an alias, namesake of the good-tempered headmaster of the government college in Chandrapore from Forster's *A Passage to India*. He only refrained from doing so at the last moment, as he feared it might have caused confusion with the crew and consternation if, by some unlikely wonder, any one of the family proved literate enough to unmask his mischievous if lighthearted deception.

He had the previous evening requested an early dinner, hoping to avoid their trying company, but meals were served at set times, and so for as long as he frequented the dining car the Prescotts were inescapable. When early in the previous sitting the young Prescott boy, distracted with as much ease as any boy his age, asked to be excused from the binding formality of the table to return to his cabin, to read or to write in his travel journal, Sebastian thought he too would have liked to have been excused. He declined the waiter's offer of an after-dinner coffee on the grounds that it didn't agree with him, though in truth it was more his dinner companions that didn't agree with his constitution.

Since then, Sebastian had done his best to avoid this family, sacrificing the diversion of the dining car for the quiet and the calm of his own quarters. He had only to ring a bell, one of which was installed discreetly in each of his two rooms, for a member of the staff to fulfill any request that might reasonably be expected from the limited reserves on board.

The train manager had called on him early this morning

already, and only minutes after the train pulled smoothly into the station at Budapest, the steward, a young man called Hamid, knocked on Sebastian's door. The steward's name was inscribed proudly on the simple badge he wore, a small metal plate whose stenciled lettering was well-worn in testimony to the employee's long service on the railway. He spoke English impeccably, though his speech was tinged with the occasional anomalous phrase and with a delicate accent that Sebastian was unable to place, but which he suspected, with little basis for comparison, as being either Turkish or Persian. He had thought it impolite on their first meeting to ask, and so despite their many subsequent interactions remained ignorant still of the steward's origins.

"Good morning, Mr. Reynolds. We have arrived in Budapest. On schedule."

"Goodness, it *does* seem a sort of minor miracle that we've been able to stay on time across all this distance. I expect His Majesty's Infantry couldn't have done any better than that. How long are we meant to remain here in Hungary?"

"In Hungary, sir, I cannot tell you; we must pass first through Kecskemét and then Szeged," came the more literal answer than Sebastian had expected. "In Budapest, we will remain five hours. Not a minute more and not a minute less. But there is much to be done before then."

"Yes, I suppose there must be. I can see there's a lot of fuss on the platform already. Will you at least find time for some rest today, Hamid?"

"It is very kind of sir to ask, but I am afraid today will be even more busy for the staff than most days. Not least since many of the first-class passengers have made arrangements to visit the city, so the crew will take the opportunity to clean the cabins from top to bottom. We must launder the linen, and we will make repairs. I will have very many things to manage today. Is there anything I can do for *you*, sir?"

"Well, I do in fact have a request, but it's only a very small one. There's a bulb in the fixture beside my bed that's gone out, which I wonder if I might have replaced before this evening."

"Why, of course. I will have one of the boys do so immediately. I know the gentleman prefers to read sometimes late into the evenings. It is for this reason, sir, that I have taken the liberty of obtaining a newspaper for you from the station-master. It is English. I am sorry it is a few days old, but I am certain it will be of some interest."

The steward, whose thoughtful gesture was most welcome and who knew he would be rewarded for it, could not have known that the paper he had procured was one of Sebastian's own, imported to the center of Europe through a complex distribution network he personally had established to serve homesick English businessmen and tourists abroad. An innovation that had become highly popular, and hugely lucrative.

Like the previous day's telegrams, the paper carried information from home, though of a distinctly less personal sort and, naturally, in an infinitely larger variety. Its columns were filled with short, pithy bulletins of interest to the widest, most diverse and subsequently most profitable readership possible. There was a heart-wrenching update of the events surrounding the recent coal-mine accident near Glasgow, and ever-more gruesome details of the disaster. Results of the by-election in Derbyshire, where the paper's endorsed candidate won, predictably, in a romping landslide. Captioned pictures of a visit by members of the royal family to towns along the Thames Valley still struggling to recover from last year's ruinous floods. There were numerous bulletins from the Olympic Games, almost thirty years since he had reported on them for the Cambridge student newspaper, and forty since last the competition was held in the English capital.

Almost forgetting the steward's self-effacing presence, Sebastian reached for his spectacles, quickly perusing the paper's bold headlines and scanning its many grainy photographs. He was interrupted only by the staff member's gentle clearing of his throat, a decorous way to signal his intention to withdraw.

"Uh-hum. Can I be of any *further* assistance, sir?"

"Well, yes, Hamid, only in that I wondered if I might take dinner in my cabin this evening. Can this be arranged?"

"Why, of course, sir. Almost *anything* can be arranged."

"Well in that case, if you can manage to have the chef prepare the same wonderful dish as was served yesterday evening, the braised duck I think it was, well that would really spoil an old man. Though such a meal might be less satisfying for the bird in question!"

Deaf to Sebastian's momentary attempt at humor, Hamid replied squarely, "Of course, Mr. Reynolds. It is always a pleasure to serve a passenger with such discerning tastes."

The steward uttered this, not in recognition of any particular discernment or refinement, but in an unambiguous bid to solicit an increase in the tip he hoped to receive. Sebastian also instantly knew this to be so, and was happy to oblige, tactfully placing a liberal quantity of coins into Hamid's open palm in a well-practiced maneuver.

As he turned to leave, depositing the heavy coins into his vest pocket, the steward stopped suddenly and added,

"The gentleman is going into the city for the day, is that so?"

"Yes, that's right."

"If I may, sir, I would advise you to keep your property safe, and most of all not to associate with anyone unknown to you on the platform. We have had trouble in this station before."

In fact, Sebastian had already come to shrink from the station platforms. For despite his initial delight in observing the barely-ordered havoc that each arrival and each departure engendered, more than once the abrupt mayhem that the train's appearance provoked had crossed into something frantic. Even alarming.

The vehicle's entrance into a station was often accompanied by an immense racket, from the dissonant shouts of the gathering crowd to the rueful cry of the braking equipment, attended by a rout of other, indeterminate sounds. Several times he had mistaken the controlled discharge of steam in the engine for a signal of the train's imminent departure, darting back to his cabin, only to find himself waiting interminably for the wheels to be set once again in motion.

Their arrival was almost invariably greeted by a swell of people, some charged by the railway with furnishing fresh supplies of some local commodity, and others who attempted during the momentary letup in the unremitting movement to secure some commerce or random profit from its ensnared passengers.

At Munich he had been accosted by a group of shifty youths looking to sell him dusty postcards, contraband cigarettes and all manner of shoddy souvenirs. He hadn't at first understood that he made himself a target by his expensive dress. Unaware of any prevailing codes that might have dictated his choice in wardrobe, out of an abundance of caution he opted in every public outing for more formal attire than would have been required or was advisable. Even for his brief appearances on the platforms, he attracted attention with his well-tailored, bespoke suits and by his fine straw hat. Above all he attracted notice by the great, Kashmiri sapphire tie-pin Olivia had sent him and that he wore always as a reminder of why, and for whom, he was making this momentous trip.

In the often dark, grubby stations where the train had stopped, the spectacular jewel acted like a flare, an ill-judged, careless announcement of his refinement, of his style and of his wealth. Wealth that attracted these bedraggled youths, numerous and unruly, interested not only in selling him their cheap goods, but in relieving him of some of his more valuable personal items. As one boy approached him with a box of wares, and another crooned a distracting tune, yet another made an enterprising, lightning attempt to lift his wallet and his passport from his jacket pocket, and in a motion just as fluid, the tie-pin itself. Were it not for the timely intervention of the train manager, who chased away the local delinquents with a stern yell and a large stick, he might easily have lost possession of these articles.

It was not his wallet or even the precious jewel, but the idea of losing his travel documents that most disconcerted him. For it was only with considerable effort and, gallingly, with the aid of some well-placed bank notes, that his solicitor had been able to obtain a passport for Sebastian in the dash of his leaving. But away from London, away from the support that his obliging staff and his important financial means could bring to bear on nearly any hindrance, he sensed for almost the first time since entering professional life a nakedness, a genuine vulnerability to unforeseen events. A powerful, unsettling recognition that he had over the course of a long and uniquely successful career been lulled somehow into a lonely life, but one of effortless, material comfort.

Long gone were the simpler days of his youth. A youth that knew no prosperity or privilege, in which his lack of resources had dictated an almost complete self-sufficiency, and a fervent aspiration to succeed. He had, however, over these many years, quite naturally and without detection, moved into a life in which money and influence meant his affairs had come to be managed faultlessly by others, and in which most challenges and obstacles would naturally be expected to fall away.

So much so that, in the heady, electrifying days before his departure for Delhi, he had overlooked many of the practical, conventional considerations of such a trip. He had not considered, and he definitely had not prepared for, protection against pickpockets on the station platforms, or for the compendium of other more immaterial, bothersome inconveniences that might still lie in store.

* *

His friend Salamon, who arrived early for their appointment at the Café Prater despite the torrential rain that deluged Budapest, recounted even more distressing stories of continental trains than simple, penny-ante thievery. Extraordinary accounts of hijackings, robberies at gunpoint and general lawlessness that had descended upon the railways immediately following the war, but which seemed to Sebastian fairly apocryphal, more like something from another era or from the untamed American West than from today's civilized, cultured Europe. He spoke too of the insidious crime that haunted his city, and the sense of desperation and anarchy that reigned in its streets. Though the city and its people showed signs of renewal and regeneration, he was nonetheless surprised at the sluggish pace with which that order was being established.

Still, it was Sebastian's plan to relocate to India that most surprised his friend, particularly as he had not known, or even known of, Olivia. He always thought of Sebastian as one to loathe the agitation of travel, to cherish the conveniences and the familiarity of home. Nor had he figured him capable of such passion and such zealous romance, to take what Salamon saw as extraordinary risks. Risks of disillusionment and of disenchantment. And he was determined to say as much.

"My dear Sebastian, I'm certain I'm not the only one who thinks you must have gone a little mad," he said in his usual plainspoken manner. "You're not a young man, prone to such hotheadedness. I expect all of London must be in a flurry about it!"

"No, I wouldn't really expect so. London's small-minded scandalmongers have long since tired of chattering about me. Or more likely, I've long since stopped bothering about it. It's funny, but in some ways, it's as if I ceased to exist as an individual long ago."

"What can you mean?"

"I mean, I've become a kind of *institution*. I've become my newspapers, and they have become me. Though in truth, the business can continue without me. The papers can grow and thrive under new direction and new management. Yes, I am no longer a sprightly young man, but *I* still want to grow and to thrive."

"How can you be so sure of yourself, Sebastian? Can you know that this woman, this Olivia, will be as you expect her to be? If I understand you, it's been many, many years since even you last met."

"Yes, it's been some thirty years."

"But that's forever! And forgive me, since I know that, like most of your countrymen, I haven't been endowed with a dreamy character, so amorous exuberances aren't in my nature, but my instinct tells me that such fantasies of rekindling youthful romances, well they seldom succeed. It's just hard for me understand your intentions."

"I don't expect people to understand. I haven't *asked* people to understand. Even you, my friend. How could you? She's completely unknown to you, and that brief chapter of my life has for many years been well shut."

"But why did you not speak of her, Sebastian? Why did you not ever tell me of this passion?"

"If I didn't speak of Olivia, to you or to anyone, it wasn't out of a lack of trust. I can think of no one, Salamon, I trust more. It was simply because it would, frankly, have been too painful for me to do so, and so alien. So disruptive to the even-keeled life I had constructed since. In part, it's also because I never once expected it to turn out this way. She had made her choices, or they had been made for her. But you of all people must be able to recognize the opportunity that's been presented to me. *You've* had your shot at a second chance, here in this city, here in this country that you love. I want *my* second chance, to pursue the only thing *I've* ever loved."

"I don't begrudge you that, Sebastian. I wouldn't want to question it either. I say that with all sincerity. You must know this to be true. I can only hope that it turns out to be everything you want it to be. That you can find the happiness I know has long escaped you."

"I can be certain of nothing. Not more than two weeks

ago, I wouldn't have wagered with you that I'd ever leave England, let alone set out for so foreign a destination. I've just turned fifty, Salamon. Fifty years in which I barely left London. Except for my time at university, I can probably count on one hand the times I left the city, and quicker still the times I enjoyed the trip."

"Not that there wasn't ample opportunity or even a compulsion for you to travel."

"That's true. Although despite my position, I found plenty of ways to avoid it. I tried terribly hard to do so. There was always a queue of enthusiastic people willing to travel in my place."

"This suited the rest of us just fine," said Salamon, with a wry, broad smile.

"I know it did. I'm grateful for it. Then one day, quite unexpectedly, I announce I'm heading to *India?* I don't blame you for thinking me mad. It's a place I know so little about. It's a place that, truthfully, both fascinates me, but also fills me with tremendous anxiety. I also know that this decision, this impetuous resolution to join Olivia in Delhi, must appear to many people, maybe to you even, like a foolish, a desperate act. But if you knew her, Salamon, if you knew the kind of joy we once had together, if the plans we once made had been your own, if anything *like* the ache, the agony at such a brutal parting were familiar to you, I assure you, you wouldn't hesitate. You *couldn't* hesitate. Not for an instant."

* *

The two men continued to converse in much the same vein for the better part of an hour, as Salamon's misgivings slowly eroded. They were interrupted only by the waiter's arrival at their secluded table with the local pastries Salamon had pre-ordered and with which he had wanted to impress and enthrall his visiting friend. The effect could not have been otherwise, and for a moment at least it stopped their talk cold.

A more decadent, more superlative selection of desserts Sebastian could not have imagined. Not even at afternoon tea at the Dorchester or at the Athenaeum. Elaborate, exquisitely-made tortes and trifles and roulades that resembled works of art. Even the Turkish coffee, like a condensed, dark syrup, was an inspiration.

Yet each man also knew that, for every sweet that was emptied from its tray, with every quarter-hour's chime of the room's enormous gilded clock, their short time together was coming closer to an end. They knew as well that likely this would be the last of their meetings.

Both men were anxious to prolong the reunion, but conscious to heed the steward's warning of the train's unfailingly punctual departure, and at the stroke of three o'clock, they grew quiet as in unison they arose. Each could sense the conspicuous hesitation and sadness with which they threw their arms around each other. In the uncounted years of their business and of their friendship, they had shared many moments of great happiness and great success. From today, however, their paths would take them in thoroughly different directions. Paths which for the afternoon had crossed so fortuitously, but which were unlikely to do so again.

As they walked reluctantly down the café's thickly carpeted hall, their arms were still entwined in an embrace as awkward as was the hollow repartee that each hoped might ease the mounting tension. Both men knew that many things had been left unsaid, and only moments later, burdened by a doleful mood, they parted in silence.

Even as Sebastian sat fretfully in the taxi on his return to the station, he reflected on the unique pleasure that a genuine, sincere friendship such as this had provided him, and how rare it had been. He didn't resent his friend's assertive line of questions or his line of reasoning, nor did he resent his suspicions or doubts of the success of his enterprise. For if anything, their forthright conversation had only underscored that he entertained the very same misgivings. Qualms about whether Olivia's interest might only have been ephemeral. That her letter had been written in a terrible moment of weakness that she might since have come to regret. Fear, as well, that she might be disappointed in the man he had become, or he in the woman she no longer was.

These doubts would linger for several more days, even after thoughts of Salamon and the raspberry cream roulade and the café's sparkling marble tabletops had become little more than a confusion of ambiguous memories added to the growing register of new sights and sounds. Especially in the quieter moments on the train, when everyone but the night crew slept and even the punctuated howling of the wheels was itself forgotten, the silence would not always be a friend. For it was in the quiet of the night when the doubts he yet harbored, the reservations he bore still, most often left their shelter.

But as the taxi reached the Budapest East Station and the regal Bright Star train came into view, for today at least, his disquiet melted away. He knew that the rails, despite curving around tight bends and cutting through irregular, rutted mountain passes, could lead him in one direction only. Closer to India. Closer to the only love he had ever known.

CHAPTER 10 • दहा

Their mid-morning arrival into Kuwait City, into the chaotic bus depot that lately had become the inevitable starting and ending point for the region's budding transport network, went largely unnoticed. Not unpredictably so, as the station was rife as always with a mob of harried, agitated people. Family and friends scrambling to greet new arrivals. Travelers scurrying to make their departure on time. All day the armada of ramshackle buses, belching sooty fumes, deposited its weary passengers, flooding in from scores of separate locations. Inestimable others were being conveyed away to a hundred different destinations, disappearing quickly into the sandy horizon.

A clang of shattering noises ricocheted off the building's high ceilings and its enormous stone pillars. The shouts of the hapless bus dispatchers competed, mostly without success, with an assortment of backfiring engines. With squealing brakes whose pads had long since worn through. With driveshafts groaning, begging to be lubricated or, more compassionately, to be replaced. Even the tired whistle of the lone besieged police officer, almost universally unheeded, only added to the bedlam, like a troubled symphony conductor warming up his orchestra but never quite able to get his players' instruments in tune.

The febrile pace of this activity was not slowed by the summer heat, which was by then climbing to its usual trying heights. Even more startling to Vikhram, it was not diminished either by the daily ritual of fasting, chief among the many consecrated rites of the holy month of Ramadan in which the entire country was still gripped. While in Saudi Arabia he had learned much about this festival and its observances. He discovered why, because of the moon's cycle, it fell on different dates every year, just as did the Hindu celebrations, and why it was so auspicious a time for Muslims. He had come to understand as well that fasting was one of its central tenets. Which meant that this morning's furious activity in the depot not only resisted the roasting temperatures, but that it was somehow being conducted by a press of people operating on little or no fuel.

Throughout his time in the oil fields, he had been astonished at how the devout laborers had managed to work so consistently and so well, barely breaking stride, despite their obligation to pause for prayer five times each day. He was incredulous that these men always knew in which direction was Mecca, no matter where they found themselves when the muezzin would make his call. He never failed either during the festival month to be awed by the strength and the exertion of these men, when he and the others, fortified by a full stomach and by profuse quantities of water, themselves felt so close to exhaustion and to dehydration. A Muslim worker from Srinagar instructed him that abstaining from food and drink was intended to educate the faithful about spirituality. To demonstrate patience, humility, self-restraint. And though he never felt the inclination to adopt or even to attempt the ritual, he felt that during his time in Al-Fadiz he had been nothing if not a paragon of the very traits this sacrament was meant to teach. Patience and self-restraint were the price that again and again had agonizingly been extracted from him.

When at last their bus came to a halt, and just as soon as the driver reached to open the door with a robust pull of the tired spring latch, Vikhram's fellow passengers rushed to exit, and prepared to disperse with some haste. They disembarked with appropriate civility. They helped each other with their bags and with onward directions, but they did so with only minimal ceremony.

Although he had spent several days in close quarters with this disparate group, despite having spoken at length with some of them and exchanged friendly words with most of the others, they paused only shortly to bid him farewell and to wish him well. He did the same, strenuously shaking the men's hands and bowing lightly in a clumsy if welcome sign of respect to the women. Though courteous, however, these strangers' hurried flight would only prove that they had spent as little time thinking about Vikhram and his welfare as truthfully he had about theirs.

The only person about whose safety and whose interests he might have bothered was Sunil. He was comforted then that, along with the boy's father Dinesh, they would remain together for some time at least, as from tomorrow morning they would travel on the same ship back home. Or at least to Bombay, the first port of call. Tonight as well, in an effort to conserve their fast shrinking savings, they had agreed to share a room in a cheap hotel.

The establishment suggested by Dinesh, where he and his son had stayed on their initial arrival, was the Bissalama Hotel, a name that in Arabic bid its visitors wishes for safe travel, though neither man knew this to be the case. Neither did the rest of the crowd, made up almost exclusively of other Indians, who loitered in the lobby, speaking amongst themselves in Hindi, Marathi, Telugu, Punjabi and other regional languages that Vikhram could not definitively recognize.

To call the entrance a lobby was to be generous. It was little more than a dingy, narrow hall, poorly maintained, with only a high wood counter from which to conduct business and a half-empty row of mounted keys behind it. Its location and its rates were about as far from the city's flashy new beachfront and bay-facing hotels as one could have imagined. A small, slipshod, insalubrious place, but one that fit well their budget. It was, in any event, an improvement over the previous nights spent sleeping out of doors, and their departure in the morning meant they would have to suffer it for but one night.

The squalid quality of the hotel didn't bother Sunil, who was elated to find himself once again in a city, synonymous for him with adventure and with excitement. A long hoped-for antidote to the tedium that had marked his joyless days away from home. Days spent mostly unsupervised in an improvised nursery, confined to the company of other, often much younger children, where he learned very little and that he liked even less. The metropolis, by contrast, was something entirely different. It held the promise of innumerable wonders, from grand hotels to refined cinema houses, even if most were only to be marveled at from afar, since the price of admission was well beyond what his father could hope to afford, or because Indian and Chinese workers were not permitted inside.

Neither of these impediments held true for the Kuwait Zoological Park, for which entry was open to all and tickets were easy on almost any pocket. The boy beseeched his father to go, without success, as Dinesh professed to have a number of indeterminate errands to accomplish. So

Vikhram, himself without obligations, agreed to take the boy. Much to Sunil's delight. The men fixed to meet again in the central square at four o'clock precisely, so that the chaperone might then hand back his charge.

The boy had never before visited a zoo, nor seen wild animals, apart from the mass of stray dogs in his Madras neighborhood and the many cows and buffalo on the public pavement everywhere else. From the very first enclosure to the very last pen, he was stupefied by the diversity and by the peculiarity of the zoo's offerings. He was transfixed by the parrots, with their distinctive apple-green plumage, ludicrously long tails and curious black rings about the nape of their necks. He might have found it amusing had Vikhram explained to him that, like himself, these birds had been imported from India, but he was interested only in their histrionic strutting and in their off-key whistling that he found so uproarious. By contrast, it was the ghoulish silence of the Nile crocodiles in the reptile cages that most intrigued him. Brooding, inert for hopelessly long periods, their eerie, remote stare might have frightened him, or frightened him more, were it not for the high chain-link fence that separated them. He liked most of all the African spur-thighed tortoises, whose scaly legs and aged skin looked much like that of their crocodile neighbors, though as these prehistoric creatures spent the better part of his visit burrowing in the ground rather than surveying the landscape for easy prey, they seemed much less intimidating.

They spent the balance of the morning and the better part of the afternoon visiting the zoo. As they ambled from one exhibit to the next, they took to mimicking the animals' odd behaviors, bestowed names on their favorites, invented stories of an unlucky creature's capture and of its eventual escape. Together they likely could have out lasted any of the institution's many other visitors.

As much as Vikhram enjoyed the excursion and the carefree time spent with this jubilant, spirited boy, his thoughts nevertheless remained elsewhere. He yearned to hand Sunil back to his father. He hungered for nothing more than to head before nightfall to the shipyard, to see for himself the vessel that would bear him home. To reassure himself that she had indeed arrived safely in port and that all would be in proper order for tomorrow's sailing. In doing so, he might imagine that the final leg of his interminable journey had already begun.

* *

On the long walk from the main square to the shipyard, Vikhram would have liked to stop for a meal, but because of the religious holiday, the stalls where he might otherwise have found cheap food, the falafel sellers and vegetable vendors that lined the city's streets, were closed until sunset, when they and the rest of city would be revived. He wasn't likely to be able to hold out as long as that.

Unobtrusively, so as not to offend his hosts, he reached into his pocket, warily unwrapping from its paper cover the last of the almonds and dried apricots he had purchased from the desert way-station at what seemed to him like a lifetime ago. He savored these treats as if they were a prodigal feast, both satisfied and uneasy in the knowledge that those around him, by choice or by coercion, were not so fortunate.

Not that anyone on the docks would have taken any note of him. The quays were overflowing with activity, an immensely fearsome display of motion that made even the city's bus depot look subdued by comparison. It was a huge spectacle. A vibrant, hectic, confusing mass of people and goods that might have alarmed the more faint of heart.

Everywhere the place was bursting with forceful energy, of men and machines racing to maintain order in the midst of turmoil. Wooden crates of all sizes and states choked the lanes and warehouses, stacked alarmingly high. The swinging cranes, incessantly plucking containers from one indiscriminate place and depositing them without apparent logic in another, posed no less a hazard.

And this was to speak only of what was essentially stationary. The cranes at least were secured to the ground, the mountains of crates at rest if unsteady, but there was also the convoy of lorries and diesel vans, scampering from one end of the wharf to the other without much regard for pedestrians or materials. Not to mention the herds of unruly, constantly shifting livestock that poured off the ships like spilled milk and that required special care to be kept in line. Care that didn't seem to be particularly forthcoming amid the mess of other distractions.

Such ordered chaos put him in mind of the regular ceremony that had been morning deliveries at the Nayā Bazaar, though it was here on a much larger scale. In fact, everything on the docks, he thought, was of a greater magnitude. The storehouses were bigger than any stockroom or shop at home. The extraordinary volume of people would have by some degree exceeded that which would have in any one day made its way through the narrow streets and alleys of the market. He felt very small. He thought himself insignificant. Of consequence to no one. And for now at least, he welcomed the sensation.

He wanted only to be inconspicuous. To slip unnoticed

onto the waiting ship, and quietly to make his way home. He had done his time. Served his sentence. He was lusting to see again his native soil, to rejoin his beloved family, to pick up the pieces of a life that had somehow gone wrong, or to start a new life altogether. One in which he wouldn't be saddled with the piercing regrets of his recent past, not diverted by the vain promises and outright lies that had tempted him to leave Bombay. India, if he was to believe what he read in the newspapers and what he often heard said, was the country of tomorrow. An assertive, free nation full of potential. He felt himself as entitled as would be any man to benefit from that potential.

First, however, he had to locate his ship, concealed among the dozens of vessels anchored in the busy port. Among them were small and large boats alike. There were fishing boats, each one crowded with a fresh catch and surrounded by a flock of hysterical seabirds circling for the scraps discarded overboard. Commercial passenger liners, with their shapely lines and sturdy forms, were the pride of the harbor. A single, domineering British naval vessel, stationed in the port as part of the protectorate's command, stood an intimidating guard over the assembled.

Mostly the quays were congested with cargo ships of every description, similar to one another only in that in unison they puffed out a cloud of pungent black smoke from their steam engines. They flew flags of different colors and shapes, hailing from well-known ports as far away as Norway, Ireland, Hong Kong. The hulls of the recently unloaded ships towered high above the water line. Others, weighed down by loads, were so deep in the water and their cargo so densely packed, one wondered what their chances were not to be lost in rough seas.

And there on the last quay, nuzzled in between a

trawler and a large freighter, stood *The Artemis*. For Vikhram, even to see her name was a kind of wonder. A miracle. She might just as well have been named *Salvation*, such was the promise she held to deliver him the following day from his long ordeal.

CHAPTER 11 • अकरा

Even amidst the flotilla of other impressive ships, she was among the most impressive and the most striking of them all. A dignified craft of commanding height and even more remarkable girth. *The Artemis* was likewise notable in that, unlike most of her rivals, she was designed for mixed use, to carry not only sizable amounts of cargo at its stern, but also to offer at its bow simple accommodation for hundreds of passengers. The ferrying of these passengers, a select number of well-off customers but mostly the shipping of contract workers to and from the labor-starved oil fields and textile mills of the Middle East, was not as profitable as the conveyance of freight, and was but a secondary industry, but it was consistently profitable all the same.

"She ain't a pretty thing, is she?" said a husky voice, that of a lone man sitting on the edge of the dock, nursing a dying cigarette and staring blankly out to sea.

His broad, distinctive accent and the long, sustained vowels in his brassy speech placed him immediately as an Australian or a New Zealander. His appearance and his clothing pegged him, even more conspicuously, as the archetypal merchant seaman.

Under a dense, grey-streaked beard, his face was ravaged from years spent in the salty ocean air and in the cruel sun, his reddish eyes and scarlet cheeks laid waste from years of consuming vast amounts of alcohol. Even the prolific tattoos and missing front teeth, lost in a brawl or from neglect, might have been drawn from a cartoon version of himself.

"Gotta be some thirty years old, this one."

"I'm no expert," replied Vikhram. "In fact, I don't know the *first thing* about boats."

"Well I do! Been sailin' 'em all my god-damned life, I have, and the first thing you gotta know, son, this here ain't no boat. She's a *ship* alright, if ever I seen one. You see the size of that main deck? You could fit three or four of them fishin' boats there on that deck and still have room for a country dance on a Saturday night."

Vikhram knew that the sailor meant this only figuratively, and that the precise number of fishing vessels that might actually fit on board was inconsequential, but he tried nevertheless to work out the number for himself.

"And I can tell ya," continued the seaman, "cause I've been with her for months. She's a wreck. A real battle horse she is, but an ugly sucker. Just have a *look* at 'er! The paint's even peelin' on the wheelhouse, for Christ's sake!"

"Surely that must be easy enough to fix, no?"

"But it ain't been, has it? That's my bloody point. The damned thing's corroded through and through. You see them beams, them kingposts? Rusted solid! Wouldn't want to be the guy has to re-weld *them* matchsticks. That's a real dog's breakfast, that is. And the capstan? That doohickey jams so often, ten-to-one says a bloke's gonna lose a couple of fingers one of these days."

Vikhram couldn't contest the inventory of the ship's infirmities. He could see for himself the damage, the injury that years of inattention had wrought. He could make out clearly the frayed ropes, the colony of rose-colored barnacles joined to the hull, the giant cables mooring the ship that from indifference had become tarnished and torn.

Still he thought, she's afloat. She's being primed for departure, so he considered it to be among the most beautiful sights he had ever beheld.

"She's alright to sail, isn't she?"

"Hell yeah! This thing could barrel laughin' through a hurricane, she could. You don't think me stupid enough to work this damned beast if I didn't think I'd see my woman on the other side, do ya? And I can tell ya, I've done my bit on a helluva lot worse than this old creaker. Last year, me and me mates sailed around the Cape on a craft held together with nothin' but glue and a couple of elastic bands. Dodged a bullet on that one, we did."

Vikhram had by now become familiar with this type of tall fiction, that of sailors who almost by rote embroidered the tale of their mostly dull existence into gripping reports of plucky heroism and of uncommon skill. He tended to admire the narrator in direct proportion to just how embellished was his tale. He knew that parables of fearlessness were part of the seamen's lore. Even another trite story of the implausibly large catch that got away would this afternoon have provided welcome entertainment, and having ascertained that this particularly amiable storyteller made up part of his own ship's crew, Vikhram would make a note of seeking him out during his voyage home.

"My money's on her bein' scrapped pretty damn soon. I reckon she must be worth a tidy sum more as bits of old metal than she would be lyin' at the bottom of the sea. I'm guessin' this must be one of her last crossings. But what stake *you* got in this game, son? You just admirin' the show?"

"No, actually. I'm also sailing on her tomorrow. I'm on my way back to Bombay."

"Good for you, mate. Best to get the hell outta this nasty oven just as quick as you can. Name's Nick. I'll be sure to look out for ya!"

"I'm Vikhram, and I'll be much obliged."

"Fancy, ain't ya? *I'll be much obliged!* They teach you that at university, did they?"

"Well, no . . ."

"Oh, don't sweat it. I's just playin' with ya."

Vikhram hesitated, not certain whether to be embarrassed or incensed by such mockery, but the sailor's broad grin and throaty laugh soon told him that the man meant no harm.

"So, Vikhram is it? How long you been in this hole?"

"I've worked here two years or so. On the oil rigs. Worked for the Gulf Petroleum Company. But it seems like a lot longer than that."

"I reckon it would. I been here just two days, and I'm already itchin' to see the back of this place. Lookin' forward to gettin' to India, I am. The girls there sure are fine."

"Oh, I'm a married man, Nick, so I don't have much of an opinion about that."

"Hell, son, so am I. Though that ain't stopped me yet!" he said, with a slap on Vikhram's back, gentle but just vigorous enough to unsettle the younger man's slim frame.

The sailor went on to describe with some specificity his most recent amorous conquests. He provided just enough graphic detail so as to make the stories he told very nearly credible. Nearly. Girls in Russian port towns who asked him, implored him to stay, at least through the long, bitter winter months. Willing, passionate girls at various points on the English coast who, he maintained, were poised to become tomorrow's magazine cover models or film stars. He was becoming as boastful in the telling of his victories as Vikhram was becoming ill at ease in listening to them.

Soon enough, however, Nick's name was being shouted from the bridge, calling the errant sailor back to his duty. So, with a shrug and a hammy roll of his eyes that communicated his displeasure, he rose and promptly melted back into the hubbub that overall commanded the site.

He was soon lost in a sea of manual laborers, most of whom, like Vikhram, hailed from the Indian sub-continent. Their simple dress and bare feet indicated their low station. In the loose jargon of their easy banter, they referred to each other as coolies. As did others, although with less charity.

Not one of these laborers was idle. A vanguard of men, linked in a chain twenty deep, was unloading the last of the crates from the gangway. Containers packed with the most refined Ceylon tea, branded ostentatiously as such on the side of the crates, that were being dispatched onto smaller boats and then to destinations unknown. Still other workers were carefully being directed to load, by crane and by hand, huge quantities of fresh merchandise into the main cargo bay.

The work was grueling. Many of the men – dirty, caked in profuse sweat – were razor thin, their stripped chests burning in the sweltering heat, their muscles straining under the weight of their task. Vikhram was staggered to see that some of these lanky men managed even to lift the heavy goods. He watched this company of luckless men, imagining the sacrifices they must have made just to get here. The same sacrifices, the same sharp choices that he had confronted all those months ago. They must have traveled here on a ship much like his own, desperate for work, desperate to better their chances of a life unencumbered by poverty and need.

A few, he thought, would succeed. They would accomplish the humble goals for which they had given up so much already. Most, however, would fall short. A long way short. They would stay far too long, accept far too much insult, unable to accept their defeat but, like Vikhram himself, loath to go home to confront those to whom their confident guarantees had so long ago and probably so casually been given.

He was profoundly lost in this contemplation when suddenly the agitated industry of the site began to cease, and within moments concluded for the evening. Vikhram had to be prodded out of his pensive fog, chased to the exit by the night guardsman to ensure that the gates of the shipyard would not be closed against him.

Unnerved to find himself back so abruptly on the city streets, he was nonetheless relieved that, with the sun having set, at least he could buy a proper meal. He stopped at the first appetizing food stall he crossed to purchase with almost the last of his local currency a skewer of freshly grilled lamb, unsparingly seasoned with pepper and coriander. He bought a handful of the dried dates that he understood to be the traditional food with which to break the fast, and which were everywhere again being sold. This, he knew, would be his last night in the Gulf. He might as well savor the local customs and the local flavors one last time.

* *

When Vikhram at last returned to the Bissalama Hotel, Dinesh and Sunil were already completing their preparations for sleep. Naturally, father and son had chosen to share the larger of the room's two beds, though neither bed was nearly large enough for an adult to sleep restfully. Nor was either particularly inviting. Like the room itself, the mattresses were grimy, sullied in parts, dilapidated from overuse and negligence. The thin sheets, though newly laundered, were stained and torn. Their porous weaves held captive within them the stories of a thousand equally impoverished, equally downhearted men. The walls, too, crumbling in spots, would have borne witness to a thousand stories as dreary as Vikhram's.

The porcelain sink by the window, for which the men had paid an extra fee, discharged only brackish water, and that only sparingly. Water tolerable for shaving, and in a pinch for brushing one's teeth, but certainly not fit to drink. Even the mirror on the door of the small wardrobe in which Vikhram had earlier placed his bag, and where on the single metal hanger he placed both his jacket and his shirt, was cracked, its spidery glass held precariously in place by a surfeit of gummy adhesive. Only the ceiling fan was a welcome feature, since though its blades created a loud, sometimes gnawing groan inside the small room, it concealed the stubborn noise of the streets below.

The state of the room was largely irrelevant. The spent travelers paid it little regard, worn out as they were by their trying tour, unsettled by the prospect of its continuance in the morning. In an instant, just as soon as the shutters were closed, all three of them fell fast asleep.

The night brought much relief. A welcome adjournment from the challenges of the waking day. But as had become customary for Vikhram, the night was also a brief one. He woke with the dawn, not troubled by the first light but reassured by it, since it brought with it the assurance of today's vital step forward in his slow, steady journey home. He rose quietly so as not to wake the others, silently opening the door to the hallway, to stretch his legs, to take in a dose of fresher air, and to provide for his morning requirements.

When he returned to the shadowy room, he couldn't quite make out the forms of the others. It appeared to him, oddly enough, that at this still early hour neither was there sleeping, that neither any longer occupied their one bed. Indeed, as he opened more fully the squeaky shutters that outlined the single window, he could see clearly that his companions had abandoned the room.

Their absence was not something that he understood at first. Vikhram didn't know quite how to react to this peculiar turn of events. Possibly they had gone for a morning meal. Maybe, as he'd done the day before, Dinesh had more of his unexplained tasks to complete before sailing. Yet a sharp sense of foreboding was not long to overtake him. There was something disquieting, something improper in this unexpected desertion.

He would prepare himself without delay, then hurry down the sinister staircase to inquire of the hotel receptionist if and when he had seen the pair leave the premises. He would dress in haste, opening first the wardrobe to get a different shirt from his bag, mindful to respect the auspiciousness of today's departure by at least sporting a change of clean clothes.

Only then did he realize that, though his canvas bag remained untouched, his blue-striped cotton jacket was missing. The jacket in which he kept his boat ticket, and in which he had carefully sewn the bulky stacks of Indian rupee notes that were all that remained of his earnings, had vanished.

Panic threatened to overwhelm him. His breathing became short and difficult. He had to sit on the edge of the bed to keep from falling, and still he could not quite comprehend what had transpired. He would not allow himself to consider the consequences. Calmer after a moment's rest, he began to rummage through the room, and then to rummage again. Then to ransack every inch of the small space for some hint as to the garment's whereabouts. He scoured his own paltry belongings, questioning whether he had been mistaken, that likely he had simply lost sight of having tucked the jacket neatly into his bag the evening before.

It was only then that he noted his companions' own bags were also missing. There was no trace of their having stayed in the room, apart from the worn straight razor Dinesh had used the previous afternoon and a number of the simple stick-figure drawings the boy had made at the zoo, discarded on the bare floor. They had not, he soon realized with certainty and with an ever-mounting sense of dread, gone out in the dawn for a stroll or to acquire last-minute provisions for the crossing. They would not shortly return to present him with a hearty, salutary breakfast in tow. They were gone. Under the cover of darkness, Dinesh had taken his son from the room. And he had taken Vikhram's jacket as well.

* *

He had no time to waste. No time to deliberate on the possible cost of such a debacle or, as he might have done in a weaker posture, to curse the gods for the string of prejudices they forever relished inflicting on him. Rather, in this pernicious moment, he could afford only to take immediate and decisive action. To race to undo this appalling misconduct, to avert its monstrous effects. His only thought was to find and to confront this cheat, and to recover what was

rightfully his. There would be time enough, and distance
enough, on the voyage home to reflect on the grave wrongs
that time and again had been dealt him.

Breathlessly, his pace barely slowed by the canvas bag
draped over his shoulder, Vikhram ran the length of the
city to the port. By the time he reached the ship, a swarm
of passengers was already boarding through the main
gangway, and a growing queue of others waited restlessly
on the dock to join them. A string of taxis was arriving
uninterrupted, bequeathing a host of additional travelers
who skirmished with the swelling masses arriving by foot
or by cart. Those who stood already in the formless, disor-
derly line jostled and elbowed each other without quarter.
The few wealthy passengers shouted instructions to their
servants. Those who had no assistance shouted at each
other.

Vikhram headed for the ticket office, located at the
base of the moored ship and in the heart of the turbulent
crowd. It was here that he knew he would have to plead
his case for passage. A passage for which he had duly paid
his fare and that he had every legitimate right to take. He
lacked only the proper documentation.

He entered the office with plenty of time to spare,
although he grew more and more impatient, all the while
the minutes ticking away, as the affluent couple in front of
him negotiated endlessly with the ticket master regarding
the condition of their cumbersome luggage and the proper
handling of their treasured pets.

When at last he reached the counter, he launched
immediately into a full-bodied explanation of the state of
his affairs.

"I've lost my ticket, sir. This morning. In the hotel."

"*Have* you really? For which ship, if you don't mind

my asking?" said the slim man behind the counter's metal grill, with a marked air of nonchalance and distraction that contrasted conspicuously with the air of concentration and consideration he had afforded the first-class customers.

"The Artemis, sir. The big one right outside. You can see it from here."

"Yes, I know which ship is which. Maybe that's why they gave me this here cap!" he snapped, pointing to the half-visor he wore, which prominently bore the shipping company's name, the very same name to be found on the side of the mammoth vessel being readied for departure just a few steps away.

"Yes, of course. I'm sorry. It's just that, well, I can't find my ticket, and I'm afraid the ship's about to leave. So I'd like to ask, can you let me on, please?"

"Oh, let's see... Can I let you *on*? 'Cause you've somehow managed to lose your ticket, is that it? Do you expect I've never heard *that* one before from your kind? Maybe you've at least got a more original story to tell about how you came to lose it?"

"It was stolen from me last night by the man I shared a hotel room with. The Bissalama Hotel, just off the Ring Road. It's true, sir, I swear to you. I swear it on the name of God. The man at the desk there will tell you."

"I couldn't care *less* where you spent last night, young man. Why ever would you think such a thing would interest me? This isn't a damn tourist information booth, you know, it's a ticket office! Says so right there on the sign. And if you don't have a ticket, you don't travel. Pretty much the standard arrangement. End of story."

"Please sir, my name is Vikhram Sukhadia. I bought my ticket just a few days ago in Al-Fadiz, at the travel agent in town. The one next to the chemist's shop. Can you please check your list? Please, sir. I'm sure my name's on it somewhere."

"I have a manifest. Right here, in fact. Updated just this morning. Got a list of the first-class passengers and the crew, or at least the crew who can stay *sober* enough on shore-leave to make it back here before she sets sail, but it doesn't list the passengers in steerage, of which I'm guessing you presume to be one? Lord knows we couldn't even *spell* half the names on a list like that! And no one, I tell you, no one gets on board without a ticket. The Crown Prince *himself* would sit here all day until he produced one."

"Sir, I've come all the way from Al-Fadiz. I've traveled for four days to get here. And I think . . . No, I'm sure, it's Dinesh Chowdhury who has my things. He's the man I told you about. The one who shared my room. He's probably on board already."

"Never heard of him, and I guess that ought to teach you to be more careful with your things, eh? I'd be more vigilant next time around, if I were you. Can't trust nobody these days."

"But what am I to do? He has my ticket. He has my money. I've just got to get it back. I've got nothing left. Nothing, sir. I *have* to be on that ship. I have to get home. My wife will be expecting me. My children will be waiting for me, too."

"Listen, boy, you're not hearing me. Listen good. Not a thing I can do about it. Only thing to do, go tell your story to the police. Maybe you'll have more luck with that lot."

But Vikhram knew the futility of a plea to the police. He knew they had little regard for the teeming multitude of foreign workers. They didn't see these hardworking, resolute men in the same way as did the ambitious and iron-fisted businessmen who hired them, as the lifeblood of the region's growing economy. They saw them only as its foul underbelly. They treated these men as scallywags, trouble-makers, rabble-rousers who threatened the calm and even the character of their land.

Besides, Vikhram had at this point barely a penny left with which he might have attempted to bribe the police. For he had long since learned that it was obligatory to pay for any successful interaction, and to avoid any barbed scrapes, with law enforcement. He had only a few loose coins in his pocket, and that would likely not even buy him a shine of his mangy shoes.

Even as he continued to argue with the ticket master, whose tone had become more condescending and ever more dismissive, Vikhram heard the whistle of the ship, the distinctive sound that announced it was drawing in its braided ropes and pulling away from the dock. Within only a few short moments, it had quit the shipyard, taking with it his ticket. His savings. And his dreams.

CHAPTER 12 • बारा

All across Anatolia, mudslides were being triggered by the heavy rains and by the unusually plentiful snowmelt. They were abetted by the frequent electric storms and brush fires that for weeks had plagued the region's precarious crops and threatened its fragile, despairing livestock. As the storms grew more violent in the rising summer heat, so too the mudflows grew in size and intensity, carrying with them the residue of all things living and dead in their grievous path. Trees and telegraph poles were uprooted, boulders consumed, houses ripped from their foundation. Nothing, not even the firm ground from which the silt and the clay drew its very life, was spared their terrible ruin.

The abundant mud was of a dusky brown hue, like a dense block of sugary caramel. The color of dirty coffee or of a four-point snooker ball. It was as thick as the colossal steel girders buttressing the triumphant, soaring towers that increasingly studded modern skylines, and when it dried, the sun-baked earth proved just as dense and just as impenetrable.

This morning, however, the mud was far from dry. It gurgled, cooed, muttered inscrutable riddles in its own secret, menacing language. Its shapeless mass shifted without end, cresting with no warning and never in the same place twice. It surged sluggishly but forcefully down the steep banks of the Taurus Mountains, like a mighty avalanche in mockingly slow motion.

The massive flows choked in their wake a long stretch of the carefully laid train tracks, swallowing whole the exacting path on which a huge number of steam and diesel engines barreled daily. The thin iron rails, now hidden and deformed, buried deep under layers of soil, sediment and rock, had become impassable. The mud even wedged its merciless way into the giant wheel cylinders of the Bright Star train, seeking desperately but vainly to advance. It spewed debris across the locomotive and into the cab car like a petulant hooligan spitting angrily into the face of a hapless passerby.

The sudden, tortured jerk of the train, and the abrupt suspension of its relentless forward motion, awakened many of the passengers from their uneasy sleep. With eyes only half-open, one by one they poked their uncovered heads out of the nearest window to see why the train's march had so brusquely been halted. Provoked as well by the sudden break in movement and by the growing commotion, Sebastian soon joined the throng in leaning out his own head from his cabin window, no less curious than the others to know the cause of this unexpected event.

With dawn still low on the horizon, he could see very little of the ghostly domain, only imprecise shapes within a few feet of the carriage. So he listened. He listened with application and with absolute concentration. Perhaps his ears could better see what his eyes could not. But he struggled, fruitlessly, to fathom by sound alone what he took plainly to be the remote place in which he and his fellow travelers found themselves. He had no experience of the echoes and babblings of the countryside, and so was at a perfect loss to comprehend.

He labored to make sense of the dramatic quiet, the swift silencing of the train's crushing engine and of its thunderous, squeaking wheels. A silence broken only too soon by the growing crash of voices. By the dissonance of a hundred frenzied exchanges. More inconsonant noise than Sebastian thought could possibly emanate from a single train's narrow confinement. These voices, the clamor that in an instant had encircled him, had risen swiftly from soft tones to full tilt, rendering it even more futile that he should try to make sense of the few dim rumblings radiating from the dark just beyond his grasp.

Only slowly did the night's gloom yield to the emerging day, revealing in its vibrant, violet-and-orange radiance a vast field of nothingness. As far as he could see, there was merely a barren backdrop of softly shimmering soil and hard, white rocks bundled into random piles like the fallen bricks of an ancient temple. The odd melancholy fragments of buckled, skeletal trees of juniper, pine and oak wrestled to emerge from the pockmarked earth. Sebastian saw the environment like a forgotten frontier or the face of a distant moon. Life here was not to be embraced. It could only exist in mutiny against the ravages of a million years of Nature's callous taunting and injury. The scant vegetation that dared to show its brow had somehow resisted. It flouted the plunder of countless volcanic eruptions and fiery storms, offering the naive spectator a false hope of vitality and resilience. The flawless blue sky, untainted by a single cloud, spoke to him of that emptiness, its increasing brilliance serving only to blind his slumbering sight against the reflection of the dazzling limestone stage below. Even the snow that capped the distant mountain peaks appeared to him like the sorrowful mourner's sprinkling of dirt on a freshly dug grave.

Sebastian could soon overhear the passengers beginning to speculate amongst themselves about the cause of the delay. Any number of explanations were being proffered, some more palatable than others. Distracted or lame animals that had strayed from the herd, and that could not be seen in the distorting blindness of the night, had been known to wander onto tracks, and their unlucky presence could cause a speeding train to be disrupted or even to derail. It was not unknown for lightning to strike a train's iron carriage, conducting its powerful force throughout the speeding cars, causing fire or electrocution. Some even spoke of the bandits that were rumored still to survey the line, striking a convoy with extraordinary precision and darting off just as quickly with its treasures, though the rail company did all it could to quiet such macabre speculation.

Yet as the day continued to emerge and to soothe the fretful passengers, word began to circulate of what was becoming only too obvious to see, that a furious mudslide had blocked the train's passage.

Such events were common in mountainous regions, but because the rail companies commissioned a battery of men to monitor and to clear obstructions at the first sign of trouble, these incidents seldom succeeded in delaying a crossing for long. The masses in Turkey recruited for such an exercise were impressive in their number and in their abilities, but they were powerless against an act of God. And such heavy rains, and the terrifying destruction they caused, could only spring from the wrath of an angry God, even if the object of his fury remained largely ambiguous.

* *

Sebastian learned from the steward Hamid that the mudslide had entrapped them in the province of Kayseri, near the Ottoman town of Çanisar, known locally as the birthplace of a once-revered saint whose fame had long since faded with time and with the diminution of religious faith more broadly. This small, celebrated town, whose very name to the Turks once evoked wealth and tradition, was but a mere three miles away, but it would be many more miles still from where the rail operator could obtain men in sufficient numbers to clear the raft of obstacles. Hamid advised that the process might take as many as two days. Two days that Sebastian desperately did not want to lose.

"Some of the passengers are gathering, sir, at the front of the train," explained the steward. "That fuss you can probably hear, those are the preparations being made to escort some of the second and third-class passengers into Çanisar, where many will stay overnight. We simply haven't enough supplies for everyone to stay here on the train."

"How can you know that there's accommodation in town, Hamid? Does the crew know this area?"

"Well, yes, I for one know this area well. I was born close to here, just a day or so's ride over that hilltop to the west. I know there are a few small inns in town."

"And should there not be room at these inns?" asked Sebastian, both baffled and awed by the speed with which this spontaneous organization was taking shape.

"Not to worry. We Turks are a generous people. Even if the hotels should not be available to us, and at this time in the hot season we should have little competition, I can assure you there will be plenty of local people who will be willing to house a passenger or two in a spare bedroom or in an attic . . . Then there is the question of the conditions of hygiene that might otherwise deteriorate if everyone were to stay on board," continued Hamid.

"Well, yes," said Sebastian, "I can imagine that to be the case."

"Oh, but *you* needn't worry, sir!" replied a vexed Hamid, concerned that his description of the worsening conditions might alarm his passenger. "Your *own* comfort will be assured."

"I'm not worried, Hamid. No, I know I'm in good hands, but I should like to get out from the train anyway. If nothing else, I'm certain fresh air and a spot of exercise would be a tonic to me, and it might take my mind off this unfortunate delay."

"If I may, sir, I would encourage the gentleman to remain here on board, and not to join the expedition into town. There, your comfort cannot be guaranteed, as it can be here."

Sebastian was tempted, instinctively, to agree. He thought the accommodations in this lost town of several thousand souls, no matter its rich history and its charitable people, would at best be primitive. He had already set his mind wandering, imagining vaguely repulsive scenes of chaos and lawlessness drawn loosely and quite randomly from exaggerated tales he had read and from early American films he had seen. A place where open-air sewage, swarming, seedy markets and boundless indigence would have been commonplace.

But a place, after all, that might be a foretaste, an unforeseen and maybe even a fortuitous preview of the challenges and trials that might await him in India, so he looked on those preparing to depart with something nearing jealousy. Not because he sought a stirring adventure. Not because he wanted to test the limits of his endurance. Not even because he wanted to anticipate and so better to prepare for his entry in less than a week's time into Delhi.

Mostly he was just dismayed at the thought of two or more dull, tiresome days trapped on a paralyzed train. He would need to keep his mind engaged and his thoughts away from this exasperating setback. Or else, he thought, with a touch of dramatic flair that would not have been out of place in one of those films from which he drew his clumsy imagery, he might well go mad.

Despite Hamid's caution, he asked the steward to organize, if not accommodation for him, then at least transport into town where he could spend the day weighing up its attractions and its miseries for himself.

* *

Although the local guide insisted that Sebastian ride into town on one of the hard-driving mules assembled for the purpose, as a special tribute to be bestowed upon this distinguished visitor, the deliberate, listless stride of the donkeys meant the advertised one-hour journey proceeded at a decidedly slower pace than if the small party had simply undertaken the short trip by foot. The irregular, unsteady meandering of the beast also meant the journey was no more pleasant than a bouncy taxi ride across London's potholed cobblestone streets. His discomfort was only exacerbated by the occasional kicking out of the animal's powerful hind legs and by its emitting of a potent bray, in a repeated act of stubbornness or insolence.

Yet the tortured pace of their progress also meant Sebastian could at last survey the terrain with care. When he had first done so early this morning from his cabin window, he could make out almost nothing, and had measured the land as inert. Closer to the ground and to its heart, he began to examine it more closely. He began to see evidence of energy. Of movement abounding everywhere. The land did not prove fallow, he discovered, but breathed steadily with ingenious life that had audaciously adapted to the extremes of this vindictive environment.

There were wildflowers whose shaky stems and muted colors were dwarfed by the great masses of rock in between which they grew. Dewy grasses, nurtured by the protective shade of those same rocks, fed a catalogue of minuscule insects and spiders, tiny life forms which themselves served to nourish the agitated lizards and the skulking snakes that so discreetly populated this realm. A closer listen, too, revealed a concourse of wondrous sounds that had earlier eluded his attention. He could hear the fierce rubbing together of the forewings of unseen crickets before the rising day would render the last of them mute. He detected the movement of a small stream, also hidden from his view, but that undoubtedly carried within its shallow depths an entirely different universe of life of its own. He heard the wind itself, racing off the sides of the mountain and down into the valley as if it were rustling leaves in a wood, though there were no leaves here to blow.

To his unpracticed eye, the unfolding scene was riveting. Resplendent. It had suddenly become a spellbinding marvel of subtlety and contradiction. From this more privileged vantage point, he saw it as timeless. The site was unspoiled by modernity, no trace of what some might call civilization and the advantages it provided or the wreckage it caused. And in the distance, obfuscated by the undulating heat and by the glaring sunlight, rose the proud, timeworn ramparts of a walled city, sculpted from the soil and the mud itself.

CHAPTER 13 • तेरा

Çanisar. From a distance, the dramatic defensive fortifications that bounded the town, still standing higher than any other structure despite the neglectful state of their maintenance, disappeared seamlessly into the desert over which they stood so imperiously. They were the very color of that desert, as indeed, remarkably, once inside the embankment and the antique outposts, was almost the whole of the town.

Hundreds of mud brick and clay houses emerged as if organically from the ground beneath, some of them five or six stories tall. And not only houses. The ruddy tint, the grainy texture of mud was everywhere. Shops were constructed from it, as was the fresh-water well, of exceptional decorative detail, which ornamented the central square. Even the tightly paved and well maintained streets themselves seemed in danger of being lost to the elements from which they had over so many years unremittingly been drawn. The town's uniform russet tone was severed only by the shock of white paint that capped many rooftops and bordered many windows, by prominent doors painted green or an intense blue, and by the tangle of wispy telegraph and electrical wires that crisscrossed its courtyards.

Though very nearly monochromatic, the town was not

monotonous. Each structure was distinctive, in height, in the symmetrical or irregular placement of its entry, in the rough stucco or smooth finish of its exterior walls. Most remarkably, the façades boasted an infinite variety of window designs and shapes that spoke of eccentric whimsy. Some were molded like portholes on a ship, many not larger than peepholes from which to spy on the animation below. Others were of an entirely more grand order. Majestic, pompous apertures that welcomed in the light and the neighborhood. Graceful teardrop ovals, massive squares, monumental arches and more exploded in fitful sequences, or in no discernible pattern at all. The effect was somewhat befuddling, and it was mesmerizing.

Sebastian's guide tied the mules to a hitching post below a cluster of particularly exuberant windows, and led him, parched and weary from the implacable mid-day sun, to a quiet, unexceptional restaurant at the edge of the main square, nestled in the gracious shade of a pair of buildings at least twice its modest height. The choice was not an arbitrary one. The guide left his visitor in what he knew would be a welcoming spot and, not least, in the one place in town where he knew English would be spoken.

The sign above the entry was written in highly stylized Latin script, but with a disconcerting quantity of vowels and symbols both above and below many of the letters that rendered the name of the establishment indecipherable to him. He could make out only the words '*kafe*' and '*sigara*', indications that, like every café in Britain he had ever visited, coffee would be served and cigarettes would be sold. Although in the cruel heat, neither was a commodity he was presently seeking.

The restaurant was little more than a small, spartan room with a half dozen square aluminum tables and chairs, and a half-hidden, crammed kitchen behind it. An austere but immaculate place, especially given the dust that everywhere governed the town, with only a faded woven tapestry on the wall for decoration beside an aging portrait of Kemal Ataturk. The latter was hung not by obligation or by devotion, but more from habit.

"*Günaydın. Hoş geldiniz!* . . ." began the woman in a pleated headscarf who shortly emerged from within the kitchen, before quickly realizing her customer was not a Turkish speaker, and so continued her greeting in flawless English.

"Good morning. What can I get you?" she repeated in a silvery, dulcet voice.

"A tall glass of cold water would make a nice start," replied Sebastian, startled that this diminutive woman, every bit what he imagined to be the emblematic peasant character, should speak his own language so impeccably.

"If it's not impertinent, may I ask how you've come to know English so well?"

"Certainly. Although I haven't had much practice to speak it recently. I was a teacher once. Literature. Composition. I taught the novels and poetry of your country. Assuming, of course, you are English," she added shyly, embarrassed by her own presumption.

"Well yes, I am most definitely English," he replied. "I would have thought my unfortunate suit would have been a dead giveaway." It was a remark at which they shared an easy laugh.

"My name is Sebastian, and London is my ho . . ., er, London is where I'm from," he declared.

"I am Leyla. Born and raised here in Çanisar. Like me, my husband Abi is also from the region, not thirty miles from here." "Abi," she called. "Abi! Come here. *Burada gel.*

I'm afraid my husband does not speak very good English. Or even speak much of anything, the rascal," she added with obvious amusement. "Some women would say this is a blessing!"

"Good night, sir," said Abi, emerging from the kitchen, his hands covered in a mess of raw vegetable cuttings, only too pleased to blurt out this foreign greeting, even though he had muddled it. A mistake that Leyla, winking affably at her customer, chose not to correct, though she was well aware of the error.

Abi stood hunched, as if he were perennially poised to take a step forward, whereas Leyla stood proudly, rigidly straight. Otherwise, so similar were they in appearance and demeanor, the couple could doubtless have passed as siblings. Despite their advancing age and their amply furrowed features, both maintained charcoal black hair, though Abi's hairline was receding markedly, and both had thick eyebrows behind the chunky glasses each wore. Even their clothes presented a kind of concord, the printed silk scarf she wore with a loose knot around her head largely complementing the vaguely floral print of his open-collared shirt. Both also wore a permanent tender expression that testified to their unambiguous amiability. They stood apart, on either side of Sebastian. Only when they shared practically imperceptible, knowing glances across the divide were there clues of an intimacy between them and that they might be husband and wife.

"You belong to the train orphans, I think?" asked Leyla, as she pulled out a chair and sat close by Sebastian. Surprising him with the lack of ceremony, and delighting him by it, too.

"Yes, I do. I'm making my way, all the way to India. Just as soon as the line can be repaired."

"Goodness. India! That is a long way from here. Though I suppose most every place is a long way from *here*. Those of us in Çanisar, we have no such ambitions. We happily stay put, tied to this land and to our heritage . . ." adding, after a long, wistful pause, ". . . although it was not here that I met my husband, but only by chance in Ankara."

Sebastian was again astonished by the immediate informality that had developed between himself and his hosts, something to which in England he would have been quite unaccustomed. He was taken off guard at the rapidity with which they could enter into such familiarity, before even a meal had been served or, for that matter, a menu had even been presented.

"So you left home, then?" he asked.

"We did. Both of us. I to be educated, Abi to find work. That we should come from so near and meet so far away, well it was a kind of miracle. Though you must understand, to go to the capital, that was not seen here as an achievement, it was seen as a betrayal. It took us many years to realize this. Loyalty and tradition matter most in a small place like this one, the place we will always call our home."

"I've left my home, too. There are those who told me that doing so, even at my age, was a kind of deceit, the kind of betrayal you speak of. Or at least an act of madness. But I know what it's like; I've learned what it is to defy the public's opinion, to ignore its judgment, and I'm no more mad than anyone else you might meet."

"In a big, lonely city like London, what can one know of loyalty? What can one know of tradition?"

"Very little, probably, especially in contrast to a small town such as this, but the metropolis has its advantages.

And despite everything, I think I'll miss many of them," he said with a muffled sigh. "You and your husband," continued Sebastian, "do *you* not miss the city sometimes?"

"*Hayir!* No city. Crowded city. *Danger* city too," said Abi, whose words might have been tangled, but whose meaning was clear.

"No, I can't say we do," added Leyla. "We have simple needs here. We have simple dreams, and that suits us. We work only so that our children, and their children, might have a better life than we have had. To not know hunger. To not know want. This is the hope of generations."

"Yet you taught literature. You know the famous tales of adventure. Of exploration. Haven't you hungered just a little for an adventure of your own?" asked Sebastian, a question that he knew to be disingenuous, having until then never tasted such escapades himself.

"We took our chances, we had our adventures in Ankara. We made careers for ourselves. Me as a teacher, Abi as a baker, and we raised our son."

"Gâwân, our son," said Abi. "He soon here. You meet!"

"Yes, our beautiful son. But only away from here could that have been possible. We went to the city for opportunity, but we only *stayed* there, in that crowded city, in that *danger city* as Abi says, for the sake of our son. My husband and I," she continued, "you see, we are not of the same faith. My family's tradition, it is Shafi'i. Abi comes from a village nearby of the Hanafi faith. Maybe like your Romeo and his Juliet, yes?"

"I suppose so, yes."

"The differences to you may seem small, but they are important enough that our wedding here would have been opposed. We could never have married in this place. God took us separately away from here, only to bring us together in his city. Finally, after many years, he allowed us to come home."

"So you defied your families in marrying?"

"We were not concerned with defiance. Such a big word! We did not think of it that way. God could see for himself, and God could accept us, but the neighbors here, they might not have been as tolerant as God has shown himself to be."

"*Tanrı büyük,*" shouted Abi, almost reflexively, as if speaking to the imam. "God is great."

"You see, our traditions, our habits run very deep!"

Sebastian, captivated by the unfolding tale, was curious to understand the circumstances that would have brought this couple and their son back to the land of their roots, despite the hostility and the prejudice they might have encountered. A tale that, by all visible cues, had ended happily.

"In Ankara, we lived almost in secret, beyond the reach of the judgments and the scrutiny we might have suffered here. It was only on the loss of my mother, may God rest her soul in peace, that we found the courage to return."

"Because, I presume, her unfortunate passing removed an impediment to your homecoming?"

"Oh no, quite the opposite is true."

"How so?"

"My blessed mother lived a long, honest life. A decent life with the man she married, my dear father, but he was not the man she loved. Theirs was an arranged marriage, as most were then in these parts. As many still are today."

"This is something we find hard to accept where I come from," said Sebastian. "In my country, one marries, mostly, for love."

"So it should be. Have you, my English friend, married for love?"

"Oh no, I haven't been as fortunate as that. I *did* love a woman once, and I had hoped to marry her. In my head I had rehearsed the speech in which I asked her to be my wife, over and over again. I had bought her a ring. Made all sorts of plans. But it was not meant to be. At least, it was not *then*. That was a long time ago, when I was still young. So much has changed since. And maybe, after all this time, love is what awaits me at the end of my journey . . ."

"Ah yes, for you, I hope this to be so. It is this love that my dear mother spoke to me about, even as she lay dying. Even as she reached the end of *her* journey. She spoke to me of many things. She told me she did not regret life's empty promises. That she did not fear the devil, that she was not tormented by her disappointments. She lamented one thing, and one thing only, that her prayer of love, to be with the man who had been forbidden her by her family and by custom, had never been answered."

"Was he a local man? A Shafi'i as well?"

"To this day, I don't know who this man might have been. I know nothing of his name, his family, his situation, but I do know, I recall perfectly what my mother whispered to me as she took her final breath. 'Between day and night,' she said, 'there is only love.' It was a revelation. An instruction to me and Abi. 'There is only love,' she murmured."

"How did you understand her message? What did you take it to mean?"

"Well of course it meant simply that we should not repeat the one mistake she had made. She was telling us to have the courage and the determination to celebrate our commitment to each other openly, and to do so, back here with our own people, no matter the obstacles. It was more than a message, it was a plea. A prayer which we took to heart, didn't we, Abi?"

190 • CLOSER EAST

"Gece ve gündüz arasında, sadece aşk vardır," he said.

"Yes, dear, that's it. Between day and night, there is only love."

Sebastian considered these glorified words again and again. The story of which they told was a universal one, an ecumenical parable constructed to announce some truth or to teach some simple lesson. The words struck him deeply. Personally. It was as if these gracious, affable people standing beside him had learned of his private story. Had somehow known that *his* only love had also once been torn from him, and to whom he was sprinting across continents. They must know too that this sprint left him struggling with stubborn doubts, battling with the uneasy gamble he was taking with, and for, his happiness. Perhaps they had unearthed his letters to Olivia, had distilled their singular, recurrent message into one consummate phrase and had read it aloud. Had not his *own* love been forbidden? Had not his *own* prayer been denied? He could as much as see the contours of the words, the silhouette of their letters suspended in front of him. This, he thought, might be some kind of oracle's pronouncement. These demure, beguiling people might be agents of the divine, a portal through which the gods had chosen to speak to him.

Such musings, he concluded quickly, were ludicrous. Çanisar was not Delphi. This simple restaurant was not a sacrosanct temple. He had not sought, would not recognize, would not welcome a prophecy. Still, he was awestruck. Lightheaded. He had to lean heavily on the aluminum table for support. He could feel the blood roaring through his veins, straining to catch up with his galloping, scrambled thoughts. The scene in its entirety seemed to him dreamlike. A surreal, delirious stream of thoughts and images, of remembrance, of nostalgia, of desire. And it seemed to him absurd. Not two weeks ago he was in a grand London home being emptied under his careful direction of its contents and of its memory. He saw himself there sifting through his art and his furnishings like an agent of the Royal Mail sorting deftly through the voluminous daily post, in the methodical, deliberate way he undertook every task. Order and routine still reigned. But today, he found himself on the other end of a jarring donkey ride. In a largely forgotten restaurant whose name he could not pronounce. In a hot, muddy, utterly foreign land about which he knew so little, his own story being conveyed to him, through simple, winsome allegory, by the perfect strangers opposite.

He could not dismiss these queer notions as scornfully or with such easy mockery as he might have done had someone else recounted to him such an unlikely episode. He knew such accidents, such overtly convenient occurrences, happened only in the eccentric minds of writers, who asked their insatiable readers to suspend their disbelief of coincidence and chance for the sake of a strong, compelling narrative. As a newspaper man, he had himself found many an occasion to apply these same tactics, to exaggerate the detail in the telling of an event in order to draw in and to entertain the public, and to sell more papers. This scene, however, could scarcely have been more real. The sweat on his upper lip was too salty to be imagined. The knot of his inopportune tie pinched too tightly. He was lost in a ludicrous but an eminently authentic reverie, and like a gripping novel, a tantalizing newspaper column or a particularly pleasant dream, he longed for it not to end.

* *

Sebastian's breezy daydream was interrupted by the entrance of a young man. A stalwart boy of some twenty years of age, but with a confident gait and a self-assured bearing that spoke of much greater maturity. Gâwân, the striking son of the establishment's proprietors. His youth spent in Ankara, he sported much more modern dress and mannerisms than his more traditional parents. Though with bristling eyebrows and bright emerald eyes, he looked every bit the carbon copy of his father.

Curious or meddlesome, the boy had been eavesdropping for some time. There were few visitors to the town in these sultry months, and rarer still was the foreign guest, and so he was determined not to miss a word of this unexpected conference.

With little introduction and even less hesitation, the boy inserted himself into the fold, instantly adding his own distinct voice to the discussion. Boasting of his language skills, lauding the merits of Çanisar, and at the very first opportunity, suggesting, nearly demanding, that Sebastian be offered a tour of the town and of its environs, with the young man serving naturally as his guide. He was anxious to share with this chance visitor his enthusiasm for his adopted home and to unveil its hidden trophies. It was a proposal to which Sebastian advanced little argument.

The trio soon set about elaborating a program for their guest, to be executed at dawn tomorrow, when adequate preparations could be made, supplies could be gathered, and an itinerary for the day agreed. They did so for hours, plotting and planning arrangements, over the uncomplicated meal that was at last being served and which, without any notion of formality, they all shared. Simple, local fare. A garnished plate of dried pastrami. Spicy sausages in which he could taste the rich cumin and garlic. Tiny dumplings rolled and stuffed right at the table, slow-cooked in the kitchen and served with yoghurt and tomato paste. They washed all this down with strong black tea served from a curious contraption of matching kettles stacked one on top of the other, and poured piping hot into small glasses with a provocative flourish from an outlandishly extravagant height. A rapturous meal, bounding with lively discussion and with goodwill, that Sebastian thought highly theatrical in its preparation and hugely agreeable in its consumption.

* *

As planned, he was met early the following morning at the head of the train by Gâwân, who had a pair of mules in tow on which to carry the day's supplies. On today's excursion the mules would not carry Sebastian, as this time he knew better to walk. It would not be long before, as promised, a succession of wonders began to emerge.

Even from the first mountain overhang, the heart-stirring view over the open, gaping expanse was spectacular. His young guide noted that, from an even higher point and on a clear day such as this, one could see with the naked eye both the Black Sea and the Mediterranean Sea, but Sebastian thought he could already see farther than that. He thought he could see halfway to Delhi, and if he closed his eyes, he imagined he could see farther still.

They passed by, and with some prodding by Gâwân, they passed beneath a sweeping waterfall, whose noisy lamentations made it almost impossible for the men to hear each other, though the broad grin each bore spoke clearly.

Ordinarily loquacious, Sebastian found even fewer words to describe his stupefaction at visiting a lava tube for the first time, a conduit through which a nearby, now-dormant volcano had in a frenzy indignantly expelled whatever had offended it, condemning it to live and to die beneath the surface in a dark thoroughfare leading nowhere. The tube was tall enough for both men to stand and to move about freely. They were careful to dodge the jagged pillars of melted rock jutting up from the ground, especially as they approached the opaque walls to study the ring-like ridges which might have been carved by a master craftsman. Though the stone was as black as tar, it carried within it a transcendental glow, a mysterious effervescence that produced the most subdued light even in the depths of the cave where the sun's rays had never been brave enough to enter. With his pocket knife, Gâwân chipped away at the stone, producing an even more intense luminosity. He handed Sebastian the knife so that he too might marvel at the effect it produced.

Yet the young man had saved the climax of the expedition for the afternoon. Beneath the titanic limestone cliffs, guarded fiercely by a tangle of impervious, prickly vegetation and by razor-sharp rocks, lay the entrance to a long-forsaken subterranean river and the glorious cave it had formed over the ages. Hardly the intrepid explorer that was his guide, Sebastian found the entrance to be a harrowing challenge. He could scarcely mask his disquiet and his fear. His suffering, however, was immediately rewarded, and very largely so. The cave was an incomparable, inimitable sensation.

Its calcite and mineral-infested walls sparkled with a million minute crystals. Sebastian thought they even put to shame the chandeliers he had seen in Lady Bedford's famed London drawing room. Dripping eerily from the ceiling was a seemingly endless series of desperately thin, supernatural shafts that to Sebastian looked curiously similar to the icicles he had often seen clinging to frozen trees in Regent's Park. Some seemed to be dripping still, while others had reunited with their counterparts on the ground to create a single, improbable column. The entire expanse was filled with a strong, mildly disagreeable odor of sulphur and of other elements he couldn't readily identify. It was the same combination of these elements – bicarbonate, calcium, magnesium – which lent the place both its smell and its brilliance. A scintillating space, made even more so by a basin of turquoise water as deep, as sumptuous as the cave itself. A pristine underground lake that Gâwân in particular found irresistible.

"Come on in, old man!" he exclaimed, hurriedly stripping off his clothes and jumping head-first into the glistening pool. "It's wonderful!"

"Oh no, no thanks. I think I'd just rather sit and take in the view from here."

"Don't be silly. A swim will do you a world of good. It's damned cold. It will brace you up for the rest of the day. And you must be stifling in that suit."

"I'll manage. Don't you mind me."

"*Manage*? You should *enjoy*. Nothing will make you feel better than a brisk swim, I can guarantee it. Besides, you've made it *this far* already, and the water here is good for whatever ails you. It has enchanting powers."

"Is that so? I presume the cave is itself haunted by a benevolent spirit?" replied Sebastian, with a lighthearted trace of false derision in his voice.

"There's nothing magical about it. It's science. It has properties. Like medicines do. Things in it that can heal. I don't know what they are, but they can restore the infirm man back to health."

"Has it cured *your* ails?"

"Not me. I'm healthy as a horse! Still, I know the stories. Of people being cured of aches and pains. Clearing up skin conditions. Even making a bald man's hair grow back!"

"I've still got quite enough hair on my head, thank you."

"Relieved my grandmother's arthritis. Or so my mother says. It might keep *yours* at bay! So are you coming in, or do I have to *drag* you in?"

"No, really, I don't have any ailments."

"Shall I count to three, then?"

Sebastian was uncertain whether the boy was serious. Whether he would have the cheek or the temerity to carry out such a threat. Though he very much doubted it. The prospect of throwing a fully clothed and by all appearances squeamish grown man into an icy pond was if anything imprudent.

But in the end, he thought, no more so than were the preposterous circumstances in which he presently found himself. An alien in an unfamiliar land. Lured hundreds of feet underground to a dark grotto. Tempted so improbably to leap into a bitingly cold lake, like a mariner drawn to his own destruction by a tempting siren. The very idea of it was foolishness itself. And it was irresistible.

"Well, for goodness sake, make way!" he exclaimed," like his host shedding his clothes and diving headlong into the frosty basin.

"There you go, old man," said Gâwân.

For well on a quarter of an hour, they splashed and cavorted like children frolicking at a summer picnic.

"You should drink a glass or two of the water, too," suggested the boy, as the pair paused to catch their breath. "In a flash, you'll be like new."

"It smells mighty awful to drink, I must say. Are you sure it's safe?"

"Safe as anything. I'll get glasses, and join you," he said, only reluctantly leaving the cool reservoir to retrieve a pair of metal cups from his kit.

Together, they took a swig of the glassy water. It was more acidic than Sebastian had imagined, but not nearly as unpleasant to taste as its smell hinted. At the young man's gingerly prodding, they took another swallow, and then another one still, like a drinking game in the Crown and Pail, until they had both consumed enough water to satiate their thirst and to indulge the boy's highly speculative calculations of what was required to stave off illness.

* *

The bounteous meal they shared that afternoon back at the café was a joyous one. Sebastian recounted the day's adventures to Leyla and Abi, brimming like a child just back from his first visit to a theme park, with excitement and with a rushed chaos of words. He described what they had seen and what they had done in storied language, as if the events of the day had passed already into legend, as indeed they had, at least for him.

His ebullient retelling of their crusade, the hazards and the action, was nevertheless cut short by the news that was rapidly making the rounds. News that the tracks had been cleared more quickly than anticipated, and that the train was preparing to depart in just a few hours. All those who had found accommodations in town were to make their prompt return. The railway, they knew, would wait for no man.

Sebastian received this news with a mixture of relief

and regret. Maybe it was the unique energy he had found in this place that had restored him. Maybe it was the sheer novelty of the experience, or the infinite kindness and generosity of this small family. Or maybe after all, Gâwân had been right, and it was the luxuriant cave water that had refreshed and revived him. Whatever the cause, he felt more alive today than he had for many years, and more convinced than ever that he could embrace with serenity the rest of his journey. Other adventures doubtless awaited him. New, astounding things to discover every day in India with Olivia. About Olivia. He would relish these discoveries as much as he had the improbable and enchanted diversion that had been his brief visit to Çanisar.

CHAPTER 14 • चौदा

The ancient Hindu scriptures had taught Vikhram many
meaningful lessons. The profound, subtle mantras, the
haunting incantations and stirring poetry of the sacred
Vedas were to him like an instruction manual, a masterly
handbook of life lessons and faithful counsel on which
repeatedly to draw. In their hallowed passages they laid
out a careful, coherent path toward contentment and
equanimity, and although he didn't subscribe to the religious authority of the texts, even in his secular reading
he knew them to contain sweet reason and great wisdom.
Besides, the stories they told and the incomparable language they employed were of such startling artistry that
even the doubter of faith was given pause to consider the
exalted source, the seemingly heavenly inspiration of
such an exquisite miracle.

For Vikhram, the most important lesson to be learned
from these canonical works was the incontrovertible notion
that every man is in command of his own future. That our
thoughts, our actions, our words add or detract from the
scales on which our fate is weighed, and on which ultimately it is decided. Just as he would later read in the elegantly recounted stories of the Christian Bible, he accepted
as truth the simple message that if we sow righteousness,

we reap righteousness, and that if we sow harm, we will in turn invite harm.

He wondered then, abandoned and overwrought at the side of the rapidly emptying quay, *The Artemis* having passed haltingly out of his darkening field of vision, who might he have wronged. What principle or command had he violated to have become the object of such cruelty, of such injustice? His had been an honest life. A faithful one. Perhaps a thorough recounting of his days would not be faultless, as it could not be for any man. It would reveal blemishes, small lapses of judgment and actions for which he harbored genuine regret. His intentions, however, had always been pure, his choices and his deeds overwhelmingly virtuous. He had shown himself trustworthy and good. Yet he hadn't reaped the succulent fruits that should have been his due, but only the spoiled fruits that might be expected of someone of an evil or of an unkind disposition.

To be unkind, to be coldhearted was not a humor that ordinarily he would recognize in himself, but this evening, his mind was full of spiteful thoughts. Poisonous meditations that weighed on him as heavily as if the hefty mass of the dockyard gates, their rusty steel bars closing against him, had fallen directly onto his faltering shoulders.

He walked aimlessly through the animated streets, advancing indifferently as if by spasm or as if blinded by drink. In front of him lay a city humming with movement and life. He took no note of the passersby whose path he crossed or obstructed, nor did they pay any heed to him. He heard nothing, only silence. He saw nothing, only darkness. And soon his mind veered to darker thoughts still.

Within him, a disturbance had been awakened. A turbulence had stirred. He brooded and he sulked. He pondered what violence against someone or something would be required to expunge this evil, to avenge the terrible, abhorrent events that lately had befallen him. A blow, clean and sharp, would be necessary to strike down whatever demon was so bent on persecuting him. Only force, he was convinced, could defeat his invisible foe and bring the universe once again into balance. Brutality begat brutality, the scriptures reminded him, and was the refuge of the lost man, but he had never felt as lost or as dispossessed as he did today, where trouble and grief had become his only companions.

He felt himself taunted on all sides, his misery and his penury mocked, not least by the lustrous objects gleaming like the nighttime sky in the windows of the city's luxury shops. Extravagant finery, frivolous prizes with which the wealthy congratulated themselves and each other. Effortlessly, he imagined, he could pilfer just one of these pricey baubles and then shrink back unnoticed into the anonymous street. Some of these shops would also have on hand a substantial reserve of cash, quite possibly in a lock-box like the one Mr. Mukerjee had kept at the Victoria Book Palace or like the more basic one he and Amit had kept hidden in their dormitory wardrobe. He knew of no law of nature that proclaimed these merchants should wield such lavish funds when he had none, and so sought to convince himself he would be right in taking his just share.

But Vikhram knew this to be counterfeit. That such thinking was false, and that it was dangerous. Crime and violence violated the intrinsic sense of virtue that had guided him always. Not least, he knew the risks associated with it could not be tolerated. He had taken too many chances, made too many compromises, to end up on the wrong side of a prison wall. If this evening he felt that all was lost, at heart he knew that there were further depths still to which he could sink. So theft, or criminality of any color, was not to be considered.

As he agonized over the lack of any discernible path home, hungry and disoriented, indiscriminate images of Bombay began to flood his consciousness. Not more than mere outlines. The sketchy edges of a place he knew well, or once did. For Bombay might as well be of another realm, so distant did it seem, so obscure his chances of reaching it. The squalor of its interminably blighted slums, its tall office blocks and manicured lawns, the discordant vestiges of colonial architecture were all a world away. So too was the great span of the coast, the alluring hotels and fabled film lots, or the unsettlingly large crowds of boisterous people who gathered nightly at sunset on Chowpatty Beach, plotting for themselves a better life that seemed always just slightly out of reach, dreaming their improbable dreams. Like them, he had been a dreamer once. He had taken his place among the nameless multitudes hoping, scheming for something better. For a way to provide sanctuary for himself and for his young family. Those dreams had long since started to fade, nearly extinguished by disappointment, by miscalculations, by calamity.

He narrowed his scope, fixed his energies on trying to imagine not the sweeping fabric of the city, but only what his own small family could be doing at this precise moment. Sapna tidying up after the evening meal. The children revising their schoolwork. His young son playing a game of pick-up cricket with his schoolmates in one of the nearby neglected fields. He could not manage it. In these two years away, his vision had been subjugated by the bitter desert's pervasive blanket of sand and sun. Irreparably, he feared. It had clouded, then broken his memories. There had been little to prod or to remind him of the happier symbols of his everyday routine at home. He couldn't quite recall whether the small space that served as a pantry in their flat was to the right or to the left of the kitchen. If the battered hoarding on the post office wall opposite advertised soap powder or tea biscuits. What, even, was the precise color of his wife's eyes, or of the children's hair? The details had lost their focus, as he had lost his way.

The cruel events of the last few days, like the monsoon's first downpour, flooded riotously back to him, though without any of the welcome release that the latter usually conveyed. The doghouse explosion. His friend Amit's blood-soaked helmet. The company manager's self-satisfied grin as he contemplated the unexpected windfall of his shameless extortion. Even a happier flashback of the young Sunil's euphoric discovery of crocodiles and tortoises was eclipsed all too quickly by wretched images of the Bissalama Hotel and the abandoned boat quay where all had somehow, and so swiftly, fallen to pieces. A string of faces, of blurry desert towns and villages through which he had sped, whispers of incidental remarks that inundated him, and only crowded out further his dwindling remembrances of home.

Yet in exhuming these more recent and these more sour memories, Vikhram's attention stopped abruptly on the exchanges he had overheard just two days prior between the rowdy men assembled at the back of the bus. Men boasting of their work, and of their large takings, on luxury trains departing from Baghdad. They spoke of excursions to Istanbul, of Sebastopol and Odessa on the Black Sea coast, of the legendary capitals of Europe. A few had spoken as well of trains that went as far as India.

He had questioned the veracity of these tales, dubious of the obvious penchant amongst these coarse men for hyperbole and self-aggrandizement. He was not competent to judge the authenticity of their stories, whether these men had ever won or even sought the bounties they claimed, but he had been left with few alternatives. Either he could suspend his incredulity and act, or he could remain immobilized. Either he could ignore his intrinsic misgivings, or be cut low by paralysis and by indecision. If only he could get to Baghdad, city of fair gardens and of golden palaces, providence might just prove merciful. She might at least, and at last, prove just generous enough to procure him safe conduct to India. First, however, he would need to get to Baghdad.

* *

He wasn't even entirely sure where the Iraqi capital was, so knowing its location, seeing its position on a map, might he thought bring him one step closer to being there, and one more vital step closer to home. Accustomed as he was to finding instruction and insight in books, he sought out a bookseller whose catalogue might include an accommodating guide or atlas.

He would not have suspected that such a mundane task could show itself so elusive. For despite the broad spectrum of shops on offer, most of whose doors were open still to account for the altered timetable of Ramadan, there was not a single bookshop to be found.

He surveyed the neighborhood's staggering medley of other establishments, all richly appointed and many of them well frequented by patrons who seemed to be parting with money with as much nonchalance as he had difficulty in acquiring it. Boutiques selling glimmering jewelry, or the finest of handmade shoes. A dispensing optician advertised

sight tests and custom corrective lenses, apparently manufactured on site. A huge emporium of furniture awarded
its insatiable customers a profusion of tawdry, ostentatious
pieces – hulking tables and beds and sideboards bedecked
in gold, in silver, in iridescent mother-of-pearl. He saw, too,
standing free at the junction of two yawning boulevards,
the elaborate marquee of a large cinema house announcing
the forthcoming projection of a Hindi film, something that
might in these most trying of hours have furnished Vikhram with a welcome distraction, had he had the time to
spare, or a penny to his name.

Though he found no bookseller, at length he stumbled
across an unremarkable pawnbroker's shop, no different
than its equivalent in the Nayā Bazaar, and in markets
everywhere. It catered to the same class of desperate people, predominantly men, deluding themselves into thinking that one day soon their luck would turn. Vehement that
they would return before long to reclaim cherished items
from safekeeping. Talking up the value of even the most
insipid of items as if they had been a personal gift from a
Russian czar or an American millionaire. Invariably, they
left disappointed at the beggarly sum offered for such abdi-
cation. The shop's thriving trade also served the buyers, the
savage vultures who fed on such desperation, looking without mercy to capture an easy bargain on the backs of the
unfortunate, to re-sell or to melt down their newly acquired
property just as quickly as possible, without a thought for
its provenance or for the heartbreak to which its presence
in the pawnshop was sad testimony.

From floor to ceiling, and in the courtyard beyond even
higher still, the ground was positively erupting with merchandise. Gazing through the derelict windows on the pavement outside, Vikhram could see huge drifts of accumulated

articles, heaps of bric-a-brac of every sort and of every possible description. The scene was one of barely contained mutiny, an assortment of goods that would take a contingent of resolute assistants a lifetime to bring to order. He spied a mighty pair of grandfather clocks, and beside them, a heap of desk clocks that were laughably small in comparison. An opulent set of barely used silver cutlery. Decorative bronze statuettes, and a parade of Chinese porcelain bowls of disputed ownership whose few hairline cracks only a connoisseur would notice or mind. Typewriters, chess sets, a brace of painted wooden boxes and painted wooden picture frames. An exhausted wireless set much less elaborate than the Falk, Stadelman model he had known in Bombay. Estranged, mismatched fabric chairs. All of this stood staring at a blank corner wall like a schoolboy being punished in class for some reckless misdemeanor.

Vikhram raked through his canvas bag, looking for items he might plausibly sell. There was little from which to choose. His shabby clothes were without value to others. So too were his tattered books and the sheepskin sandals he had long ago bought, wrapped still in wax paper. The tiny silver-plated elephants that Sunil had so admired might fetch a decent price, but they were the only mementos he had managed to secure for his children, and he couldn't, he wouldn't part with them, even if it meant he were to go hungry. By contrast, the gold bracelet he had long ago procured as a gift for Sapna, masterfully crafted and elaborately inscribed with what was to him an unknown Arabic verse, might well be ransomed for a modest figure. Its surrender would also mean torment, for it would mean he would return to his wife with truly empty hands, but he set his mind nonetheless to conceding it.

Out of apprehension, and out of embarrassment, he

entered the shop only after its last customer had gone. From behind the counter the aloof, dour owner inspected him, appraising Vikhram as if he too were an object to be sold or bartered. Measuring his chances at swindling this latest prospect, or of at least stripping the young man of his effects at the lowest achievable cost, estimating the degree of Vikhram's distress and eagerness to sell as the determinant factor of his opening bid.

He could see Vikhram's hunger all too clearly; he could nearly smell his discomfort. So the price he advanced for the bracelet was derisory. Disdainful. It spoke conspicuously of the contempt in which he held his despairing customers. The amount proposed would hardly buy Vikhram more than a few proper meals, and would certainly not compensate for the loss of the one favor he might present his wife. He appealed to the owner to reconsider. He begged him. He used every argument and every tactic he could muster, rational and emotional alike, of the type against which over the years the shopkeeper had developed a near-perfect immunity.

But in making his high-spirited appeal, the owner could not but notice the gold watch that adorned Vikhram's gaunt wrist and that peeked from under his shirtsleeve. A watch that Vikhram had worn for so long that he no longer noticed it. He had purchased it those many months ago, early in his tour in Al-Fadiz, as a solemn sign of his triumph, or at least of his ascendancy. He had worn the object proudly as the first indication of his early good fortune. He could not have known then that it would also be the last, that the assurances he received of prosperity and of abundance were as slight as the gilt on the device's heavily polished case. Like so many of the empty promises that had been made to him, he had soon forgotten about it.

Rarely had he used the timepiece for the purpose for which it was intended, for he had learned that there were innumerable other, equally reliable ways in which one could ascertain the hour. The change of shift on the rigs or the end of the mid-day break was announced by a sharp whistle. The muezzin's astral voice called out with unbending regularity five times each day. Even when there were no thundering bells or roaring sirens, there was always someone nearby instructing him, snapping terse commands at him about where he needed to be, and when.

The gold plating on the watch was undoubtedly thin, though not nearly as thin as the shopkeeper asserted. What was without contention was the excellent condition of the piece, and its overall appeal. For which, and with conspicuous reluctance, the pawnbroker proposed to Vikhram a respectable amount. It was considerably less than he had paid for it, and less than he might have hoped. It would, however, be more than sufficient to provide him a few square meals, and not least, a bus ticket to Baghdad. It was a surprisingly honorable offer, and in any case it was not one he could afford to refuse.

* *

He wasn't twice going to lose his money, even the much depreciated sum to which he now laid claim, and so he stashed the small bundle of banknotes in his shoe, where he knew it would be safe from the pickpockets and swindlers he was inclined to imagine were everywhere about him.

Despite the temporary boon, Vikhram avoided renting a room in a hotel, both because of the expense, and because of the still raw, dismal association it held for him. He sought refuge instead under a disused railway bridge, where tonight he would once again sleep rough. The underpass would serve to protect him both from the unceasing noise of the streets above, and in its obscurity, from the redoubtable patrolmen who roamed those streets methodically looking for vagrants and, in every sense, looking for trouble.

Even after all this time spent in the mournful desert and in the thriving cities it had somehow miraculously disgorged, he was confounded still by the contrast between the despotic heat of the day and the numbing cold of the dry, tempestuous night. The strong wind, channeled tight into the narrow passageway, blew him asunder like a weathervane on a high cathedral roof. It pummeled his lean frame. Cast-out, neglected, battered by the successive blasts of the night air, cowed by the foul darkness, he was a ghost. An unseen, obliterated ghost.

But ghosts cannot feel. They cannot hurt. So though tonight he never felt closer to the somber spirits of the dead, Vikhram knew that he existed still. He was not an apparition or a hallucination. Neither dream nor figment of imagination. He was flesh and bones. His quivering limbs were proof enough. His rumbling stomach only confirmed it. He had persevered, held firm against so many temptations to submit. Sustained himself through tests and contests even more formidable and more intractable than this. He knew he would prevail. To give up now, to renounce this fight, would be an unpardonable act of weakness. An apostasy. All he needed was warmth and bread and courage. All of which, he felt certain, tomorrow would surely bring. For tomorrow, he repeated to himself over and over like one of the Veda's angelic mantras, a change would come. Yes, tomorrow a change would come.

When morning did break, before even the new day

had been confirmed, Vikhram had already taken his place
aboard the first bus bound for Baghdad. Not a full day's
travel away, the city was well out of reach of the desolation
and the despondency that had defined his previous night.
Unlike on his bus trip from Al-Fadiz, an odyssey filled
with memorable characters and encounters, this time he
spoke to no one, and no one spoke to him. Even his books
remained unopened, as he fixed his vacant stare out of the
window for the first sign of the city. He would not have long
to wait.

* *

The bus arrived at the mighty Central Railway Station,
the centerpiece of Iraq's burgeoning transport network, at
the height of the afternoon. Like the bus depot in Kuwait
City, this station too was heaving with people, not least
by the inexhaustible workers scattered across the grounds
like debris on a storm-battered beach, racing to finish the
building's much delayed construction before the expiration
of yet another elusive deadline. These shifting goal-posts
would time and again reveal themselves to be pure fiction,
as the initial work on the station would require another five
years to finish, and its chronic maintenance would be found
forever wanting. For despite the great strength and durabil-
ity of the materials chosen to line the huge domed structure – the crystallized white marble imported from Spain
and the smooth grey, locally-sourced granite – the damage
inflicted on it by the unrelenting climate and by the infer-
nal volume of people who daily passed within it meant the
building would never quite achieve its longed-for air of per-
fection, or even an air of completion.

Still, few could fail to be impressed by its thrilling

architecture, by the dramatic statement of exultation and ambition that the building was designed to make. A proclamation that no passenger traveling to and from it could ignore. The central dome soared a hundred feet above the ground. Around its base, a dozen or so massive archways had been carved, each two or three stories high, leaving the main concourse awash with brilliant sunlight. A huge marble double staircase, the likes of which Vikram had never seen before, led to a more moderately proportioned second floor of additional departure platforms and an endless series of identical, unmarked doors behind which he could only guess at the kind of dreary work that took place.

He paid only sparing attention to the design of the building. He was not concerned with the majesty of the structure, of its trompe-l'oeil frescoes or the massive clock that embellished the central hall, a blazing ornament which, like the station itself, was a gift from the country's rulers to celebrate or to flaunt their new found oil wealth. He sought only two much more prosaic things: the timetables for a train to Bombay, and the station-master's office, where he would need to address his case for work.

Affixed like advertisements at various points around the entry hall, the published schedules were easy enough to find, though their codes and symbols were maddeningly difficult to understand. He considered the litany of places whose names were unknown to him, unsure in many cases even in which direction the trains would be heading, toward his destination or away from it. Not one of the many schedules indicated Bombay itself. Within the crammed register of listings, he could make out only one line that appeared headed to India, a train that passed through Baghdad Central twice a week, en route first to Karachi via Iran, then north into its terminus, Delhi. This he knew must be his target, his best and his only chance to get at least to the Indian capital, and from there to get home. Even the line's name resonated with promise and with enchantment, and spoke to him with confidence. Bright Star.

Deciphering its timetable was demanding enough. Finding a way on board would be much harder still. He possessed only a fraction of the price demanded for a third-class ticket, and so, as expected, he would need to find work on the train, to take up the challenge revealed to him by his fellow bus passengers and with which they alleged to have had such success. He was not seeking their same reward. He aimed not for easy wages or for rich tips. He sought only passage. He did not fear failure, for he had found himself in such a position more than once before, confronted with such improbable odds, and had overcome them by sheer determination. It was, after all, with nothing but a dogged tenacity that once he had won his cherished place in Mr. Mukerjee's handsome bookshop. It was the same course he would pursue again today.

* *

The object of Vikhram's campaign was Mr. Taman Ansari, or so the brass plaque on the station-master's simple office door indicated. A veteran of the company, he had been engaged by the railway for the whole of his long professional life. He had joined the lowest of its ranks as only a boy, part of the initial, ardent wave of employees recruited at the turn of the century by the German government, whose funds and know-how were building an almost unrivaled network of rail links across the region. Not particularly interested in the Germans' grand efforts to supply their colonies, he was never concerned with the complex polemics of imperial influence, or the outsized role that control of shipping from the Middle East would soon play in the outbreak of war. He had been lured only by the promise of a job, and when he learned that the Ministry of Public Works had granted a concession to extend the railway to Baghdad, he was amongst the first in line to benefit from the largesse that everyone presumed would follow directly.

With more than half a century spent in the company's employ, he had come to know its people well. Through his decency and constant consideration, with a willingness always to lend his hand and his favor, he had earned his colleagues' esteem and had won their countenance of his steady advancement. He came to know as well every inch of the Baghdad station, in all of its sundry iterations, from the earliest backwater outpost it had been to the stately edifice it would soon become. He oversaw the current construction as if he were its chief architect, as if the building were his own. In some ways, it might just as well have been, so integral had he become to the company and to the station.

Vikhram could see the manager's hazy silhouette through the tinted glass window of his cluttered office, fixed for hours to his desk. He studied the faint relief of this man's form and the blurred line of his movements. In the process he drew himself a loose portrait of the man, persuading himself, satisfying himself that somehow he could divine in these movements telltale, compelling hints of benevolence, of humanity, of pity. For he would need the manager to possess some of these qualities, or all them, to succeed. All the while, like a hunter crouched stealthily in the underbrush, patiently stalking his prey, he waited for his furtive target to surface, as inevitably he would be required to do.

"Mr. Ansari. Mr. Ansari, sir. Can I speak to you, please?" he asked excitably, as the manager finally emerged for one of his regular site inspections.

"Well, hello son. Do I know you?"

"No, sir. No you don't. I only know your name from the sign on your office."

"How can I help you?" he asked, though he had already guessed at the all too conventional request that likely would follow.

"I'll be frank, sir, and I'll be brief. They told me that *you're* the man I need to see for work. And you see, sir, I'm very much hoping to find work on a train."

"Work on a train? There's nothing but heartache and loneliness there, son, I can tell you. Traveling all the time, being away from your home, from your family. That's no life for a young man like you. Better to find a regular job here, something in the city, something fixed. There's plenty of work around these days. Or so I'm told."

"You see sir, it's precisely *because* I'm desperate to get home that I want to work on the train. The one train I could find that goes to India. That's where I'm from, and that's where I want to go."

"Oh, you must mean the Bright Star. Comes next into the station . . . when is it? Must be Friday morning, I think. She's been delayed in Turkey by a mudslide. The poor souls on board really have had to be patient! Always a bit of a ruckus when she comes in, that one, and I expect it'll be even more so this time," said Mr. Ansari.

"Do you have something waiting for you in India?" he continued, in a tone that to Vikhram sounded genuinely solicitous, and evinced a disarmingly gentle and magnanimous character.

"My wife, sir, and my children. A beautiful son and

daughter. I've been away from them for a long time. Much too long. Working on the Saudi oil rigs."

"Goodness, away from your family? That's a load no man should have to bear. And on those blasted rigs! They can break a man. So I can't say I blame you for wanting to get home. If you don't mind my asking," continued Mr. Ansari, "do you have any savings? Have you managed to put anything by during your time away? Can we arrange to buy you a ticket?"

"I've lost everything I earned, sir. Absolutely everything. Stolen from me just yesterday. The scoundrel took my boat ticket home, too. Didn't even have the dignity to leave me that . . ." he just managed to say, before his words trailed off into a stifled jumble of emotion and anguish.

The anxious, crestfallen expression that came upon Mr. Ansari's face was unexpected, and it spoke volumes. He reacted instinctively, with obvious compassion and with demonstrable concern.

"Oh, I can't *tell* you how often I hear stories like yours," he said. "Such appalling stories of insult. There seems no limit to some people's cruelty."

The manager placed his hand softly on Vikhram's shoulder, in a small but eloquent gesture that moved the young man deeply, so unused had he become to even the most meager sign of affection, as indeed he had to any manifest interest in his welfare.

"Sir," continued Vikhram, eager to get back to the substance of his initial and his only material question. "I was hoping I might be of use to the railway, and that in turn it might help me get home to my family. Do you know of any jobs on that train you mentioned?"

"I wish I could help you, my friend, but that train's fully staffed. Seems *all* of them are nowadays. Got a surplus of folks on board the trains at the moment, including the Bright Star. A fine train *she* is, too. Little wonder everyone seems to want to work on that line. You'd be surprised at the number of requests I get. Young men, fine men just like yourself, lining up in the hall here early in the morning, sometimes four or five deep, for their chance. But my hands are tied. If the company says there isn't any need for men, then I've no cause to supply them. I wish I could help you, but there's little I can do."

"Surely you can use *one* more person. Just *one* more on a big train like that. There must be so much to do. And I'll do anything, sir. Anything. *Any* job there is to take. I promise you, you won't be disappointed. I work hard, and I'm an honest man."

"Oh I can see that, son. You seem like quite a decent young man, and you do seem determined. I like that, and I like you. But if there's no place, I can offer you no help."

For the next few minutes, the two men danced around this fruitless, circular conversation as if they were partners in a whirling, quick-time waltz, until ultimately the manager was compelled to take his leave. It was a conversation that, articulated only slightly differently, repeated itself numerous times over the subsequent two days. Vikhram waited outside Mr. Ansari's office in perpetual anticipation. At every fleeting interaction, they greeted each other with something akin to friendliness, or at least with increasing familiarity. Each time, Vikhram would alter his tack, taking always a somewhat different bearing, emphasizing his ordeal, his hurt, introducing humor or flattery. He wasn't above bribery, though he had precious little to offer and even less reason to believe that such a grotty course would be entertained. He took to stalking the station-master as he made his daily rounds, trailing him like a benign shadow, offering to run errands for him, or to provide any practical, credible sign of the vigor and commitment with which he was willing to serve the railway.

He slept where and when he could manage it, on the muddy ground behind the station and later, when he felt certain that he had gained Mr. Ansari's protection, on a bench in the main waiting room. When his money ran out, as too soon it did, he took to filching scraps of food leftover by rich passengers who had abandoned their expensive meals in one of the station's cafés in a hurried dash to make their departure. He washed in the public lavatory, read snippets of the daily English language newspaper on display at the kiosk, but otherwise spent the balance of his long days planted firmly, unmovable, in front of the manager's office.

* *

On the third day, when the routine had become truly wearisome and, despite his staunch convictions, his confidence had begun to fade, he was awakened from an uneasy sleep by a gentle pull on his shoulder. All around him, the station was in a kind of systematic uproar, preparing to meet the Bright Star train, whose arrival from Aleppo at the top of the still-early hour had set off a chain of frantic arrangements for its extensive provisioning. The tug at his side was that of the station-master, who urged Vikhram to rise.

"Wake up. Wake up, my friend! Listen. The next train bound for Delhi arrives here in just thirty minutes. I've got word that two of the cabin boys, a pair of Iraqi brothers, I think, intend to leave the train and to stay on in Baghdad. If you can get your affairs together, if you can get yourself cleaned up in time, one of those places is yours. It will be the most menial of work, hardly any pay at all . . ."

Mr. Ansari's remarks went on for a few moments more, but Vikhram heard little of it. All he had heard, and all that mattered, was that this kindly, soft-spoken man, a man of position and of authority who was still only a well-known stranger to him, had shown himself compassionate, had secured for him, before all other contenders and against his diminishing expectations, a coveted place on a train to India. He nodded his head avidly in affirmation, as he could not readily find the words, even as he robustly shook the manager's hand in unbridled gratitude.

With fantastic speed, he made his way to the back end of the assigned platform to receive his instructions. He was given a faded but clean uniform. With a thick pen, he was directed to scribble his name on a blank nameplate, and without any other ceremony, he boarded the Bright Star now idling restlessly in Baghdad Central Station.

Within moments, he was once again, and this time emphatically so, on his way home. This time, nothing could obstruct him. Not theft. Not deceit or trickery. Nothing. He would not have hesitated to blow on the wheels if he thought this might help to accelerate their turning. Above all, he would demonstrate through diligence and industry that he was worthy of the station-master's trust and of his beneficence. Just as he would need to re-earn the trust of his young family, whose faith he had so sorely tested by the sad tale of his interval in Arabia. An interval at last coming to a rapid close.

PART THREE

GRACE

CHAPTER 15 • पंधरा

All morning, the venerable train trundled up through the thickset cloak of drowsy rain clouds, advancing unhindered along the sharp, naked mountain walls of Western Pakistan. Its thin frame pierced the heavy fog with self-assurance, breaking forcibly, heroically through the swollen haze.

In these last few days alone, the aged vehicle had demonstrated immense stamina, confronting with vigor and with strength a procession of unnerving adversaries, each one more wily, more insidious than the last. It had shown itself to be as redoubtable as its hard-won reputation had long suggested, proving itself again and again to be resilient. It had been delayed but not defeated by the mudslides in Turkey. Rattled but not deterred by the pummeling, crippling temperatures and the punishing sandstorms of the infinite Iraqi desert, and even less so by the corrosive menace of Iran's dry salt lakes that threatened to maul its varnished skin. It had not even been put off by the taunting insults of the newer, sleeker, faster diesel-electric locomotives, which with the arrogance of their youth mocked the fits of steam its tired, coal-burning lungs periodically exhaled.

Yet as it drove up the sheer, spine-chilling hillsides, the

massive train at last started to lose its steely nerve. With good reason. The climb was wearily steep, the drops vertiginous and abrupt. The towering passages on the range's western front were noticeably more modest than in the Hindu Kush or in the celebrated Himalayas to the north, but they were daunting nonetheless.

As the steam from the Bright Star's timeworn engine escaped its fiery incarceration, wheezing out in increasingly desperate puffs of white and grey smoke, it let out as well a terrible sound that for miles ricocheted off the cliff sides, like a ferocious beast cautioning all others to yield. But in the supreme emptiness of the terrain, this forewarning sounded less like the roar of a proud lion and more like the wail of a wounded cub. These cries were in any event wholly unnecessary, as the sustained, repeated echoes across the valleys spoke of the fearsome height, and of the total oblivion below. A deadened, frozen backcloth of only dry, scrubby undergrowth and of bloodless volcanic rock into which the black steel of the train's lumbering carriages melted like perfect camouflage.

Sebastian had left open the windows of his cabin throughout the long, torturous ascent. Not because he wished to admire the view. Majestic and as unearthly as he first thought it was, the scene had soon become lifeless and ever more monotonous. He did so because, despite the cool air that outside held sway at this great altitude, he felt himself stifled, suffocating. The thinning sky left him groggy and light-headed. For a brief moment, as the train bent its stiff skeleton around a perilous bend, he found himself close to fainting. Gently the room spun around him, whirling lightly as if he were on a children's carousel ride coming gingerly to its long, measured close. Despite the chill, he was plagued with a profuse sweat on his brow, and would have wagered heavily that it was much hotter in his cabin than the mercury might have indicated.

He was not, however, especially troubled by these displeasing sensations. He had learned early in this expedition to expect as much, if not worse, at such heights. Already, in passing through the Alps of Austria and Switzerland he had felt the lethargy and the distraction of that exalted elevation. He had understood that this was the price one paid for admission to such rarified places. He had learned too that the tiredness and the incapacity he experienced would likely pass just as soon as the train again reached a level closer to the sea, just as the Bright Star would soon make its descent into the Karachi plateau.

What he needed most, as the train continued to wind its way down the mountain's hazardous ridges and edges, was fresh air to steady his tattered nerves. He would need rest too, if only he could manage it. Chilled water to drink and to splash on his perspiring temples and neck would also prove a welcome antidote to his discomfort.

For the latter at least, he had only to ring the bell in his cabin for the steward or for one of the cabin boys to appear, ready to answer this and all requests, conditioned only by the chance that language might interfere or that the item or service he required could not readily be procured. Constraints he had happily yet to encounter.

* *

When Hamid heard the bell's distinctive chime – for to the trained ear every cabin's signal was slightly different – he was engaged in supervising the progressively more panicked arrangements for lunch in the dining car, where supplies were running alarmingly low. Unable to extract himself from the current worried predicament in which he found the preparations, it was Vikhram whom he sent to fetch fresh water for the Englishman.

He did so with confidence. For three days Vikhram had received sporadic, indiscriminate assignments from the Turkish steward whose cramped quarters he had been assigned to share, to fill in wherever and whenever additional manpower or muscle was necessary. In every task he had proved himself worthy. He had worked briefly with the women in the laundry, washing the linens from the first-class cabins, pounding them with stones over and over against a hard baseboard, choking out the soapy water with his strong hands. He helped out in the kitchens, chopping vegetables, boning fresh fish when on occasion it could be found aboard, plucking feathers from newly slaughtered birds. He had even infiltrated the tight ranks of busboys in the dining car when one or more of them was accorded a day of rest, folding napkins just so, polishing the silver until the waiters were satisfied it could shine no brighter, making certain the warming candles under the tins of coffee and hot water remained alight.

* *

Vikhram was surprised by many things upon entering the Englishman's cabin. Most striking was that the windows in both rooms were completely ajar, drawing in the angry, biting air of the mountain without restraint. He thought this a folly, and a dangerous one at that, but he would not dare to meddle with the passenger's clear, determined intent to bear or maybe even to relish the monstrous cold. How queer, how unpredictable, he thought, this curious race could be. He had known his quota of eccentric, capricious

Englishmen, whose irregular habits and tastes would always remain a mystery to him, and this one must have forfeited a princely sum indeed to have such a splendid cabin as this reserved for him alone.

Besides, here was a passenger quite unlike the others he had observed. Not least, his cabin was in a state of impeccable order, as if he had not quite had time to settle in or was preparing to leave. Both of which Vikhram knew not to be the case. In the open wardrobe hung the man's numerous suits and trousers, white cotton shirts well pressed and stacked one on top of the other, his other affairs all aligned in fastidious, precise rows. Belts, cufflinks, a generous pile of silk socks and cotton drawers, black and brown lace-up, highly polished pairs of shoes. Several newspapers, whose titles he didn't know, lay carefully folded on the side table, as if unread, on top of which lay a pair of folded spectacles, which suggested just the opposite. In the bath his effects were equally well organized. The contrast with other first-class cabins could hardly have been more acute, where clothes and towels and half-eaten trays of food were often strewn wildly around the room without care, in a reckless, indifferent presumption of someone else tidying up.

Many of these same passengers, who paid so little heed to the negligent way in which they flung about their belongings, also paid scant attention to the occasional presence of the personnel in their cabins. Nowhere was this more vexing than in the indecency of their attire, for which they made little or no effort to respect a minimum amount of modesty. Many never bothered to don suitable garments or even to get out from their comfortable beds when the staff appeared, as if the crew were simply insignificant enough to be thus inconvenienced.

But here was a man, despite being alone in his cabin,

who was clad in immaculate dress. He wore a smart linen suit, one that showed barely a crease. His collar, though opened, was starched, his silk tie loose around the neck but the knot flawless just the same. On his wrist he sported a fine watch, but even the allure of that delicate instrument paled in comparison to the prominent, dazzling tie-pin he wore. A pin that held in between its silver clasps a blue gem-stone whose hard, glittering brilliance seemed less to reflect the light than to be drawn in directly from the stars above.

And there were books. Many books, stacked in neat piles on the desk. On the sitting room's single shelf. Beside the armchairs. He would have liked nothing more than to examine these treasures at leisure. He could see by their bindings, some in cloth and especially those in calf-leather, that they were of a very good quality. Many had thick decorative spines and rigid paperboard dustcovers, and which he knew would be stitched together tightly with fine string. A few folio-sized volumes drew his particular inter-est, since he had become well accustomed to admiring the magnificent illustrations and the riveting stories he knew they were likely to contain.

He would not be offered the time to survey this anthol-ogy, since his duties and his station compelled him, with the utmost discretion and with the least disruption, only to replace the jug of water in the cabin as requested, and eventually as circumstances demanded, to make up the bed of this retiring passenger.

A passenger who appeared quite lost in his thoughts. To Vikhram, the Englishman's temperate but stalwart countenance bore an irresistible fascination. He imagined Sebastian might be a teacher, beloved by his fervent pupils despite the firmness of his methods and the severity of his discipline. Or maybe an eloquent, persuasive lawyer or a powerful man of politics, respected in his profession, beyond reproach and incorruptible, feared by those unlucky enough to have engaged him as an opponent, esteemed by those more fortunate to have benefited from his counsel and from his sponsorship.

Yet there was also something overcast, something dark in the man's face and in his absent stare, wavering between either contemplation or concern. Vikhram had perhaps mistaken a look of weariness or of abstraction for a kind of sorrow, but he thought he could nonetheless discern a private regret to be the principal feature of this reserved man. A feature he could only too well recognize in himself, not as native to his character, but as an obstinate quality that had only lately emerged, clumsily, agonizingly, from his years of rout and injury. He had become familiar with melancholy and misfortune, those gloomy twin syndromes for which the cure was forever in principle promised, and that always proved elusive in practice. He had most mornings these past two years in Arabia glimpsed them squarely in his mirror. He was not then altogether surprised when he sensed, immediately and forcefully, the same maladies entrenched in the Englishman's kindred spirit.

What he did not yet know was that Sebastian at least had begun, from almost the moment he had left the rocky coastline of his England, to reach for a remedy, to which every mile they travelled east was bringing him closer.

* *

The hard-driven, industrious crew shoveled coal incessantly into the locomotive's ravenous ovens. They swept its floors of that coal's wreckage, battled to keep clean the train's fevered facilities and the remnants of a thousand footsteps up and down again the length of the carriages. Vikhram had easily melted into this anonymous, frenetic mass, so well obscured behind the outwardly placid scenes. Part of an unseen, unspeaking band of women and men whose unacknowledged contributions ensured the train would advance. Whose presence the customers they served so scrupulously would only suspect, but seldom be required to witness.

Since most of the tasks he had been assigned had failed to put him in contact directly with any passengers, he had received no gratuities, and still had almost no money to his name, besides the inconsequential daily wage he had so far earned.

Today would be different. As Vikhram completed the few simple duties required in the Englishman's cabin, he bowed respectfully to his passenger, his hands clasped together in a traditional sign of respect and of reverence. As he did so, edging backward toward the door, Sebastian reached his hand nonchalantly into the wooden bowl that lay next to his newspapers and into which he had throughout the journey tossed loose coins. He grabbed a handful of these coins as a tip for the cabin boy, whose good name, as Vikhram would refer to it, only now did he learn, offering his own in return.

Vikhram was startled by the heaviness, by the bulk of the tip, and thought it must represent an important sum. Likely a trifle for the Englishman, who for certain dispensed with these coins with practiced indifference, but a windfall for those who served him. Out of habit, for in his many small jobs and errands in Bombay over the years he had become familiar with this custom, he immediately placed the lot in the front pocket of his uniform, without pausing to look at its contents, anxious to avoid any sign of embarrassment on the passenger's side, or of any disappointment on his.

Once outside the cabin, however, at the extreme end of the long, tight hallway that led from the lounge car to the service quarters, he dug earnestly into his pocket, eager to examine his reward. He was not disappointed.

He held in his hand a half-dozen coins. The objects were themselves of as much interest to him as they were of value. These coins of the Realm spoke their own language, told their own astonishing stories, held their own secrets and surreptitious confidences. They would already have passed from hand to hand many hundreds of times, leaving only the faintest suggestion of their application, each time to travel just a tiny bit further away from their source and toward another destination that could never be known or anticipated in advance. They were tiny pieces of a long, unbroken chronicle. A worn, burnished manifestation of a country's civic and economic posture. An expression of how England was to be perceived, or wished herself to be. To consider them, to inspect them, was to stroll breathlessly through a double-sided museum of art and of history that fit smartly in the pocket of his uniform. It was almost to be in the mythical land of England itself.

Many of the coins he recognized from tips he had received in Bombay. A farthing. A shilling even. He admired most the half-crowns, in his youth made of silver but struck today from nickel, which carried on their face the stern effigy of King George. An image sketched in strong, exaggerated profile, like the familiar gouache paintings of Indian princes, freshly produced, that the hawks of the city sold to tourists as antiques, for shameful sums in shops tucked away in the shelter of the finer hotels. On the reverse side of the coins, he found himself sauntering suddenly, unexpectedly through lush English forests, replete with a meticulous depiction of prickly flowers he didn't know, and of a three-leafed clover that he did. A smaller, brass threepence took him even farther into this cool woodland, surrounded by oak sprigs and firm, bristly acorns and by a signpost around its grooved edge in Latin that was utterly undecipherable to him, apart from the letters GEORGIVS REX, which he knew meant the King, and IND IMP, which he didn't know meant Emperor of India.

He was still jangling the collection of coins in his hand when the bell for lunch soon rang out again from Sebastian's cabin, solidly consistent in the hour of its call from the first day he had chosen to take his meals alone. Once again it was Vikhram who was sent, cementing a quickly established if unstated agreement, for the time being at least, especially as Hamid continued to struggle to keep order and to assure a wider service elsewhere, that this passenger would become the young man's ward. An instruction that Vikhram could hardly have been more pleased to oblige.

What struck him most on his second call to Sebastian's cabin was not that there had been much movement or much change since his first visit, but that there had been so little, and especially that the books that decked out the room, and which were quite clearly Sebastian's chief occupation, had not been opened. Not one of them had been moved. Nor, for that matter, had Sebastian. But whereas earlier in the day his passenger seemed to fix his languid regard on no particular point within the sitting room, he was staring closely this afternoon out of the picture window, seated in the same roomy leather armchair, but his gaze more alert, more animated than it had been earlier.

Indeed, as the train made its way out of the spectral mountain terrain and onto the arid flats below, driving through a landscape of pulsating, vibrant villages and towns, Sebastian sat for hours spellbound. For only now did he come to understand that the succession of fanciful, captivating images in front of him were those of his only objective. His singular goal. They were images of India.

* *

He knew that the official border had not yet been reached, that their passage into Rajasthan was still some twenty-four hours away, but he knew too that this boundary was an arbitrary one, the object of considerable strife and contention, and from his vantage point at least illusory. The impressive mass of people working, walking, milling about just outside the train cared little about the political context in which the lines on a map had somewhere been drawn, by men in starched white uniforms, each with rows of self-congratulatory medals and most with almost no interest or consideration for the place in which these commendations had been awarded them. What mattered to the crowds only were the traditions, the customs, the everyday ways of life that had for centuries defined what the sub-continent was. Those customs and practices had suddenly everywhere become visible, and in rampant abundance, from Sebastian's cabin window.

And the images flooded in like a tempest. A series of elaborate, splashy illustrations he thought at first surprisingly faithful to his raw, one-dimensional vision of what the country must be, fashioned by the endless photographs he had reviewed for his newspapers. By hours spent marveling at classical and contemporary Indian paintings in London's high temples of art, and from the acutely detailed, highly personal and highly romanticized picture Olivia had pro-filed for him in her letters.

A whole world, a new world began to lift its latticed veil, and to show Sebastian its exquisite face. A grimy, cha-otic, fractious, miraculous face.

All along the train's route he could see a continuous progression of villages, many not bigger than a tiny cluster of rickety thatched-roof and packed-clay huts, bookended by food stalls, tea-sellers, shoemakers, dispensaries and other shelters of fortune whose usage and even whose form remained mystifying. He made out hints of the byzantine network of busy, crudely-paved roads that snaked between these settlements, pockmarked by torrential rains and by palpable negligence, where packs of listless, vagrant ani-mals of all sort seemed to enjoy the right-of-way more than did the rare rusty vehicles that barked at them.

From these minor townships, from their mud-spattered arteries, emerged a complex picture of astonishing diver-sity. A perplexing, jumbled picture that destroyed at once the clumsy, convenient idea of the region he had created for himself. There was nothing uniform, nothing subdued or, for that matter, little observably structured about it.

Even the skies above were agitated. By late afternoon, as the train pulled into the remote depot at Asanpur, the nimble cotton wool clouds that all day had been hover-ing overhead had arranged in secret to convene, closing together into a single portentous mass with a power that alone escaped them. Conspiring in an instant to bring a violent deluge onto the land. But their rage only lasted an instant, and in its wake, when the vehemence and the hos-tility receded and calm once again ruled, they left the land even more splendid, even more seductive than they had found it, washed clean of its leaden, dusty pall.

The wait that afternoon at Asanpur would be a lengthy one. The Bright Star was just one of a long queue of trains that needed once more, and for the final time before crossing the approaching Indian border, to replace its engine in order to accommodate a different gauge of rail. Time enough for Sebastian, despite feeling marginally indisposed still, to descend from the train and to stroll around the area.

With the train's engine cut and the raucous steam temporarily interrupted, Sebastian could hear more plainly many of the conventional sounds he knew to be indigenous to the countryside. Not the quiet, pastoral songs of England's Arcadian provinces, though here too there were crows and cows and howling dogs, many of whom had taken shelter already under the train's shaded, idling canopy. The pitch, the accents of the symphony here were much more piercing, more sharp. They sang tales not of halcyon manors or of extravagantly fertile earth, but of a stormier, more impetuous land, fulminating with exertion and with strain, and to his untrained ear, with far less poetry. He heard as well the sounds he would more easily have ascribed to the city, those of motorcar and motorbike horns, of diesel generators, and a chorus of a thousand muscular voices.

The depot itself, erected in what was once and on its edges remained an inhospitable marsh land, did not boast a proper stationhouse or even a passenger platform, at least not in the customary way to which Sebastian had become familiar. The lack of a proper stage, however, did not prevent the crowds from assembling in large numbers. And the numbers seemed to him staggering.

They had congregated in their multitudes, huddled mostly in small, discriminate factions but some alone, watching, laboring, dozing, each with his own reason for being there, but many for no apparent reason at all. They stood inert against the iron gates and against the other parked trains. They sat cross-legged on the chalky ground in the lotus style he had often seen in sculpted images of a meditating Shiva or Siddhartha, and that he thought would crack his own splintery knees if he were to attempt it. Everywhere else, there was movement. A permanent, chronic stirring that seemed always on the point of organizing itself, but that never quite managed to do so. Not as much a tumult as a low bustle, a dull flurry that swayed and that peaked fitfully and without giving notice, like an unpredictable wind.

The presence of such an immense crowd did nothing to help keep the site ordered or clean, though the acute disorder did not offend him, as it might well have done. It was strewn with prodigious piles of household waste, in which quick-tempered chickens and testy pigeons found easy sanctuary. In which half-naked but blithe children scampered for scraps from the baking rubbish. The very ground battled to breathe under its heavy, teeming carpet of litter.

The cramped outpost where documents were checked and where small talk among drivers and officials was tirelessly, lustily exchanged, fared no better. Somehow, despite the battery of people employed to care for it, the place was permanently unkempt. Outside, a group of young women stood crouched over, each with a too short, coarse, spiny broom in hand, pushing the dust from one side of the stone entry hall to the other, without much conviction and with even less effect. Inside, he could see a pair of thin women squatting on the floor, mopping the hard surface with brackish water, wringing out the mops with their bare hands, and every few moments leaning with those hands against one of the whitewashed teak pillars, leaving them dirtier than they had been before.

Just beyond this rudimentary building, and once again in the savage, glassy heat, there were many more people on the move, carrying all manner of goods. They did so on carts, on their backs and, most astonishingly, on their heads. Sticks of wood, kerosene canisters, bags of grain and of gravel, bicycle wheels, even stone bricks made for the curious helmets of this spry army. They hauled these goods from one end of the site to the other and, he felt nearly certain, back again, at what seemed to Sebastian like cross purposes.

To the clamorous sounds of all this stirring and flux was added the range of smells that wafted over him with authority, not always recognizable and not always pleasant. Punchy reminders of the area's distress and of the discipline that eluded it. The one smell he could not mistake was that of frying food, a familiar, nostalgic sensation that came over him like a potent blast. He would know this sublime perfume anywhere. As a child in England, almost his entire, unwholesome diet had been prepared this way. Fried eggs, black pudding covered in batter, fish and chips served with an unselfish side of mushy peas. At school, the staples for breakfast had been fried bread and baked beans. Eventually he had left behind these simpler tastes for a more refined, balanced regimen, under the watchful, guarded supervision of his housekeeper. Though he would often regret it.

The menu here consisted only of the light, triangular fried *samosa*, the same tantalizing pastry he had seen elsewhere at other recent points along the route. Their shells were filled with lentils, cabbage, peas, curry leaves or spiced potatoes, but it was the onions and the chilies he could make out most clearly.

"There's no better way to understand a place," his friend Salamon had said to him back at the Café Prater in Budapest, over the plate of luxuriant patisseries they shared, "than through its food. People travel for many reasons. Maybe they'll keep in mind an image of the unique sites they visited. They might recall a person they met by chance. Perhaps they'll buy a souvenir for a spouse or for a demanding mistress. But it's the food they remember most."

With his friend's words resonating in his ear, it would have been impossible for him to forgo the temptation, and so he purchased one of these spicy treats from the first of the food vendors, unwittingly paying double its going price. He found it just as greasy, just as sloppy as the fish and chips of his youth. Which is precisely why he found it so irresistible. He could taste in the oily dough the rich, soft happiness of his childhood, and he could taste in it a whisper of a happy future, too.

Still, not even the peppery flavors or the strident sounds brought as forceful an impression to his senses, straining as he was to take it all in, as did the eruption of colors that were addressing him on all sides. Such a contrast, he considered, from the blank sand dunes and the black hills they had just exited. Not to mention from the London he had left behind, where the somber weather, the smoldering factories and even the dreary outlook were all but a shade of grey. Here, even in the squalor of the anguished shanty-town that lined the grounds around Asanpur, the vibrancy of its colors, a huge palette that jutted out from every shapeless home and on every improvised rooftop, was astonishing. The walls of these homes, constructed from whatever materials had been most readily at hand, were painted the vivid blues of the spirits, of harmony, of peace. The greens of Islam, for vigor, health, fertility. Electrifying reds for strength, yellow for joy and for divine inspiration. About these tottering structures and the flimsy tarpaulin tents that abutted them, from every possible line and on every free surface, were hung a swarming kaleidoscope of colorful clothes, like streamers at a Christmas fête. They competed for space and for attention with the equally arrogant advertising hoardings, political placards and ubiquitous film posters, whose reflection in the stagnant pools of water around which the houses were carelessly arranged only amplified the impressive effect.

He had thought that many of the implausible, extravagant postcards Olivia had sent him from India had been doctored, the intensity of their brilliant tones embellished in a photographer's studio, but this was clearly not so. Color here seemed to be an indispensable way for people to influence their world. To elevate it. There were whole festivals, he knew from his readings, dedicated to celebrating the exuberance of color, and here he saw its everyday expression far and wide.

Nowhere was this more so than in the attire of the people among whom he now moved easily. The draped, hand-woven, often flamboyant saris of the women, and the bright, resplendent patterned dhotis of the men. Though he assumed falsely that he would see more of them, he noted just a scattering of turbans like the one atop the self-effacing Sikh man who had delivered Olivia's portentous letter and the jewel it contained to his London townhouse. These garments were all made of yards and yards of lustrous fabric and, he suspected, required considerable proficiency to fold, then to tie them tight. It must take years of learning, he thought, lessons from mother to daughter and from father to son, to come to wrap them so effortlessly. Yet it must be something that, over the course of time, becomes quite mechanical. Just as, soon enough, seeing all this handsome, sumptuous clothing would become habitual to Sebastian. There were a thousand million such turbans and saris and dhotis in India. Before long he knew he would cease to notice them.

The more Sebastian delighted in the enthralling, seductive details of the land that were unfolding freely in front of him, the more tangible his meeting with Olivia was becoming. A once faint, amorphous destination, the abstruse foreign land she had long described, was not far away. It was within his grasp. Traces of it were under his feet already. One week ago, standing on the summit of a mountain range in Turkey, he thought he could see halfway to Delhi. He thought today, and with his naked eye, he might see all the way there. The great capital of the proud, promise-filled young country was less than a day away, and with his arrival into Delhi would come their long frustrated, and their potentially hazardous, reconciliation.

It was that hazard, for a brief moment at least, that persecuted him. Faith, desire, resolution alone had propelled him thus far. They had encouraged him to take his fateful decision to leave his prominent, enviable situation in England without the slightest hesitation or apology. His colleagues, his solicitor, banker, housekeeper, his friends, all had cautioned him against such imprudence, such lunacy. He had dismissed them all with respect, but with determination. He knew, however, that the misgivings, the apprehensions of others were within him too, and they were not buried deep.

He needed to brace himself for the last, long leg of the journey, and to fix his concentration only on the initial, precarious moments of their imminent reunion. The rest, he was convinced, or he told himself anyway, would find its own natural, happy level. Anything else would be unacceptable. Unthinkable.

So what, then, he wondered anxiously, would the first moments of their meeting be like? Would embarrassment or discomfort or prudence mean they would keep a distance, or would they shake off any reservations and, like the young lovers they once were, embrace? The moment would be fraught, and as he returned to his cabin, tired out from his long walk, it was the prospect of that sweet embrace on which he focused most.

* *

Vikhram too would soon have a reunion, and it was just as fraught with uncertainty. There had been no time to alert Sapna to his return, and no way to know how he would be welcomed. He had found no words that might appease her or prepare her for his shattered promises, and even less a plan to look after her and the children.

Last night he had suffered the same two, difficult dreams that for days had rattled his already precarious sleep. In the first, he found himself at sea, swimming against the roaring tide of the ill-tempered ocean when a tremendous wave rose like a horrid beast, dragging his helpless body under, back to its sequestered lair. Behind it he managed to escape, to rise on the crest of a second wave, glimpsing from that airy height the safety of the shore just beyond, only to be dragged down even farther when the second wave crashed against the seabed. He cried out, he waved his arms for help, but there was no one to hear his call, no one to throw him a line.

The second dream brought him no less violence,

and had even darker tones. The creature this time was not a watery dragon, but an invisible phantom, somehow offended and hateful, that came to him in his bed. It enveloped him. It pushed hard on his chest to prevent him from breathing and from crying out, and just as quickly as it came, it fled, leaving him alone, stiff, breathless and afraid.

Such malevolent visions were only a symptom of the lingering fears that haunted him. Fears especially that he would never break free from the binding limitations of his class and caste. Never to escape from a bitter fate in which he and his kind were to be kept weak, close to the ground, permitted to occupy only the most unsavory, the most unwanted of places, and certainly not to enter the merchant trades or business. They were the teawallahs, the street cleaners. They were the cabin boys on the trains.

He knew the received wisdom, that he would remain enslaved within this abject group, follow always its prescriptive rules. He had no ambition to do otherwise, and no expectation that his children could do so either. He had hoped only that the money he earned on the oil rigs would provide an abatement of his family's sentence of poverty, and the time he needed to find prospects for them that were more decent, more tolerable.

But steaming back to India, Vikhram would not let the darkness defeat him, no matter what form these night terrors took. There was ample evidence of hope, of change, at every corner. In his youth, for one, his people had been kept apart from others. Like the exhaust of the motorcars that polluted Bombay, the affluent, educated castes feared his people might infect the very air they breathed. He had not been free to enter the same places of worship or to drink the same water. No longer. In a free India, he would be free as well. To work, to love, to live. He believed this.

He *had* to believe this. His whole world was subordinate to this thin tenet of faith.

* *

In the tight room they shared, Hamid presented Vikhram a cigarette, which he welcomed, and the opportunity to converse at length, which he prized even more. They spoke of their respective families. Of their surprise at the many amusing, exasperating, endearing traits that their children seemed to have in common, as they concluded must children all over. They spoke too of the lands from which they came and of those they had visited.

Hamid told of his many sojourns in New Delhi, courtesy of the railway, and even of his one glorious visit to the Taj Mahal in Agra, but he admitted to never having made it as far as Bombay, or even of having the ambition to do so.

"It had always been a dream of mine," said the steward, "to see the Taj. They say it was built as a tribute of a husband who grieved for his dead wife. Goodness, how excellent his devotion must have been! Have you been there, my friend? Does every Indian visit it, like every Muslim goes to Mecca?"

"I've never seen the great Taj," replied Vikhram. "Maybe one day I will. But I *do* know the Haji Ali Mosque in Bombay, which if you believe the guidebooks is just as nice, and it also has a remarkable story to tell."

"As remarkable as a king who empties his country's treasury to honor his dead wife?"

"Well, to begin with, the mosque comes right out of the sea. It's built right in the middle of the water, like a tiny island just off the coast of the city. The walkway must be a mile long, but you can only get there when the tide is low. Otherwise, the path is drowned by the sea. And I can tell you, the tides are very strong just at that point, so you have to be really careful. The whole thing is a bright white. It shines like a lighthouse from miles around, but once you get inside, it's a different world. There is marble and stone and glass of every color."

"Was it built by a king?"

"Oh no, it was built by the people a long time ago to honor a local man, a Muslim businessman who everybody in Bombay knew, but people of all religions come to the mosque, not just Muslims. They come because they think, if they visit it, their wishes will come true."

"So it's like the wishing wells in our Turkish tradition? A sacred place where the waters house the Gods, and who might answer any spoken wish. Do you throw a coin in as an offering?"

"Oh no, no. The legend of Haji Ali, that was his name, his story is very different. He was a rich gentleman who helped lots of people, especially the poor. He did lots of things for them. He was a very generous soul. He helped them buy food, to fix their homes after a storm. He brought doctors for the sick. And the people loved him. One day he stopped to help a local woman, a very poor woman who couldn't even afford to buy oil for her home. So he helped her to find this oil. But he didn't do it by buying it at the market, as you and I might do, but just by bending down and sticking his finger into the earth, on the spot where the mosque is today, and the oil just flooded out. Imagine that! A miracle."

"A miracle indeed! So the man built a temple on that spot, out of gratitude to God?"

"Well, no. If you'll just let me tell my story . . ." said Vikhram jokingly, at which they both laughed.

"Sorry, sahib," sulked Hamid, "please continue, your Grace."

"Thank you! So, as I was saying . . . This man was very generous, but he was also very sensitive. Very spiritual. He could read the forces of the universe more than most people. Soon he became so upset about the damage he had done to the earth, taking its oil without even asking, that he cried and cried for days. Only a few days later, he died from grief."

"Well that's just a *terrible* story!"

"The very next day," continued Vikhram, unflinching, "his body was thrown out to sea, but it washed back ashore to this *very same place*, and *that's* why people go there. Because it was a miracle, first that he made the oil come out of the ground, and another miracle that his body came back home to the same place. People want to give thanks to this saint, and they want their own miracles, too."

"You've visited this mosque?"

"Oh yes, many times. Once I went out there with my children when they were very little. I wanted to show them its beauty and to tell them the story of its miracles. And yes, because I *know* you want to ask me, I *did* stick my finger into the earth, and do you know what happened?"

"No. What? Oil gushed?"

"A sand crab bit me!"

"Ahh ha ha!" laughed Hamid. "Sounds like I ought to avoid this spot. I could either get stranded by the high tide, or bitten by a crab!"

"Oh no, it's wonderful, I can tell you. Just like the city of Bombay. *Do* come, Hamid. I promise you won't be disappointed. The city's just filled with places like this to visit. The Gateway of India. You *have* heard of that, haven't you?

The Hanging Gardens. The Elephanta Caves. I'll be your guide. No one knows the city better than me."

"So tell me then, friend, why should I come to Bombay before I see other parts of India? Like the mighty Ganges at Benares. *That* must be something."

"Because Bombay is the City of Gold, where anyone's hopes can come true. People come from *all* over to try their luck. Which means it's filled with all *different* kinds of people. There are the very rich and the very poor, and people from so many religions. There are Hindus like me, but also Muslims like Haji Ali, Jains, Christians, Buddhists, Zoroastrians . . . I'm sure I've even forgotten a few. With people from so many places, you'd be most welcome, Hamid, and you can try your luck, too!"

* *

Even as he continued to extol to his roommate and fledgling friend the supreme virtues of his home town, where fortune and serendipity might cast their custodial shelter over anyone willing to take risks and to brook hard work, Vikhram was thinking only of his *own* fortunes, and of the years he had wasted away from this City of Gold, chasing a hollow, contrived fantasy. The sudden recognition, aching and comforting both, that the answers he long sought, across continents and across time, could never have been found anywhere but at home.

He didn't resent this merciless conclusion, or of having shown himself so credulous, so callow in succumbing to the foolish temptations of easy success. He didn't consider his time away from his family and his city to have been anything but necessary, even if his travels led him back only to the very place from which he started, no richer perhaps but more solemn, more sober for the traveling. He would allow himself, impose on himself a renewed confidence in the future. He would carry that new confidence, a new optimism, with him on his return into Bombay, just as he carried it everywhere this afternoon as he completed the balance of his duties.

It was to be an afternoon no less full than the previous several had been. For the days on the train were long and they were taxing; the demands were insatiable and the time always too short. He went about his tasks with his usual consideration, attending to the cabins while their occupants were out loitering in the café car, reading salacious novels in the lounge or playing endless games of backgammon with an unnerving competitiveness. He made their beds, dusted their furniture, rearranged the mayhem they had left. He did his second tour of the day in the kitchen, where his presence was especially welcome, particularly among the young women who enjoyed the male company and the friendly attention they willingly mistook for flirtatious advances. An impression he never bothered to correct.

Though he hadn't been instructed to do so, he took a tray of tea and biscuits from the kitchen to offer Sebastian. For if there were one thing he had learned about the English during his brief time in the employ of their Colonial Service, it was that late afternoon tea was sacrosanct, revered like a saintly ritual afforded by the angels. He grabbed from the pantry the last of the Earl Grey and the only remaining tin of ginger biscuits, stamped "Fortnum & Mason, London."

By then, Sebastian had little appetite, but he accepted, and happily, this simple gesture. He couldn't fail to be moved by the thoughtfulness of its envoy, just as he had all along been touched by the courtesy and the hospitality shown to him by the rest of the train's obliging crew.

He couldn't fail either to notice Vikhram's buoyancy, despite his ashen, drawn face. Mainly, he thought he saw in the young man an uncanny amalgam of every other face he had just seen at the rail station, those staring blankly or those staring fixedly straight back at him. The hardened, grinding faces. The honest, decent, forthright expressions of an entire people. He saw in Vikhram the personification of an immense country, his new country, for this was so far all he knew of it. He saw too in the cabin boy's undoubted positivism the faith he had long ago lost, and was trekking across thousands of lonely miles to reclaim.

This was a hopefulness, an expectation, thought Sebastian, that defied the impoverishment that must penetrate this young man. A man whose patently bankrupt condition was itself a reflection of the privation and vacancy, the tremendous abjection through which Sebastian had walked only a moment ago at the depot, and through which he knew Vikhram and millions of his kin must be condemned to walk every day.

Like so many first-time visitors to India before him, he wished he could erase the baneful scourge of that poverty, about which he had been counseled, but for which he knew he would be little prepared. Even if it had been his intention, he knew that any charity he might eventually bestow, drawing on his significant wealth, could do little to ameliorate the plight of so many. The few menial jobs his new household with Olivia might generate would not correct the course of that mighty river, just as the loose change he had given the cabin boy would not alter this young man's trajectory.

But then and there, all he could think to do was to

thank Vikhram, and in so doing to thank by proxy the millions. To demonstrate to them all through these shallow gifts of small coins that he, a man who lacked for nothing, was grateful for what they were offering him. For what they offered was a chance to start anew. And to Sebastian, this was the most precious gift of all.

What he didn't know, what he couldn't know, was that Vikhram too wanted only the same thing, to begin again. To dress the wounds of his failures. To scratch out all record of his misadventures. To pick up simply from where two years ago he had left off.

That new start for both men lay just over the approaching frontier, to which they were racing now, unimpeded, at full speed.

CHAPTER 16 • सोला

No matter how well or how often his cabin was cleaned, the dust continued to accumulate in accursed quantities. Not without surprise, given the forbidding amount of earth the train's vigorous passage kicked up. The rattled soil, beleaguered and parched despite the dawn's driving rain, mixed freely with the exhaust of the region's squalid, chaotic textile mills and foundries. It tangled with the pitched dirt of the ever-present construction sites, and with the powdery grains of the season's pollen. Together they produced a venomous cocktail. To make matters worse, Sebastian's cabin was toward the front of the train, where ostensibly the ride was smoother than in the rear carriages more prone to being tossed about like a child's rattle, but also just downwind of the marauding locomotive, whose engine day and night spit out particles of burnt coal and pungent smoke with contempt. His bleached white washcloths were quickly sullied with the soot and grime. With his finger he could trace his initials in the skin of ash on his books, on the wooden furniture and on the paneled walls of his cabin that attracted the dust like a magnet.

This, thought Sebastian, must account for the rising difficulty he had in breathing, for the persistent, maddening cough that with every awkward convulsion left him more short-winded and just a little more drained. This too must explain why his lips were so dry, so brittle. Why the outline of his mouth had cracked in places like the most fragile Venetian glass, and why it smarted so. He had no balm or ointment or petroleum jelly in his kit with which to soothe his injured lips, and had only the vaguest of notions of the old wives' tales about how to treat such a condition. Nor had he at hand the cucumber slices or beeswax that these folk remedies might have called for.

Besides, the irritation that had come upon his mouth had begun to proliferate more generally, and had steadily gained his arms, his elbows, his neck. Scaly in places, his skin peeled like that of a molting snake, and it began more to burn, to sting, as if he had been attacked by a swarm of irascible flies, though he could see none. The raspy, inflamed itching drove him to distraction, and prevented him from thinking of little else. The more he sought to ignore it, the more it taunted him.

In a predicament such as this, he knew his mother would have enjoined him to soak for hours in a hot bath. She had done so that autumn day when he had come home from school covered with the telltale bumps and blisters of poison oak. He hadn't known, of course, that what made the berries so enticing also made them so dangerous. But tonight, he feared, the strangling heat of a bath would have been an even more baneful enemy than the itch itself. The blistering fumes would only add to his stubborn fever, and they would only render him more faint than he already was, especially as the dizziness he had experienced of late had not yet dissipated. If anything, it was only more aggravated. Like a novice sailor, he felt himself seasick, queasy from the motion, trapped by the close confines of the room that increasingly hemmed him in. That room spiraled around him whether he kept open his eyes, training them on a horizontal line as sailors were taught to do, or whether he kept them closed, when he felt an even greater sense of falling. It was impossible to know which attitude was more unpleasant.

What he did know was that the condition in which presently he found himself – flushed, perspiring and weak – risked ruining his upcoming entrance. He would be in a terrible state tomorrow to meet Olivia. Not that he imagined an especially triumphal or exuberant arrival. There were no plans for trumpets or elephants to parade him in like a maharaja, or for sentries to announce him like that of the Prince Regent at a state dinner. He wanted only to be presentable. Dressed in a neat suit, well-shaven, affecting a slapdash air of insouciance, though he would be terrified, as he knew she would be as well. Not, in any event, wilting from fever, green from nausea. First impressions, even the second time around, and even after some thirty years, mattered to him, and so he would need to summon all his strength and all his fortitude to restore himself to form.

Ordinarily, Sebastian was a man of robust health. He was seldom off his feet, and never for long. As a boy, he had contracted chicken pox at the same time as the others in his class, and had suffered his share of the common cold, though these weren't anything that a dose of magnesium and a few cups of strong black tea hadn't been able to chase away. At school he had broken his collarbone, roughhousing on the playground, having fallen victim to his own laughable attempts to impress the girls with his physical prowess, but even that injury he had worn as a trophy, and extracted from it the maximum sympathy it warranted, and even a bit more. Otherwise, he was quite unaccustomed to illness, and for a man of such exceptional energy and action, he was especially unaccustomed to the fatigue that had come to hang on him.

And an appreciable fatigue it was. Listless, dulled, he lacked the vitality to walk about his cabin. To read. To eat. He lay prostrate in his bed, unable to summon the force even to sit up properly, though not for lack of trying. Every effort he made to lift himself only made it harder for him to breathe, and only exacerbated the aches he felt building in his raw, billowed abdomen, as if he found himself suddenly on the losing end of a prize fight.

* *

Though he was loath to do so, Sebastian asked that the staff medic pay him a visit, in the hope that he might be administered some trenchant tonic for what ailed him. His reluctance stemmed less from hubris and more from the uninspiring figure he knew the practitioner to be. He had seen this colorless man in the corridors a number of times, disheveled, distracted, always looking as if his meal had just been interrupted, with hands that weren't always clean and an unlit cigarette that dangled clumsily from a corner of his mouth. He wasn't what Sebastian had expected in a medical professional, and definitely not what he hoped for.

As he might have guessed, the medic's examination was a cursory one, and not one to inspire confidence. He listened briefly to Sebastian's chest, measured his temperature, appraised his general state. The advice and the medication he dispensed were equally suspect, suggesting only that the patient regularly down a fistful of cure-all tablets, drink copious amounts of water, and stay in bed. Even the first-year student nurses at the Royal Chelsea Hospital, thought Sebastian, could have suggested a more robust course of action, or at least have done a better job of making a show of their concern. They might have queried him about his recent diet, teased out of him the folly of having drunk mouthfuls of water from an underground cave, then plied him with the latest in powerful antibiotics.

On leaving the cabin, the medic whispered a muted comment to the train manager who had accompanied him, but one that Sebastian managed to overhear, and one that set his mind reeling. The patient's condition, he said softly, called for more attention than could be provided for on board. A visit to a clinic would be required, and it would be required urgently. There would likely be one in the city of Jaisalmer, just over the Indian border that they would reach by morning.

Though the celebrated name of Jaisalmer might have inspired Sebastian, the idea of the clinic there did not. For his thoughts went straight back to Asanpur, his substitute for every Indian town. To the flimsy, dilapidated depot and slum houses that masqueraded as modernity. He began to imagine what a medical facility, lost in time and far from any contemporary amenities or resources, might resemble in such a place. It would be primitive. Archaic. And it would be grim. There was no reason to think that a clinic in rural Rajasthan would be any different. He envisaged it devoid of anything but the most basic of supplies and medicines, if any medicines could be found there at all. He wondered whether he would find among its decay any running water, any trained staff, and in his gradually more clouded, more troubled mind, any instruments other than the harrowing, medieval implements of medical torture he'd once seen on display at the Tower of London.

Yet his going there seemed increasingly inevitable. If only to avoid the alarm and the anxiety of the clinic, he attempted to convince himself that his condition was slowly improving, but he was quickly disavowed of this deceit by the specks of blood he saw on his handkerchief. His chills were getting worse. His cough was getting worse, and he was finding it harder and harder to draw in the evening air.

He craved most of all just to sit up in one of the leather armchairs in the next room, so as to be able to look out his window, to admire more fully the continuous spectacle outside. Even at this late hour, he saw hints of silvery light emanating from the indefatigable villages along the train's tracks.

He rang the bell for assistance. When, only moments later, Vikhram arrived, he was startled by the Englishman's drawn features and by his obvious, disquieting weakness. Shocked at the swiftness with which it had overtaken him. He hastened to help Sebastian get up from his bed, and delicately, discreetly he helped him to dress. He implored the older man to let him provide other service. To run him a bath, prepare him a simple, soothing meal or to call again for the doctor. All these propositions his passenger gently refused, and once dressed, well installed in an armchair, asked only that his picture window be opened even wider. An impossible request, as it was plain enough to see that it had been opened fully already.

What was more plain to Sebastian was that the grand ambitions with which he had begun this day had by nightfall become pathetically mundane. They had narrowed, absurdly, to not more than sitting upright in a comfortable chair. Having achieved that small victory, for a victory nevertheless it was, he wanted most of all to be alone. Abandoned to his complaint.

He wasn't ungrateful for the companionship, and certainly not for the relentless kindness being shown to him.

Quite the opposite was true. This unassuming servant, who for several days had attended to him so abidingly, had not flinched in the face of his infirmity, as others might have done, or recoiled at the sight of his growing vulnerability. For this, for the respect and the restraint with which he continued to serve him, Sebastian could only be indebted, and was eager to demonstrate his gratitude. He could not, however, suffer as easily his own feeling of humiliation. A self-inflicted sense of indignity that this unexpected, uninvited fragility bestowed on him, on a man unacquainted with such defenselessness, and one even more ill-equipped to cope with the risk this posed to his guarded modesty.

Once again, he provided the cabin boy with a generous tip, and that as usual Vikhram placed directly into his jacket pocket. But for the first time Sebastian also reached out to shake Vikhram's hand, as robustly as he could muster, holding it there just a little longer than protocol would have demanded. Long enough for him to communicate his own, incontestable message of sympathy and compassion. One simple motion that, among the wealthy men for whom Vikhram had once run countless errands in Bombay, would have been unthinkable.

* *

When the door closed behind him, Sebastian closed his eyes, too. He was finding it near impossible to concentrate, to keep his thoughts clear. The fever was bringing on a kind of delusion. A delirium. The long, agitated night begat a run of driftless, promiscuous images and sounds, like a waking dream. Hurried snapshots of events that had happened, or that never quite did. The distant echoes of things he had said, or wished he had. He heard the lonely, poignant cry of a cello or oboe reverberating down the long nave of a candlelit church. He saw blurred, broad representations of childhood, his own or invented. Fine, groomed horses on a velvety track, going nowhere. Going nowhere. Wilting blades of grass. Newspaper printing presses, illicit library books, the Dean and anonymous dons at High Table, his foot snarled on a wire like a rabbit caught in a trap. Flashes of color and light and hazy forms, from every possible direction and on every conceivable course. Jumbled images, confused images that appeared entirely dissimilar. Unconnected. Except that they all shared one thing. In the near-ground or in the far-ground, in brilliant Technicolor or in black and white, somewhere in every frame was Olivia. Radiant. Her smile as broad as he remembered. Her soft voice whispering mutterings he couldn't quite hear. Her arms held wide apart to welcome him.

Slowly, he opened his eyes. Might Olivia even now be in front of him? No, he had lost her, but still he could see the landscape out of his window, and in the distance, in the emerging light, he thought he could just make out Jaisalmer. A string of bonfires illuminating the honey-colored sandstone rising abruptly out of the thirsty desert. The massive hilltop on which he knew at this hour the palaces and the sanctuaries of legend would be sleeping. One day, and with Olivia, he would come back this way, to take in the extraordinary beauty of this place. There was so much he wanted to visit with her, so much he wanted them together to do.

But he would never see Jaisalmer. Everything was again becoming dark. And just as the fires on that distant hillside burned out with the new day, the fire within him burned out, too.

CHAPTER 17 • सतरा

The railway station-manager, flanked by two scruffy police officers, each with more than a hint of malice in his bloodshot eyes, tried to beat back the rabble with the help of a wooden stick. He struck the men, hollered at them for calm, and still they surged forward like a rolling column of ocean waves. The throng had become assertive. Unruly. A hundred pairs of hands reached in every direction, grabbing their neighbors' shirttails, pushing sharply up against each other to secure a more favorable vantage point.

The crush of people that had crowded around to see what the upheaval was about had themselves only created even more of a commotion. Like rowdy spectators at the gladiator games, they bayed for a good contest, for an exploit. They sensed it. They wanted some reward for their patience and their fidelity. To satiate their appetite for danger, convinced there was sure to be amusement in it. Or at least an excellent diversion.

Even the presence of the police, always spoiling for a fight, excited the restless mob, but the sudden arrival of the British Counsel in Rajasthan, who entered in a convoy of pompous automobiles and with a retinue of subalterns in tow, threw them into a veritable frenzy. They were expecting a well-known dignitary to emerge from the standing train, or for some other noteworthy event to occur that would explain the attendance of officials and the general mêlée of the unfolding scene. Yet the longer the bureaucrats conferred with the station-master, exchanging forms, dictating telegrams and generally keeping the fitful pack waiting for something, for anything to happen, the greater their distemper became.

So when at last by late morning the body was taken off the train, the well-primed men broke out into near pandemonium. They pushed and shoved each other to get to the front, knocking the makeshift gurney sideways with such force that the corpse risked falling off the narrow plank. Even a single close-up view of the body would have sufficed to compensate for their long wait, though no one in attendance had any idea as to the man's identity, and most were at this point wholly indifferent to it. It was the spectacle that mattered most, and not the object of it.

Vikram had often seen such spectacles. Large gatherings, both peaceful and violent, had always been integral to the India he knew. He had stood frequently on the margins of heated public rallies, especially as the calls for independence had grown louder and louder. He had fallen in line behind the fiery pickets demonstrating against the vile working conditions of Bombay's factories and, only days later and at those same sites, in the determined queues for jobs left vacant by the blacklisted agitators and known sympathizers. Just as frequently, he attended festivals, religious celebrations, elaborate weddings that lasted for days and involved stage-managing hundreds if not thousands of people. Often he would sneak hidden through the chaos of those weddings, their noisy marching bands and ululations, to snatch a free meal, unnoticed by the gay, inebriated and already exhausted revelers.

But standing this morning atop the elevated steps of the train's carriage, he felt himself not so much above the congregation as removed from it. He had trouble seeing himself reflected in their faces. Though they were recognizable, something in him had changed. He was one of them, but different now. Not better, just different. Quietly, imperceptibly. He might be wiser than before. Maybe he was diminished. Certainly he was changed.

A minute or two passed before Vikhram identified the source of the agitation, before the masses divided, like a tremor opens up a schism in the angry earth, revealing in the parting before him the inert body being led away. In a flash, the crowd closed in again behind the cortege, swallowing it as swiftly as it had been revealed. He knew instantly it was Sebastian they were carrying. He deduced this well before he saw the hired lackeys off-loading the passenger's distinctive red leather trunk, spilling its contents, carelessly dribbling its books onto the ground with negligent respect for the objects, and almost as little respect for the man's spent, lifeless form.

Racing to the cabin, he saw it empty. Stripped bare, as if it were not occupied, or never had been. As if the dead man had been erased, or never existed at all. The bedclothes were removed, his belongings gone. The room was being readied for the next passengers, and for the countless ones after that, oblivious as they would be to its previous occupant and to the sorrowful circumstances in which he had left it. The only evidence that remained was faint. Outlines of dust where newspapers had rested. A half-empty pitcher of water. A pair of folded reading glasses. There was no hint of a man closely tracing his course across continents on the cabin's ornamental map. Of the hours he spent looking through the windows, knowing that out there lay a succession of unbounded days. Or of the contagion, the disarray, the fever that so quickly delivered him. There was only water and dust. The fate of every one of us, thought Vikhram.

Almost immediately, he was overcome with a blunt, forceful sense of distress. He felt the ground unsteady beneath him, and he was, nervously, awkwardly, disconcerted by it. For he wasn't certain why he should react so strongly to this man's death. He couldn't possibly mourn for him. He had hardly known him. They had spoken very few words, exchanged only the smallest of conversations and courtesies. He had never even learned why the gentleman was traveling to India, though privately, and not without an abashed sense of presumption, he had from the beginning felt they were on a similar journey.

Which is why he struggled so furiously to countenance that journey's untimely conclusion. As with the death of his friend Amit in the blowout not a week before, he wrestled to conceive of a lesson to draw from this. To comprehend why the gods had spared *his* life, despite all the obstacles they daily threw up against him, when they seemed so intent on taking others near to him.

In Amit's demise he had seen an admonition. A stark, unambiguous message to go home. Not to wait to be the man he wished he could be, but simply to be content with the man he was. He would always remain grateful to his friend for that legacy, even if it came at such an unbearably high price. But in Sebastian's death, he saw nothing. He had no way to understand it. No clear instruction or motive could be discerned. He suspected the gods only of provocation or of derision, or worse.

* *

Vikhram, however, would not allow himself to be burdened by the weight of such thorny philosophy. He wanted to act, not to think, for thinking of such things was far more perilous, and could only eat away like a ravenous tumor at his shivery confidence. A confidence he maintained resolutely, but in truth was so fearful of losing, especially as his paramount goal was so close at hand. Besides, his duty and his humanity compelled him to action. To go to the dead man's side. To offer his respects. To serve him still, as witness, guardian, friend.

Pushing his way through the assembly with impulsive, conspicuous authority, he was horrified to see the body exposed, robbed of the conventional decorum of being wrapped in a sheet or in an expedient covering of any kind, to spare him the ignominy of the collective stare and the annihilation of the torrid heat. To Vikhram, such an assault on the man's dignity was intolerable. It deprived the departed of the nobility in death that he obviously had earned in life. An assault all the more galling as it befell him in a foreign land, with only the detached, impotent British Counsel to look after him and his interests.

Yet somehow, despite the slander of his treatment, despite the maelstrom and confusion swirling about him, Sebastian's grace and his honor remained intact. There were no traces on his person of the carnage that had desecrated Amit in the rig explosion. No grisly blood stains or mangled features vandalized him; there were no signs of struggle or of violence. His slightly opened, parched lips gave off a soft expression that was almost peaceful. A fair, gentle smile even. His panama hat placed in his tightly clasped hands, he was dressed just as Vikhram had left him, as if he were napping, and would rise up at any moment and go about his important business.

With one notable exception. Vikhram noticed at once, with fury and with indignation, that the bejeweled tie-pin the man wore so proudly was gone. The one item he knew the Englishman cherished most. He had seen him fumble absentmindedly with the perfectly round gemstone. He had stroked it, rotated it, meditated on it as if it were a talisman. It must have held great store for him, and not only because of its inestimable monetary value, worth manifestly more than any of these desperate men could ever have hoped to earn in all their days. Or could Vikhram, for that matter. It must have carried great personal sentiment as well for the traveler to have dreamed on it so, to gaze within its endless geometry as if it were poised to reveal a long-held secret or some penetrating truth. It had been pirated from him. Plundered by someone who didn't know the man, who couldn't know the value the object held for him. Taken with as much speed and insolence as the man's life itself. And Vikhram was outraged by this affront.

Maybe, he considered with wary resignation, this is how the world works. There is not today, nor had there ever been, anything sacred about it. Sacredness was a fraud, a sham word conjured up for poetry and for song, not compatible with or germane to the lives of real people. It had always been, and forever would be, every man for himself. You take what you can, when you can, without regard for others, and without concern for the consequences. This, after all, is what allowed his country to progress, the pitiless determination of individuals to succeed at all costs, but it was also what stifled his country, since this progress of the individual was so often consummated at the expense of so many others. He recognized this, and could only be offended by it. Ashamed at the irreverence, the profanity he had today again seen.

Defeated, disconsolate, he made his slow way back to his cabin, and as quickly as he closed the door, sank into his bunk, his head in his hands, a parade of gloomy, aggravated emotions threatening now to overwhelm him.

His calm was restored only by the thought that this, after all, was native land. Even if it is flawed, at least he had reached India. The scratchy red soil just outside, the heady, intoxicating scents were well known to him. If he put his ear to that ground, he might just hear it pouring out its heart to him, in a language he knew perfectly, and tomorrow, or very soon after, he would be home. The coins in his pocket, the small gifts of the gracious Englishman, would be more than enough to buy him a train ticket from the capital to Bombay. This much he knew. Soon enough he would bound across the threshold of his tiny flat, to take his beloved, patient wife into his weary arms with a force that would broadcast urgently, and without any doubt, his joy, his relief. He would embrace his dear children, too, as if he had never made the ill-advised, calamitous mistake of leaving them. As if he hadn't squandered all this time away. And slowly, over time, as he settled into old routines and into new combats, as he found a different path and a different dream, his wounded pride at his failings, like the calluses on his hands, would heal.

Vikhram put those callused hands into the pocket of his jacket, to feel the coins he had placed there. To feel their weight, to rub their polished metal like one rubs the votive brass statues in the temples for good luck. He would need all the luck he could muster.

But he was soon jarred out of his stupor, for he felt not just the smooth, round coins, but also a prick that stung his hardened skin. As he took out the coins to see what was assaulting him, he thought his tired eyes were deceiving him. He knew then that neither the crew that had cleared Sebastian's cabin nor the crowd that had carried him away had done the Englishman any wrong or any disservice. For there in the palm of his hand, mixed in with the coins that were so familiar to him, was the glorious, shimmering tie-pin, its radiant, layered, deep purple sapphire drawing in ever stronger the brilliant light from the skies above.

Lightning Source UK Ltd.
Milton Keynes UK
UKOW050659200911

178969UK00001B/6/P